A DUKE WON'T DO

DUELING FOR DUKES

JESSIE CLEVER

SOMEDAY LADY
PUBLISHING, LLC.

For Kayla.
Because you are freaking awesome.

CHAPTER 1

*L*ady Gwendolyn Bounds had just taken a bite of her eggs when she learned her father had sold her to a sheep farmer.

That wasn't precisely how it went, but that was certainly how it seemed.

Because it wasn't only her father's news that was so unsettling but also the fact that Gwen and the word *marriage* had never been uttered in the same sentence before. In fact, it took all her strength not to involuntarily touch the smallpox scars that marred her cheek the moment her father spoke the very word.

Marriage.

Impossible.

It was enough that it felt as though everyone's eyes drifted to her, that briefest of moments when their faces registered disbelief and not a small degree of pity—for Gwen or for her prospective husband, should he be saddled with a disfigured wife, she couldn't be sure.

When it had become apparent that people of society were repulsed by Gwen's scars, her family had closed ranks around her, protecting her from the outside world, and assuring her she would always have a safe place within the family. Although no one ever spoke of it aloud, it was a tacit understanding in the family that Gwen would remain unwed, a spinster and comfort to her mother in later years. Even though she understood and appreciated her family's protection, she couldn't help but feel as though she were missing something important. She had not even had a season, and now at the age of six and twenty, only extraordinary circumstances had led Gwen's mother, Nancy Bounds, Countess Stoke Bruerne, to consider presenting Gwen to the *ton*.

Because if the gossip were true, there was not one but *two* dukes looking for a bride that season.

As the mother of three unwed daughters, Countess Stoke Bruerne would have been branded an utter failure as a matriarch had she not immediately decamped the family from their country home in West Northamptonshire and proceeded directly to their London townhome to begin preparations. But now, it seemed, it didn't matter so much as far as Gwen was concerned.

This was probably why Gwen's mother spluttered in her tea when her father made the announcement of Gwen's impending marriage over breakfast. Because if a Bounds daughter should marry anyone that season, it was going to be one of the dukes on the Marriage Mart and certainly not some obscure sheep farmer in the far-flung regions of England.

"Henry, you cannot mean it. You've signed a wedding contract for Gwen?" Nancy asked as if her husband had just announced his intentions to join a Bavarian circus.

Henry Bounds, Gwen's father and Earl Stoke Bruerne, was unfazed as he spread marmalade on a piece of toast. "Yes, it's all settled. You needn't thank me, Nancy. The opportunity arose, and I took advantage of the situation." Stoke Bruerne had just passed his sixtieth year, but his dark hair remained largely untouched by gray, and he still wore it in a severe style, swept back from his forehead where two horizontal creases appeared every time he made a pronouncement such as this one. Today the creases might have been a pair of moats protecting a medieval castle.

Gwen set down her fork and looked across the table to where her youngest sister, Eloise, sat, hoping to gain comfort from her sister's ubiquitous smile, but Eloise was looking at their mother, her face decidedly drawn.

Gwen shifted her gaze and felt an immediate spike of concern. Her mother's mouth was open, her jam knife forgotten in her hand, her eyes huge pools of disbelief. Horribly, Gwen was fairly sure her mother wasn't breathing.

She reached out a hand. "Mother," she said softly, placing her fingers against her mother's wrist.

The woman jerked, and Gwen was only too glad she hadn't been touching the wrist of the hand that held the jam knife.

"Henry, what have you done?"

Gwen turned, casting her gaze down the length of the breakfast table to where her father sat at the opposite end. This afforded her a view of her other sister, Annie, who poked at her sausages, clearly hoping not to be noticed and drawn into the conversation at hand, and Grandmother Bitsy who continued to shovel clotted cream on her scone as if the conversation around her had nothing to do with her. Which perhaps it didn't, but at least the woman could show some support.

Henry touched his napkin delicately to his lips although Gwen was certain the man never allowed a crumb to stray into his bristly mustache. "What have I done?" He gestured vaguely in Gwen's direction. "I've reduced the number of daughters for whom you must find husbands from three to two. I am sure you will appreciate the effort."

Finally Nancy set down her jam knife. "I certainly will not appreciate the effort."

Henry Bounds was not one to react to such an affront, but at his wife's words, he set down his napkin beside his clean plate with the precision of a naval captain plotting a defensive maneuver. "I beg your pardon, Nancy."

"She said she doesn't appreciate your meddling, Henny." Grandmother Bitsy didn't look up from her plate as she scolded her son. "If you pulled your head out of your newspapers for once in your life, you would know what's going on this season." She stuck a fork in the direction of the Bounds daughters. "There are two dukes on the auction block this season, and you've just reduced Nancy's chances of securing a duke by ninety percent." Bitsy waved her fork in triumph and returned to her sausages.

"I'm not sure that's correct, Mother," Henry stated in a low voice as he adjusted the placement of his knife and fork at the rim of his plate. His careful movements and casual tone revealed just how timid he was when it came to his formidable mother.

Even at eight and eighty, Bitsy Bounds was still prone to pinch her son's ear.

But this wasn't what had Gwen's attention then. It was the slight tremor in Annie's hand as she moved her fork amongst the sausages on her plate, the way the silver cut across the porcelain and made an unbearable sound should anyone have been listening. Gwen wanted to reach out and take her sister's hand into her own, assure her that their mother wouldn't force Annie to marry when she was still grieving for the husband she had lost the previous year, but Gwen couldn't make that promise. Her mother was on the hunt, and Gwen feared no one would be spared.

Henry looked down the table at his wife again. "I am sorry if I meddled, Nancy," he said, his mustache twitching. "I was unaware of the possibility of one of our daughters courting a duke this season." He gestured again at Gwen. "At least I've had the presence of mind to secure a match for the unattractive daughter."

Gwen didn't flinch at her father's words. It wasn't as though she were unaware of her scars. But her physical appearance hardly mattered. She had no say in what had happened when she was only eight years old, and the physical scars were hardly the ones that still plagued her. Besides, there were far worse fates than an arranged marriage.

Her eyes drifted to Annie again and away, suddenly feeling as though her gaze itself intruded on Annie's grief.

Nancy closed her eyes briefly, and when she opened them, the heat there matched the firmness of her jawline. "What's done is done. When can we expect the wedding, Henry? Perhaps I can use this to our advantage. A wedding so early in the season will get us unparalleled attention. That will put a bee in Rosemary Hayes-Martin's bonnet," Nancy said with far too much relish as she spoke of her nemesis, Viscountess Bowes.

The last time Nancy had gone toe to toe with Viscountess Bowes, the Bounds women had been banned from Spalding's on Marlborough for three years.

"Excuse me," Gwen managed to find her voice. "I should like to know who it is I'm to wed." It was funny to hear the objectiveness in her voice, as though she were speaking of someone else's impending marriage, as if all of this wasn't happening to her. As if her entire life hadn't changed with a single statement from her father.

As if her stomach weren't at that very moment fluttering with anticipation. No, no. She mustn't get her hopes up. Not yet.

Her father blinked as though her question were unexpected. "Oh, right. Logan Bender, the Earl of Gracey."

Bitsy's fork clattered against her plate. "Henny, no," she breathed.

Gwen's momentary bubble of hope dissolved at the stricken look on her grandmother's face. She had been right not to let her hope grow. Life had taught her not to have such expectations, and suddenly learning she was to be a countess when only minutes before she had fully expected to remain alone for the rest of her life was a far too beautiful thing for Gwendolyn Bounds.

But then as Bitsy continued to stare at her son, her lips parted and her eyes narrowed in something akin to real sadness, Gwen felt something different flutter in her stomach, something very much like fear, and when Annie took her hand beneath the table, she jolted in her seat.

Henry picked up his napkin only to set it down again. "Lord Gracey is a respectable member of the *ton* and checks into his background and financial standings show a man of character and sound investment. Gwen should be thankful for such a match." Only then did he finally look at her and even then, it was only a sideways glance as if he knew how hurtful his words might seem, but he was only speaking the truth.

And he *was* speaking the truth. That was probably what hurt the most. Gwen should be thankful for any kind of match. Her father was correct on that point.

Gwen had already resigned herself to remaining her mother's companion. It wasn't bad really. She would have pin money and still come into town every season when her father was required at Parliament. There were worse lives to live. She had even nearly convinced herself it was what was meant for her. That her mother should never be alone in her old age.

Her heart pinched though, just the tiniest bit, every time she thought about it, how boring and small her life would be. After surviving smallpox, she had always believed she should live a life of purpose and meaning. After all, why had she been spared otherwise? It turned out such grandness was denied to an outcast like her. It made her feel as though she had squandered the second chance she had been given.

But now that she might actually have a chance, her grandmother's concern had her worried.

"An earl?" Her mother's eyebrows disappeared into her auburn fringe. "Why, Henry." Her eyes narrowed much like Grandmother Bitsy's. "What's wrong with him?"

Gwen didn't know how it was possible, but this hurt more than her father's statement. To infer that something should be wrong with the man for him to accept Gwen as his wife. It hurt. It hurt deeply.

"Do you know the earl, Grandmother Bitsy?" It was Eloise who spoke, her tone direct and accompanied with a glare in her mother's direction.

"I know the family, dear," Bitsy said as she sank back in her chair. The old woman looked like she'd wrestled a bull instead of simply having broken her fast. "They hail from Yorkshire, I'm afraid." She turned her head then, meeting Gwen's gaze directly. "They're sheep farmers."

Nancy knocked over her teacup, brown liquid sloshing across the pristine linen tablecloth as Eloise jumped to her feet to staunch the flow with her napkin. It was several seconds before Gwen realized what was happening and rose to add her own napkin to the pool of spilled tea.

She looked over her shoulder at her grandmother even as she helped Eloise gather the sodden napkins onto a discarded plate. "Why do you say it like that, Grandmother Bitsy?"

Bitsy had closed her eyes, and Gwen worried the woman

had fallen asleep at the table again. But then she said, "Just that, shortcake." She shrugged, her crocheted shawl riding up against the back of her chair. "They farm sheep. Dedicated bunch they are. I've never known a person to carry on so about wool." She opened her eyes then and found Gwen's gaze. "At least you won't have to worry about the man mistreating you. You'll likely never see him. Sheep farmers rarely leave their herd."

"Mother." The word was quickly spoken but hardly of a harsh tone. Still, it was the closest thing to a reprimand Gwen's father had ever said to his mother, and for that, Gwen felt a modicum of warmth for her usually distant father.

"Surely you exaggerate, Bitsy," Nancy said then, fanning herself with one hand as though the revelation that her daughter was to marry a sheep farmer had elevated the temperature in the room. "A sheep farmer is not what I would have chosen for my daughter, but he is an earl. We must take comfort in that."

Grandmother Bitsy's eyes sharpened. "I had a friend once. Lilith. I thought her a spinster until I met her husband one day. I asked him where he'd been, and he said he couldn't leave his flock." Shakily Grandmother Bitsy leaned forward. "Do you know when it was that I met him? What extraordinary reason could pull him from the flock?"

Gwen watched her mother swallow. "No, Bitsy. I can't imagine. What was it?"

"His wife's funeral," Grandmother Bitsy uttered and collapsed back against the chair, deflated.

Gwen picked up her head and met her father's gaze, ready to break the chill that had descended over the table. "When am I to marry Lord Gracey?"

"You'll leave for Yorkshire tomorrow. He's already

arranged for the license, and you can be wed as soon as you arrive."

Nancy stood up at this so quickly Eloise lurched to her feet to save the butter dish from near doom.

"Henry, no. I must protest. I will not allow my daughter to marry without having me in attendance."

Henry stood far more calmly than his wife, holding up his hands in a placating gesture. "Then go to Yorkshire. I'm not stopping you."

"Henry." But Henry had already left the breakfast room. This did not stop Nancy from going after him. "Henry, come back here. We must discuss this."

Before her mother's skirts had even made it through the door behind her, Eloise was coming around the table as Annie reached over and gripped both of Gwen's hands in her own.

"You mustn't worry, Gwennie. We're here," Annie said, her tone unflappable if soft, but Gwen couldn't help but see the uselessness of her sister's words.

Annie had no control over Gwen's future any more than she had control over what the queen might wear that day.

Eloise knelt beside Gwen's chair. "Gwennie, my heart, it will be all right. You'll see."

Gwen managed a wobbly smile. "It looks like I must leave it up to the both of you to catch one of those rumored dukes this season."

Eloise smiled her sunny smile, but Annie looked away, and Gwen regretted her words.

"We'll catch both of them. I promise." Eloise shrugged, her mouth lifting ruefully on one side. "Just think. A Bounds sister could be a duchess by the end of the season. Have you ever heard of anything more impossible?"

Gwen felt her smile wobble and moved her gaze to Grandmother Bitsy who snored softly now in her chair. If her grandmother were correct about Gwen's future husband never leaving the barn, then how was Gwen to have her second chance?

* * *

SHE WAS LATE.

Logan Bender, the Earl of Gracey, had received Lord Stoke Bruerne's letter informing him of his bride's impending arrival. Stoke Bruerne had written that Logan was to expect the carriage on the third of March. It was now the morning of the fourth of March, and with every passing hour, he felt his annoyance growing.

He didn't want a wife, and having to be constantly reminded of her absence was vexing.

"My lord, Miss Haversham wishes to speak with you."

It was convenient that Logan reached the door to the kitchen garden at the moment his housekeeper, Mrs. Rehnquist, spotted him. He ignored her, sailing out the door into the kitchen garden as if he hadn't heard her.

Only to find the gardener's assistant in the kitchen's bean patch. "Lord Gracey!" the gangly lad shouted across the rows of cabbages, pushing the felt hat that was far too big for his head back as if it would help him be heard. "Miss Haversham—"

But Logan was already through the garden gate.

"Ah, Lord Gracey. I was hoping to run into you. Miss Haversham was in the stables again."

Logan finally stopped, his booted feet kicking up a cloud of dust in the yard. He turned, planting fisted hands on his hips to face his stable master. "Piven. It looks to be a lovely day. What do you think?" He squinted against the sun that was just beginning to rise off the hill to the east. He couldn't stop his gaze from picking out the dots of white against the hillside, counting as he went.

"That it is, my lord, but we can't be having a lady in the stables. One of the lads tossed the manure he had just mucked out back into the stalls thinking it was the hay, he was so distracted. The lady is causing a right mess, my lord." Piven scratched at the top of his forehead where his brown-blond hair had receded.

"Noted, Piven. I'll be sure to speak with her."

"Will you speak with her now, my lord? She's a right persistent one. I don't want any more hay ruined, you see."

Hay. He was standing in the yard speaking to his stable master about hay. He turned, his gaze going down the drive that led from the main road, but there was no sign of a carriage in sight. Drawing his watch from his waistcoat pocket, he paused ever so briefly, his thumb going over the polished surface. It was the briefest of pauses, and he pretended as though he hadn't done it at all before clicking the mechanism to spring the latch. Half seven.

Where was his bride?

He snapped the watch shut and replaced it in his pocket. "I'll speak to her as soon as I am able," he answered and strode off before the stable master could trap him into something more specific.

He had just reached the pole barns they'd erected the previous summer that they now used for lambing when his steward found him.

"Lord Gracey—"

He held up a hand. "I'm aware Miss Haversham wishes to speak with me."

The steward, a Mr. Hatrick, was a small man, barrel chested and with unkempt graying whiskers. His chubby fingers were dotted with various knots of red string, a reminder system that seemed to work because the man was the best damn steward the Gracey estate had ever seen.

"I'm sorry, my lord?" He shook his head, his whiskers scraping along the frayed scarf he had tied about his neck. "Miss Haversham?"

Logan paused, his hand involuntarily, and perhaps impatiently, going to the waistcoat pocket where he outlined the bulge of his watch. "You're not here to speak to me about Miss Haversham?"

The man's eyes skated left and right. "Eh, no, my lord. I am here about the pens in the east paddock."

"Right," Logan said, lifting his head fully for perhaps the first time that day. "Let's have it then."

He spent the next several hours in blissful ignorance of anything else about him except for the care and keeping of the flock and the running of the farm. He even forgot he was expecting a bride. He visited the new mothers and lambs, inspected ears and hoofs, and even reviewed the feed stock with Hatrick.

It was midafternoon when he found himself outside the ram pens with his steward. They had borrowed a ram from the neighboring Bartlesfield estate in the hopes it would impregnate a portion of the herd. As Logan's plan to build the flock progressed, he was finding it necessary to borrow more rams. He would need to discuss this with Hatrick as at some point they would require a longer-term solution. For now the borrowed rams would do.

Except perhaps the one they were monitoring just then.

"And he's been acting like this all morning?" Logan asked as the ram in question head-butted the wooden stockade enclosing his pen.

Hatrick nodded. "Seems so, my lord. It must be the other rams setting him off. He was docile before we brought in the two beasties from the Browning estate."

Logan scratched at the back of his neck as he considered the animal. The rams were penned too closely together here, but it was all they'd been able to manage at the time. With the dowry from his impending marriage, they'd be able to expand the facilities and position the estate for the robust breeding he had planned.

Dowry.

He swung about in the direction of the drive only to find it empty as he had every other time he'd eyed it that day. He groped for his pocket watch now.

"See that the ram is kept separated. We don't want him injuring himself or the other rams while he's in our care."

He managed the spring on the pocket watch just as the faint sound of carriage wheels reached his ears.

Half two.

Bloody late indeed.

He need only fetch the special license. The vicar in the village had already been notified of his intent, and he would be expecting them. Logan wouldn't let the woman disembark. She had already made him far too late in this endeavor, and it would be best if they were to get the deed done that day. The transfer of funds would occur according to the marriage contracts once the vicar sent verification of the marriage to Lord Stoke Bruerne, and Logan could begin planning for the next phase of the flock building.

He paused, his feet skittering at the edge of the drive when his thoughts strayed to the other necessity his plans required, but he would worry about that at another time. For now, he must simply be married.

Hailing the carriage to a halt, he stepped forward without greeting and wrenched the door open. It had taken some time to find a man willing to marry off his daughter to him without an in-person negotiation. London was too far to travel during the lambing, and he knew it was a risk he was taking, but it hadn't mattered what the girl looked like or how she carried herself. His only requirements had been that she come from fine breeding, be well trained in the duties required of a titled gentlewoman, and have a sizable dowry.

It took a moment for his eyes to adjust to the dimness of the interior, but once they set upon the object of his focus, he felt an instant, and quite unexpected, flicker of relief.

She wasn't attractive in the least.

It hadn't been a requirement when he'd gone in search of a bride, but he couldn't ignore how pleased he was to see she wasn't beautiful. His first wife had been beautiful, and he couldn't help but wonder if that had been the reason for the turmoil that followed.

He cleared his throat. "Lady Gwendolyn?"

She nodded and made to rise as if she intended to leave the carriage. As she tipped forward, sunlight struck her face, and he could see her fully now. She had a plain face with an overlarge nose and thick lips. Her brow was heavy, and her hair was a dull brown lying limp along the crown of her head under her bonnet. But that wasn't what drew his attention.

Deep pitted scars marked her cheeks and the flesh above one eyebrow, the marks unmistakable for what they were.

Smallpox.

An unexpected and sharp pang of sadness struck him, his mind grappling with what she might have endured, and he resolutely looked away.

"Stay," he barked and turned to the driver. "I'll be only a moment," he said. "Then I'll require you to take us into the village."

The driver's mouth opened, but Logan was already turning away when he heard the crunch of gravel behind him. He spun about, surprise widening his eyes. His bride stood on the drive, her arms clinging to the wrap about her shoulders. Her bonnet caused a shadow to fall over her face, but he was too busy studying the rest of her to notice.

The momentary relief he had felt at her plainness evaporated at the sight of her. At the *curviness* of her.

He hadn't been with a woman in well over two years, and the length of his celibacy suddenly mattered like it hadn't before. Lady Gwendolyn filled out her gown in all the appropriate places. She wasn't the sickly thin waifs he had seen the last time he'd been in London. Not at all. She was…something he hadn't wanted.

Well, there was nothing for it. He would simply not look at her.

He lifted his gaze and pointed to the carriage. "Get back in the carriage. We're leaving for the village at once."

There was only a second for her eyebrows to lift in question before shouting behind them drew his attention.

Hatrick stood by the pen that housed the ram they'd been reviewing, his arms swinging wildly in the air as if trying to get Logan's attention. Logan dropped his gaze long enough to take in the broken fencing, the stampeding, mad ram, and the direction in which the animal traveled.

Logan moved, throwing himself forward as there were only seconds before the ram would meet his target, the target being Logan's newly arrived bride. He registered the shock on her face the split second before his arms came around her, and he lifted, tossing both of them into the carriage. The impact of the floor against his shoulder reverberated through him at the same moment the ram struck the outside of the carriage, the cracking of wood echoing through the air as the conveyance rocked around him.

Vaguely, he heard Hatrick shouting orders outside, a bleat of protest from the ram before the sounds of a scuffle, the scraping of gravel as the beast was led away. But none of it mattered. The only thing he truly heard then was the pounding of his own heart, the way his breath suddenly matched hers.

She smelled of fresh air and something wilder like spring rain. His fingers flexed into her back before he could stop them, as though his body was laying claim to something his mind wouldn't allow.

But when she looked up, and her wide frightened eyes met his, the last of his resolve vanished.

Catherine had never looked at him like that, with such uncertainty and need. With such expectation.

He shoved the thought aside. He didn't want to be needed. That was something else his first wife had taught him.

But he wondered for a moment if he could get lost in Lady Gwendolyn's eyes. They were so big and brown and fathomless. He'd never noticed a woman's eyes like he did then.

"Are you all right?" His voice was gruffer than he'd intended, and he blamed the dust from the gravel drive, but then her lips parted, her tongue darting out nervously to lick her lips, and something deep inside of him, something he thought long dead, clenched in anticipation.

He got the hell out of the carriage even before he heard her reply. Once his feet were safely on the ground, he turned back to find her sitting up now on the floor of the carriage, her knees drawn protectively to her chest. She looked so vulnerable then, and horribly, he felt protective of her.

"I'm sorry about the ram," he said. "They can be quite aggressive when it's time for mating." He nodded in the direction of the house, determined to get back to task. "I'll just fetch the marriage license and then we can be wed. Welcome to Scarcroft Manor."

He slammed the carriage door shut and strode away.

CHAPTER 2

Gwen sat on the forward-facing bench of the carriage, her hands curling against the hard seat.

It had been decided Nancy could not be spared at such a critical time in the season for the other Bounds daughters, and the family could not afford to be parted from their own carriage for Gwen's journey north, and so her father had rented this less than desirable conveyance for her trip to meet her future husband and enter her new life. Somehow she doubted a more comfortable carriage would have made a difference now.

Her shoulder ached from where she had met the floor after her soon-to-be husband had lifted her—*lifted her*—and thrown her—*thrown her*—into the vehicle just before that animal had attacked. Well, attacked the carriage really. But they had been inside the carriage.

With her betrothed's arms around her and her hands pressed to his chest, she could feel the outline of every hard muscle and the rapid beat of his heart, smell the intoxicating aroma of clean sweat and masculinity.

She had spent a lifetime not being touched and now he had touched *everything*.

She couldn't think, her mind utter blackness as her body hummed. She unclenched her fists, and stripping off her gloves, held her hands up for her inspection as though she might suddenly have inhabited a different person. But no, the faint outlines of smallpox scars were still there along the backs of her hands, along the ridge of knuckles. She shoved her hands back into her gloves.

She couldn't stop the thought from coming even as she tried to stop her hands from shaking long enough to get her gloves back on. Her mind traveled back to the last time she had been thrown into a carriage. She'd been eight, sick with fever, her very body burning with disease, and her mother had made the difficult decision to banish Gwen from the house lest she give the illness to her sisters.

Frightened and sick, Gwen had been bundled off to the gamekeeper's cottage where she would be cared for by the gamekeeper's wife until she could safely return to the main house. That was, if she lived. It would be a long time before she would be touched again, and then only by her mother and father, her sisters, and Grandmother Bitsy. Their touch was always light as though they feared hurting her even long after her scars had healed.

But never—

She made a noise then, a strange gurgling noise as if she were drowning.

She must get a hold of herself. This was it. This was her one chance to make something of her life.

She hated feeling so helpless, hated to think she might ruin this second chance too, so when her betrothed had told her to remain in the carriage, she had refused. She wanted to see her new home for herself as if by taking in Scarcroft Manor it would help to quell the uneasiness

inside of her. Her mother had only given her two instructions, one pertaining to her wedding night, which Gwen
was trying very hard to forget, and the other that Gwen
must host a dinner or soiree where she would introduce
herself as the countess. With only those two bits of information, she was feeling lost, and the thought of seeing her
home beckoned. She'd barely gotten her feet on the ground
when there was a cry of surprise, a shout of warning, and
then—

It seemed her future husband was incredibly strong.

She waved a useless hand at her face as heat flashed
through her. Sucking in a breath, she stared at the carriage
door as if focusing on something else might calm her. She
didn't dare step foot outside the vehicle, not until Gracey
told her it was safe to do so.

It wasn't that she was frightened of rams. She'd seen
plenty of the creatures rendered in numerous landscapes. It
was just the suddenness of it. A ram where she hadn't
expected one. A husband throwing her to the floor to save
her from injury.

A husband.

The carriage door flew open, and he appeared in the
doorway then as if summoned by her thoughts. She sat back
against the bench, sliding as far away as possible to give him
room to sit on the bench without touching her as she was
used to doing.

He hesitated, and for a horrible moment she wondered if
he had changed his mind now that he saw her scars. But he
took the seat next to her, and she forced her gaze out the
opposite window as he snapped the door shut, and the
conveyance sprang into motion.

"I expected you yesterday."

His words were short, his tone clipped, and for a
moment, fear welled up inside of her. But then she remem-

bered Grandmother Bitsy's words, and the fear receded somewhat.

"I'm terribly sorry, my lord. The carriage lost a wheel outside of Leeds. We were forced to stop for the day to have it repaired." They were turning back onto the main road when she finally gathered the courage to look at him. "Where are we going?"

She had caught something about a license, but in the melee, she hadn't understood completely what was happening.

"We're going to the vicar to be wed." He spoke as if he were telling her how he liked his tea.

Her throat closed, trepidation washing over her, pounding in her ears and smarting at the back of her eyes. She swallowed. "Today? We're being married today?"

He'd had his head turned to the opposite window, but at this, he looked at her. "Is there a problem?"

His eyes were green. He was close enough she could see the gold flecks in the green, but the intensity of his stare was unbearable, and she had to look elsewhere. At his unshaven cheeks, the dust that lay like a sheen on the felt hat he wore pushed back on his head, the thick black hair that escaped it. He wasn't wearing a coat. He was in shirtsleeves rolled to his elbows. His waistcoat was torn on one side. His trousers—oh God, was that mud or…something else?

Suddenly looking into his eyes didn't seem so impossible. "You're not dressed for it, my lord."

"Logan," he said.

"I'm sorry?"

His eyes narrowed. "Is there something wrong with you? I mean, with your wits? You're not addlebrained, are you?" He started looking her over the way she had done to him, but his gaze was far more calculating. She tugged at the edges of her wrap as though the thin crochet could shield her. But it was like all the other times someone had cataloged her scars, and her chin went up.

"I am not, my lord." She involuntarily sank back into the corner as if she could escape his scrutiny, but he only reached out a hand and pulled her closer.

The shock of his touch made her flinch, and her body heated all over at the memory of him pressed against her. She forced her body to realize what was happening. There was nothing loving about his touch. In fact, he seemed to be inspecting her as if she were one of his sheep.

She tugged at her arm, hating how degraded he made her feel while reveling in the feeling of human contact, but he held fast as he turned her arm this way and that.

"I was promised you were of fine breeding. I will not be swindled."

She gave one last tremendous tug, and her arm sprang free, sending her elbow into the side of the carriage. She winced at the pain that shot through her arm and cradled it against her.

"My lord, I promise there is nothing wrong with me. I am simply not aware of what is happening. I only learned of our impending marriage five days ago, and I am still attempting to catch up."

He sat back. "It's really quite simple, I should think. We're to be wed. You'll be the Countess of Gracey, and I expect you to fulfill the duties as countess and represent the Gracey title with extraordinary care. What is so difficult to understand?"

Her lips parted in mild shock as his harsh words struck her, but not wishing for him to think any worse of her, she spoke to hide her reaction. "Five days ago, I wasn't even aware I was to be wed, my lord. In the span of only a few days, my entire life has changed, and it would be kind of you to understand that."

He tilted his head, his eyes narrowing again. "You're to be a countess. That's hardly a burden. Have some courage."

She was grateful he looked back out the window then and couldn't see the shock that was likely written across her features. Breathing was suddenly difficult, and she used the hand holding her wrap together to push against her furiously beating heart. Was this truly happening? Was she truly to be wed to this...brute?

She had thought this was her second chance. But was a second chance truly a chance at all if this was how it would be?

The carriage stopped abruptly, pitching her forward as if in answer.

"Wonderful. We're here," Gracey said and flung open the door before the coachman could jump down.

The earl stepped from the carriage and...disappeared.

Gwen blinked at the opening where he had been only seconds before, expecting him to offer her a hand down, but when he finally reappeared, it was only his head, and his face wore a grim, assessing expression. She was beginning to worry it was the only expression he possessed.

"Aren't you coming?" His eyes narrowed further. "You're sure you're not ill?"

She didn't answer him. Gripping the edge of the door, she pushed forward, nearly smacking him in the head with her elbow as she exited. If only she had.

They were standing in front of a small cottage, its thatched roof dappled by the shade from two benevolent elms that marked the front yard. Looking around, she realized they were on a lane of similar small cottages, and she wondered if the village was near here. She hadn't seen the village that would be her home on the way to Scarcroft Manor, and her curiosity rose.

She wasn't to have time to ponder this though as Gracey took her elbow and pulled her in the direction of the cottage.

"Ow." She yanked her elbow free, rubbing it softly as it still hurt from hitting it in the carriage. "I can walk perfectly fine on my own, my lord," she said.

"Prove it."

He was exceptionally tall, she realized as she had to peer up at him. Again, she didn't bother answering and instead followed him mutely to the door of the cottage. The door was opened after the earl's brief knock to reveal a diminutive woman holding a feather duster.

"Oh, my lord," she nearly twittered, blinking furiously behind silver round spectacles. "You weren't expected."

Gwen glanced at the earl to find the same accusatory expression he had inflicted upon her.

"Yes, I was," he said and pulled a sheaf of papers from his trouser pocket. "I had informed Simons about my impending marriage. He knows to expect me."

The woman in the doorway twittered again and pressed her free hand to the apron straining over her round belly. "Oh, but my lord. We didn't expect you *today*. The vicar—"

Gracey didn't wait for a response. He stepped through the door of the little cottage, pushing past the woman with the duster at the same time he grasped Gwen's arm and pulled her with him. She didn't jerk her arm free. There was no time for it. The cottage was indeed small, and soon they were standing in a square, nearly barren room that contained little more than a desk, two chairs, and a man bent over a thick tome. Gwen saw the man's nearly bald head first before he looked up, and she saw the same round silver spectacles as the woman in the doorway.

"Dudley! Dudley, my darling!" This from the woman with the duster who had followed them. "I tried to tell him—"

The man held up a hand, and a small, sad smile came to

his lips. "Lord Gracey, a pleasure." The man's tone didn't match his words. He held out a hand. "I'm sure you're here to be wed."

Gracey pursed his lips and cast a knowing look back at the other woman as if to say he told her so. The woman crossed her arms with a harrumph and held the duster in one hand like a dagger she wished to use on the earl. Gwen wondered if she might borrow it from the woman.

"Delilah, won't you offer our guests tea?" the vicar said. "I apologize, my lord. My sister is not herself today."

"I'm perfectly myself," she grumbled but left the room.

The vicar opened the sheaf of papers Gracey handed him, but Gwen couldn't see what was on them from where she stood. She surmised enough to understand it likely contained the marriage license her father had mentioned.

It was suddenly real. She was getting married. Today. Right then. Like this.

Once more her gaze traveled to her soon-to-be husband, and she took in his bare arms. She could see now in the light from the windows beside them that they were streaked with dried mud, his boots and trousers faring much the same, and he still wore his hat.

This was not the second chance of which she had dreamed. This was not the shimmery wedding she had longed for, the groom she had imagined who loved her despite her scars, this was not the beginning of a future filled with possibilities. This was the fulfillment of a contract.

Her eyes unexpectedly met his, and something in them had her stilling.

His expression had changed. The cold, assessing gaze had been replaced by something else, something softer and wondering. It almost looked like he felt sad about something.

There was no further time to think about it because at that moment the vicar began their wedding service. It was brief and perfunctory, and in it, Gwen learned the entirety of her husband's name was Logan Alexander Matthew Bender, the Earl of Gracey.

Logan.

He had been trying to tell her his name. Yes, of course. Her father had told her as much that morning at breakfast when he'd made his announcement. She had just been too overwhelmed to remember.

Sadness unlike any other she had felt before swamped her then, and the last of her tethers let go, sending her spiraling into a life she hadn't expected to live and one she was coming to fear she didn't want despite how desperate she'd been for a second chance.

The vicar smiled, but there was something heartbreakingly knowing in his eyes when he looked at her before turning to Gracey and saying, "You may kiss your bride."

"Right," Gracey said and turned to her.

Her body went instantly rigid, her heart thumping wildly, so loud she knew they could hear it. This was it. She would finally be kissed.

But instead of kissing her, Gracey patted her on the shoulder briefly.

"Right, well, that's done," he said and left.

She looked at the vicar as if he could help, but the man's befuddled gaze held nothing but sorrow and pitiful understanding.

"I beg your pardon," she mumbled and went after her— she swallowed—she went after her *husband*.

The carriage ride back to the manor was silent, terribly so. She wasn't even sure the horses made any noise. This time the carriage made it to the front of the manor house, circling the front steps before stopping. Gracey alighted, but this time she didn't wait for him to offer her a hand. When she stepped down into the drive though, she found another woman standing in front of them.

And she was holding a baby.

To say the woman looked frazzled was an understatement. Her hair was falling loose of its pins, the apron pinned to her gown was covered in a rainbow of stains, and even from where she stood, Gwen could smell the faint odor of a full nappy.

"My lord, I must insist—" she began, but Gracey held up a hand, cutting her off.

"Ah, Miss Haversham. I've been looking for you." He gestured to Gwen. "Allow me to introduce my wife, Lady Gwendolyn Bender, the new Countess of Gracey. She'll tend to the baby now." With that, he walked away.

CHAPTER 3

Gwen watched him go.

He'd been her husband for all of a half hour, and he was leaving her there. With a baby.

Her husband's baby?

She swung her gaze around to the beleaguered woman standing in the drive. She was older than Gwen had first thought with honey-colored hair, delicate features, and a long, thin neck. With a sharp stab, Gwen realized this could have been her. If her father had not sold her to a sheep farmer, she could have been this woman. The poor, unmarried spinster relation come to care for someone else's children.

Gwen reached out, her arms going forward of their own volition. "Give him to me," she said.

Miss Haversham hesitated, clearly as unsure as Gwen was. "It's a girl actually."

Gwen eyed the bundle in the woman's arms, concern creeping over her. The baby on second glance was older, perhaps almost two years old, but still in the pudgy, squirmy state of babyhood. The babe wore a frocked gown in navy with a straight collar meant for a boy.

After another questioning look, Miss Haversham finally handed the baby over. "She's called Felicity," the woman said, her hands lingering on the baby, suddenly reluctant to relinquish her it seemed.

Taking the child into her arms had the effect of rekindling a memory. Gwen had cared for each of her sisters. By the time Eloise had arrived, Gwen was old enough to change her nappy and rock her to sleep. Nanny had often quipped she would soon no longer be needed thanks to Gwen's natural ability with babies.

Until that was, the day Gwen had been forced to leave the house.

She dipped her head, her nose finding the soft fuzz on the top of the babe's head, inhaling the familiar baby scent she hadn't known she missed. She knew this. She understood this. An invisible tether snapped into place, and the unpleasantness of the past hour drifted away.

She glanced in the direction her husband had disappeared, recalling Grandmother Bitsy's words. She had feared the potential absence of her husband, but now her grandmother's words gave her comfort. Perhaps Gracey would stay in the barn with the sheep, and Gwen would be left with—

She peered down at the babe who had taken a great interest in the crocheted loops of Gwen's wrap.

"Felicity." She said the name aloud and looked to Miss Haversham. "And whose babe is this?" She asked the question, hoping she was wrong about her assumption. It wouldn't be unheard of for an earl to take in the child of a poor relation or even a dead one. The possibility that this was her husband's child, that the earl had been married previously, wasn't necessarily the only explanation.

And why did Gwen feel an odd pang at the notion that her husband might have been married before?

However, it was as though she'd slapped the poor woman before her. Her jaw dropped, and her eyebrows shot up. Gwen felt that single tether she clung to wobble.

Shaking her head, Miss Haversham said, "I'm sorry, my lady. It's—"

But she was stopped from saying anything else when an exclamation rang from somewhere behind the stricken woman. "Dear heavens, my lady. What are you doing here?"

Gwen looked up sharply at the words, momentarily forgetting the shocked look on Miss Haversham's face, to find another woman at the top of the steps leading up to the front door. The door was open now, and it framed a woman of late middling years with small, round eyes and a button nose, her face rimmed by even, tight graying curls, her hands grasped tightly around a chatelain of keys.

Finally. Someone in charge.

Gwen hefted Felicity into her arms and began to climb the steps, taking in the edifice before her as she did so. The manor house was comprised entirely of stone in grays, browns, and some reds, and she was surprised by the clean lines and sparse ornamentation, realizing she had expected a grander estate for someone with a commanding personality like that of her husband. She pushed that thought aside as she took in the front facade with a single door and five windows stacked. There were no wings visible from this angle, and Gwen thought the house must extend to the rear.

She nodded when she reached the woman on the top step. "You must be the housekeeper. I am Lady Gwen Bounds." She stopped. "I'm sorry. I suppose it's Bender now. Lady Gwen Bender, the new Countess of Gracey."

The housekeeper's eyes darted between Gwen and Miss Haversham who was now coming up the stairs, her skirts balled into agitated fists. "I'm so very sorry, my lady. I wasn't informed—"

Gwen cut off the woman with a shake of her head. "It's quite all right, Mrs...." She let her voice trail off.

The woman seemed to come to her senses because she straightened then, her shoulders going back and her chin going out, which only accentuated her button nose. Gwen realized this woman would have been pretty once before hard work and age had made their mark on her face, but the smile lines bracketing her mouth were deep, and somehow Gwen knew she would like her.

"Mrs. Rehnquist, my lady," she said with a bow. "His lordship did not inform the staff of your arrival. I promise in future—"

Again, Gwen cut her off. "I have learned of the earl's preference for brevity, Mrs. Rehnquist. No apology is necessary. I am afraid, however, I am in need of something far more delicate."

The woman's eyes snapped together in concern. "Anything, my lady." She gestured to the front hall where a pair of footmen waited. "I'll have your trunks brought in immediately. Your coachman can take the horses to the stable for the night. He's welcome at our table, of course."

"That's very kind of you, Mrs. Rehnquist, but I'm afraid it's something more urgent than that." She held up Felicity. "I need you to tell me whose baby this is. I wish only for you to relay the facts, Mrs. Rehnquist. I would never ask you to report on your employer." Here she gestured to the baby. "Am I to understand that this is Lord Gracey's daughter and that the earl was married previously?"

The housekeeper stood paralyzed on the stoop, her eyes darting frantically to Miss Haversham and back. Gwen knew she was towing a fine line. A loyal servant would never gossip about her employer, even to said employer's new wife. It was why she'd worded her inquiry as she had.

The woman swallowed, her button nose bouncing slightly with the effort. "Yes." The single word was soft and timid, and that single tether that had snapped into place at the familiar sensation of holding a baby nearly split in two.

But Gwen held to it fiercely, the yawning sense of being utterly lost looming over her. Babies she understood. Babies she knew. Running a house? She'd been trained for it as it would be expected of her to aid her mother in household matters one day. Perhaps if she thought of the things that were familiar to her, she wouldn't feel so overwhelmed by the things that were not.

"So Lord Gracey intended to find a wife to raise his child and care for his home." It wasn't a question. Gracey had told her as much in the carriage only she'd been too blinded with hope to see the truth of it.

She glanced at Felicity. Well, he had told her part of it.

It was funny and a bit sad then, the twinge of regret she felt in her chest as she came to understand what it was she was really doing here. Even though she knew her place in society, she had hoped this would be a fresh start or at least the start of something different and unexpected. But it wasn't to be. She'd been sold to be the caretaker of a baby, a manor, and a title. Nothing more. Instead of being her mother's companion, she would be steward to a baby and a house. It would need to be enough.

"Your ladyship, I..." The housekeeper's voice faltered.

Gwen waved her off and stepped into the manor house. "It wasn't a question, Mrs. Rehnquist. You're safe from any further implication." She swept her gaze upward at the two-story foyer with its wrap-around wooden staircase. It was beautifully if quietly appointed, as though the home had been designed by a man without a wife. Still, it was opulent, safe, and warm.

She turned about to face Mrs. Rehnquist and Miss Haversham standing just inside the front door. "Mrs. Rehnquist, I've been traveling for four days. I should like a hot meal and an even hotter bath. I will go with Miss Haversham to the nursery to see to Felicity, and then I should ask that you come and fetch me when my room is ready." She turned to the nanny. "Miss Haversham, as I am unfamiliar with the house, I should like your assistance in finding the nursery."

This was met with relieved expressions from both servants, which was both comforting and concerning. They seemed more at ease with direct orders than with kindness, and after her brief introduction to her husband, she wasn't at all surprised by this.

Miss Haversham gestured to the stairs. "After you, my lady."

The nursery was on the top floor of the manor house. It was spacious and bright with cushioned benches nestled into the dormer windows. Bookshelves crammed with leather spines and overflowing with sketching paper lined two walls while a fireplace took up a third. A door in the far corner likely led off to the nanny's rooms. And the entirety of it looked as though the ram she had met earlier had had its way with the place.

She turned a questioning glance to Miss Haversham.

The woman cowered, her cheeks flaming. "I'm a governess, my lady, not a nanny. I'm not skilled in caring for babies." The woman's shoulders drooped as though a great weight had been lifted from them.

Governess? Gwen eyed the baby in her arms. Just what was happening here at Scarcroft Manor?

Gwen took pity on her. "It must have been quite a shock

to arrive here and realize you were expected to care for a baby."

Miss Haversham smiled then, a soft gesture, that had Gwen realizing the woman was likely feeling as untethered as Gwen was.

She set Felicity in the basket by a toppled-over stack of books and began unfastening the child's gown.

"Miss Haversham, I suppose you'd better tell me what's going on here. I know Mrs. Rehnquist must abide by certain rules, but as a governess, you exist somewhere in between where the rules are far more flexible." She looked up from her work to pin Miss Haversham with a knowing gaze. "So perhaps you can tell me what it is I should know to be better prepared to be mistress of this manor."

The woman stood perfectly still for a moment, but Gwen could see when she came to some conclusion. Something warm and understanding passed over her features, and then she was moving. She went to a cupboard beside the fireplace and retrieved a clean nappy and a different gown.

She knelt beside Gwen and offered her the clean garments. "It's Rachel actually, my lady." Her smile now was friendly, and Gwen could see the confident woman that was likely under the frazzled and overwhelmed temporary nanny.

She returned the woman's smile. "It's Gwen. You mustn't call me *my lady*. I have the sense that in different circumstances we might be friends." She was busy pulling the soiled nappy out from under a squirming Felicity, so she didn't notice the other woman's look of surprise until it had almost faded.

Gwen handed her the full nappy, making the woman laugh. "I suppose you're right. Gwen." She spoke the name carefully, and Gwen wondered how long the woman had been at Scarcroft without a true ally as she hovered in the odd space between servant and gentlewoman.

They worked in silence for a few minutes, Gwen holding Felicity up so Rachel could give her a proper washing from the bowl and pitcher kept in the corner. The baby squealed when the cool water touched her skin but was easily distracted when Gwen blew softly in her face. Soon the babe was giggling, her pudgy hands squeezing Gwen's cheeks.

The tears came hot and fresh, stinging Gwen's eyes, and she pressed her face into the baby's soft tummy to hide them. Her heart yearned for this baby. She hadn't even known the child had existed that morning, and yet the feeling was real and vibrant. How could she feel such a strong rush of emotion for a baby that wasn't hers?

Because she had always wanted a baby, and she had learned to cradle that longing deep within her where no one would see it. Picking up her head to look into Felicity's innocent face, Gwen knew.

This was her second chance. Not the dashing husband who would overlook her scars and sweep her off her feet. This motherless child needed her, and Gwen had been put there to help. It was so cruelly simple.

She glanced in Rachel's direction as the woman put aside the dirty things. Maybe there were other signs of her second chance if only she knew where to look for them. Perhaps soon she would no longer feel she had squandered the life she'd been given.

She stood, a clean and fresh Felicity in her arms. Rocking the baby gently on her hip, she turned to Rachel. "Am I to understand the earl's first wife passed on recently?"

It felt cold asking the question so bluntly, but it was a common enough occurrence for a man to take a second wife when the first had passed, especially if children were involved. A man was expected to attend to the business matters of the estate and not the complexities of the nursery.

Rachel turned only her head as she poured fresh water into the bowl to wash her hands. "I understand she died shortly after giving birth, I'm afraid."

Gwen studied Felicity's round cheeks, her perfectly formed ears and little nose, feeling the injustice of such a thing. To carry a babe for nine months only to never truly meet her. To have one's life ripped away like that. It hit far too close to home.

She swallowed. "And the boy's clothing?"

Rachel wiped her hands on a clean towel before taking Felicity so Gwen could wash her own hands. "I'm not sure exactly, but I've heard the servants whisper as one does in a house like this. They say the countess was convinced it was going to be a boy and had all the clothing made with such an expectation."

"And the earl didn't think to have it remedied in the past two years?"

Rachel looked at her swiftly. "How do you know it's been almost two years?"

Gwen dried her hands and took the baby back. "When you've had as many sisters as I have, you start to be able to tell these things from sight."

Rachel shook her head. "I truly am not suited to be a nanny."

Gwen laughed. "I hope you'll stay long enough to help me settle though, and then I would be happy to write you a reference for your next post."

Rachel laughed now. "I hope it doesn't take me back to a nursery. I'm far better in a schoolroom."

This made Gwen pause. "How is it that you did end up here?"

Rachel's expression dimmed. "I answered an advert for a

governess. It wasn't until I got here that I learned the truth of the situation. It seemed the housekeeper's only choice was to advertise the posting as such. The household had already gone through the eligible nannies in the county. Gertrude, the upstairs maid, says they've had eight nannies in the past year alone."

Gwen nearly dropped Felicity. "Eight nannies come and gone? But…why?"

Rachel looked her dead in the eye. "Because of the earl, of course."

* * *

HE'D DISAPPOINTED HER.

When they'd stood in front of the vicar, he'd seen the disappointment register on her face, and it hurt him. He didn't wish to feel anything for the woman or because of the woman, and yet somehow he couldn't prevent it. The mere sight of her *did* things to him.

He quickened his pace if only to increase the distance between them. He walked briskly in the direction of the lambing barn, hoping some sweaty, hard work would settle his roiling emotions.

It wasn't supposed to be like this. He had executed a marriage contract with a respected member of the *ton*, and in return, he should have received a wife for whom he felt nothing but who fulfilled the expectations of a countess, and a dowry that would fund the expansion of the flock. That was all.

Well, perhaps not all, but he would worry about the rest of it at a later time. A *much* later time.

But those scars.

His step faltered as he recalled the deep pits slashing her cheeks. What had she endured? What had she overcome? He remembered the way her chin had gone up and wondered just what it was he might find in his new wife.

He had hardly stepped through the door of his office in the barn when Hatrick confronted him.

"My lord, are you well?" Hatrick said from his table in the corner where he had clearly been going through the stock ledger before Logan had entered the room.

It took a moment for Logan to sort through his thoughts to understand of what the steward spoke. He wasn't sure it was possible, but somehow his entire life had turned upside down in the span of less than an hour. He had almost forgotten his near death at the hands—or horns, rather—of a stampeding ram.

He tugged at the front of his waistcoat, his fingers absently finding his watch. "Yes, quite well, Hatrick. Has the ram been secured?"

"Yes, my lord. We put him in the east wing of the horse barn. Piven is letting us use the old stallion's stall for now. It seemed the best option while we have the pen repaired."

Logan pushed at his sleeves as he took a seat at his desk. "See that the pen is reinforced this time. I don't want the ram escaping again."

"Of course, my lord," Hatrick said.

There was a heavy beat of silence then as Logan rummaged through the post that he'd left on his desk the previous day, letters from fellow farmers, the quarterly review from the Agrarian Society of Yorkshire, and a message from his solicitor in London informing Logan he awaited confirmation of his marriage to see the rest of the contract carried out.

His fingers curled around the solicitor's note, the events of the past hour roiling through his mind like a swollen stream in spring. It was a moment before he realized Hatrick was staring at him.

He met the steward's gaze, and as was his character, the man did not look away. If anything he turned further in his ladder-back chair to face Logan.

"My lord, am I to understand you've just been wed?" Hatrick asked.

Logan set down the solicitor's note. "Yes. I've just seen to the matter in the village."

Hatrick hesitated for only a moment before standing and approaching Logan's desk. The office in the barn was small, and the idea that it was used for something so robust as managing the intricacies of the flock seemed absurd if one were an outsider observing the room for the first time. Bags of feed they were testing were stacked in one corner while the cot Logan used to snatch some hours of sleep during the height of the lambing season was shoved in the opposite corner under the single window in the room that was thick with dust, letting in very little light. Beside Hatrick's table were the crates of old stock ledgers and above it on the wall were pegs filled with forgotten tack when previous earls had focused on horse breeding instead of sheep.

Logan loved every bit of the mess because he'd spent countless hours in this room with his father when he was a child and even now Logan thought he could still smell his father's pipe there.

"It's just that when I married my Sue, it was customary for the groom to spend the rest of one's wedding day with the bride. I had thought not to see you in the barns again today." Hatrick played with one of the knotted strings on the index finger of his left hand.

"Why would I spend the day with her? Mrs. Rehnquist and Miss Haversham will see to her."

Hatrick blinked. "If I may speak freely, my lord, you make it sound as though you've married a sow instead of a lady."

Hatrick tugged at the scarf at his neck. "And from the little I've seen of her, the lady is no sow."

An image of Gwendolyn standing on the drive by the open carriage door flashed in his mind then, the sun highlighting every one of her devastating curves.

Logan frowned at his thoughts more than his steward's words. "No, she is not."

Hatrick stood in front of his desk then, and he leaned forward, knuckles against the wood. "My lord, I've worked for you for a very long time and your father an even longer time. I hope you will take my words as I intend them. Not as criticism but as something which might aid you in your future relations with your new wife."

Logan's body tensed, his hands going to the arms of his chair as if bracing himself. "What is that?"

Hatrick's mouth screwed up on one side in some kind of commentary Logan couldn't understand, but then the man said, "I hope you will only keep in mind that your new wife is not Lady Catherine. It's a terrible thing to treat a person in a manner deserving of someone else."

Logan had nothing to say to this as he knew perfectly well Gwendolyn was not his first wife. Why on earth would he treat her as such? He recalled her behavior in the carriage, the way her chin rose with every one of his statements, and wondered if he shouldn't treat her with greater care than he had Catherine as she was clearly made differently than his first wife.

Logan pushed to his feet. "Thank you for your counsel, Hatrick. I shall keep it in mind. I think we should update the stock ledger with the lambs born last night."

He didn't wait for his steward. He exited the office in the direction of the lambing pens, hoping work would eradicate thoughts of his wife from his mind.

He spent the next several hours there with Hatrick and

his stock ledger. Triplets had been born the previous night, and Logan was concerned for the mother after birthing such a large litter. While it was good for his goals with the flock, the ewe's health was paramount to any profit margin, and he wanted to see she was comfortable and strong and caring for her lambs. He found her on her feet in her pen, her head all but disappearing into the bucket of feed in the corner while her lambs nursed, and some of the tension eased from his shoulders.

God willing, the flock would grow this spring. After several years of setbacks, he may even see the flock increase in numbers by midsummer, and with Lady Gwendolyn's dowry, he would have the resources to expand the barns and perhaps acquire one or two well-trained sheepdogs.

If only his father were here to see it. It would be the next generation of Benders who would see the flock truly flourish but so much had been done. So much had been *repaired*.

He pushed the lure of self-recriminations away and spent the evening hours back in his office in the barn with Hatrick going over the progression of the lambing, the number of lambs predicted, and the rotation of rams within the herd. The fence had been repaired around the ram who had tried to impale the new Countess of Gracey, and accommodations for other borrowed rams were being made a priority.

He wasn't sure who was more startled when Mrs. Rehnquist appeared shortly before seven in the evening, he or Hatrick. The sun had long set, but the sky was the pink and orange of twilight through the single, dirt-smudged window when the housekeeper appeared in the door of his office. Blissfully it wasn't until he laid eyes on the housekeeper that he recalled he had acquired a wife that day.

"Ma'am," Hatrick said as he half stood in greeting, clearly unsure and unsettled at the arrival of the housekeeper.

"Mrs. Rehnquist," Logan said. Whatever the woman had

to say, it was best she be out with it. Typically the house-keeper sent a footman with any questions, and the presence of Mrs. Rehnquist herself suggested something dire or something of which she disapproved. He had a niggling feeling it was the latter.

"My lord," she said with a nod. "Will you be joining Lady Gracey in the manor house for supper?"

Ah, it *was* the latter indeed.

"I'm afraid not, Mrs. Rehnquist. Matters here require my attention, and I am unable to break away." And he didn't wish to see his bride's deep brown eyes warmed by candlelight.

Mrs. Rehnquist shared a look with Hatrick then that Logan was unable to grasp.

"Very good, my lord," she said. "Hatrick," she added to the steward with a nod and left.

The woman's brevity and ability to get right to the point was the reason Logan had hired her, but now he felt chafed by such a gruff dismissal. He shook his head and went back to the ledgers.

It was full dark when he let himself into the manor house through the kitchen. He raided the larder as was his custom, selecting a hunk of ham, bread, and some cheese, which he ate as he made his way above stairs. He wiped his hands free of crumbs before slipping into the nursery.

He knew exactly which floorboards squeaked, the precise location of every piece of furniture in the room, and the direct route to Felicity's bassinet in the dormer window to the left. He knew because he'd crept into the nursery like a thief every night since his daughter's birth.

Tonight moonlight fell through the window, illuminating his daughter in ethereal light, and he wanted nothing more than to reach out and stroke the chubby curve of one cheek. But he knew it would wake her, and shattering her peaceful sleep would break his heart. So he sat in the chair he had placed by her bassinet that night so long ago now and reclined, propping one foot over the opposite knee.

"A lamb was born today, Felicity," he whispered, his words hardly more than breath.

The babe didn't stir. Her breathing remained even and deep, her face relaxed.

"Hatrick is calling her Pudgy because she's a squirmy little thing. A lot like you were when you came out." He laughed softly at the memory, feeling the weight of the past two years press against him. He drew a deeper breath and went on. "I found you a mother today, darling. I promised I would, and I did. I know she will be good to you." He didn't realize he meant the words until they were out.

For a moment in the carriage earlier that day, he had worried his bride was dim-witted, but when she hadn't cowered at his shortness, when she had stood toe to toe with him in front of the vicar, he had known she was made of sterner stuff than he had first believed. She must have been to survive smallpox.

But as his thoughts wandered he couldn't help but remember Hatrick's warning, and he wondered what the steward had meant. Catherine still haunted every decision Logan made, but surely she wouldn't influence how he treated his new wife.

He watched Felicity sleep for several more moments before lying his head back against the hard wooden chair and closing his eyes. Sleep didn't come for some time, but when it did, he welcomed the completeness of the dark.

CHAPTER 4

*R*achel's words reverberated in Gwen's mind long after Mrs. Rehnquist had come to bring her to her rooms.

Eight nannies in one year was surely impossible, but with her limited knowledge of the man that was now her husband, it was too easy for Gwen to manufacture every kind of reason for the nannies to have quit the position.

Her heart broke for little Felicity. She had spent a couple of hours that afternoon with the baby and found her to have a naturally happy and inquisitive disposition. Gwen had sat on the floor while Felicity explored tower after tower of blocks, pawed through any number of books, her wrinkly hands tracing the illustrations as she made sounds of approval over the depictions of cows and rabbits and even honeybees.

Felicity was more than capable of pulling herself up as she did several times with the help of a chair or a cabinet, using the piece of furniture to steady herself. Gwen was surprised how her heart leapt at the sight of it the first time, of Felicity's tenacity when she wobbled, at the determination in her little face to one day take a step.

Gwen tried to remember when her sisters had each taken their first steps, and she worried Felicity may be behind a bit. If she was truly nearing two years of age, she should be walking already and not merely pulling herself up. Perhaps it was the inconsistent care that was holding her back.

It was this that plagued Gwen's thoughts as she wallowed in the hot bath Mrs. Rehnquist had had brought up for her, and she worried her lip now, wondering what could be done.

A real nanny must be secured, of course, but she knew it would take more than that. Felicity needed direct and consistent care to reach the milestones she should be reaching at her age. And poor Rachel.

When Felicity had pulled herself up for the first time, Gwen was sure the poor woman would have a fit of the vapors as if the child were attempting to climb a tree instead of reaching for the doll on the shelf. Clearly the governess was suited for much older children, and it would be better to let her secure a more suitable post.

She was just toweling her hair dry when she heard a brief knock, and the door to the countess's rooms opened. A woman appearing a few years older than Gwen stepped in and gave a deep curtsy.

"I'm Jean Kent, my lady," she said as she rose from the curtsy. "Mrs. Rehnquist has assigned me to be your maid. She noticed you didn't arrive with one. I hope Mrs. Rehnquist's decision isn't too forward."

The woman was perhaps a little more than thirty, but her face was marked by deep lines showing just how difficult those thirty years had been. Her skin was clear though, and her dark hair was pinned neatly at the nape of her neck. Her apron was pristine and starched, and her carriage was commanding. Gwen liked her immediately.

"Kent then, I suppose, if you're to be the maid to the lady of the house," Gwen said as she continued to towel her hair. "I've never had a maid of my own. My sisters and I always shared a maid. Do you have sisters, Kent?" Gwen discarded the towel with the others she had used and turned in time to see a small smile fleeting across Kent's face.

"I have four sisters, my lady," she said.

"Then you have my condolences," Gwen returned, and Kent laughed, a hand going to her mouth as though to stop the sound. "I do beg your pardon, my lady. That was—"

"Honest," Gwen said and made her way over to where her trunks had been left. "I think we should start here, Kent. I've been traveling for too long, and it would be lovely to wear something other than my traveling gown."

Kent nodded, her smile steadier. "Yes, my lady," she said and bent to work.

Together they unearthed Gwen's gowns and hung them to air in the countess's dressing room. Much like the rest of the house, the countess's rooms were fine and plush if the attention to detail was sparse, and she couldn't shake the feeling the whole house seemed to be lacking something.

It was while Gwen was unpacking her personal effects— the few books she had brought with her and her brushes and such—that she thought to ask Kent, "Did you grow up here?"

Kent sorted through Gwen's underthings, placing them on the shelves of the armoire on the other side of the bed. "Oh yes, my lady. Grew up in the village. My father owns the apothecary there."

"It must have been quite a boon for you to get a position here at Scarcroft Manor."

Kent glanced in her direction, a curious expression on her face. "That it was, my lady, and I'll be forever grateful. Papa has already apprenticed my brother and one of my brothers-in-law. He couldn't take on another child. He cried the day I told him I got a post here."

Gwen smiled. "Then I'm sure he'll be delighted to hear you've been promoted to lady's maid."

The woman stalled in putting away Gwen's crinolines, her eyes going soft as if in wonder. "Yes, he will, my lady."

"Kent, do you happen to know anything about who built Scarcroft Manor? I find its design tasteful, but it lacks the usual ornamentation found in country homes."

Kent bent to pull a stack of stockings from the trunk at her feet. "That's likely because it was built by a gentleman who made his fortune smuggling brandy in the last century."

Gwen had been placing her brushes on the dressing table, but she turned at this. "Truly?"

Kent's smile shone. "Oh yes, my lady. It's told he gave his best stock to the king himself, and that's what got him the title of baron." She wrinkled her nose. "But he wasn't seen as truly a member of the peerage, having bought his title and all, and he thought if he could catch himself a refined wife, he would be accepted into society."

Gwen sank onto the dressing table stool, enraptured by the maid's tale. "And so what happened?"

Kent gestured to the room with the piles of stockings in her hands. "He built Scarcroft Manor in the hopes of attracting a refined lady." She shook her head. "But he lost everything when another smuggler pushed him out of his route. He was forced to sell the manor house to the then Earl of Gracey to cover his debts." She shook her head. "Such a terrible story, isn't it? I'm not sure I feel sorry for the baron. How obtuse to think it would only take a nice house such as this one to win a bride." Kent stopped abruptly, her hands and their piles of stockings stilling in midair. "Begging your pardon, my lady," Kent murmured, and even from where she sat, Gwen saw the twin spots of color on the maid's cheeks.

Gwen laughed. "No need to beg my pardon, Kent. I'm afraid I didn't even know about the manor house when I agreed to marry the earl. It seems I'm a sight worse than any of the baron's prospective brides."

Kent's smile was quick, but her eyes were far away as if she were thinking of something else when she said, "I'm glad you agreed to marry him, my lady. I think this place needs you."

Gwen wished to ask her what she meant, but the maid turned back to the armoire and the moment was lost.

Gwen knew she should take the few hours before supper to write Eloise and Annie, but she still wasn't sure what to say. Instead she found her eyes traveling to the lavender and green gown Kent had hung on the front of the armoire for Gwen to wear to supper.

Her mother had insisted on it at the start of the season, and staring at it now, Gwen felt a tightening low in her stomach. Would her husband join her for supper? Would it be another battle? Must she remain always on her toes should he choose to question her as he had earlier? She was far too tired for such a thing and wondered if she could claim a headache and have a tray sent up to her rooms instead.

But even as the thought entered her mind, her eyes drifted to the four-poster bed that dominated one side of the bedchamber. It was hung with emerald curtains and festooned in pillows and quilts in hues that complemented the bed curtains. It looked terribly inviting, and she wished for nothing more than to sink within its depths and fall directly to sleep.

Except tonight was her wedding night, and her mother had instructed her that Gracey might have certain expectations of her. Her hand involuntarily went to her collarbone, exposed at the edge of her dressing gown, and traced the familiar pitted scars there. She swallowed and looked away.

Kent emerged from the dressing room then, Gwen's traveling boots in hand. "I shall see to these, my lady, and when I return we can dress you for dinner," the maid said and left.

With no other excuses, Gwen found her traveling desk among the things placed on the rosewood table under the window, and soon she was penning a letter to Eloise. Much as she had expected, she couldn't think of what to tell her sister.

That in coming to Scarcroft Manor she had not only found a husband but a baby as well? She had almost written a *daughter*, but somehow she couldn't quite pen the word. How could she claim Felicity as a daughter after only a couple of hours? Gwen had only been married to the child's father for less than a day. It seemed impossible that they should be some kind of family.

Her heart squeezed, and she set down her pen at this. In leaving her family in London, every connection to the future she had thought she would have had been severed, but that was the point really. She was supposed to find a new start here in Yorkshire, the very thing she had always sought. But instead she found herself married to the Earl of Gracey, a man so cold and unfeeling, and she felt more lost than ever.

No, the earl was not unfeeling. There was that one moment during the ceremony when his face had changed, and she wondered about it now. She shook her head. She mustn't look for rainbows where there were only clouds.

She wasn't sure how long she sat there, but it was long after the sun had set, and the sky had turned pink. Mrs. Rehnquist had brought up a tea tray earlier with the bath, and Gwen sipped at the last of the tea that had now grown cold, her gaze lingering beyond the window at the green of the Yorkshire hills, spotted with little white dots she knew were sheep. While she was tired from traveling, it was a different kind of calmness that washed over her then, and she sat, watching the sky turn from pinks and oranges to purples and deep blues, the letter to Eloise unfinished before her.

The knock at the door startled her, and Kent came in, Gwen's traveling boots, now perfectly polished, in her hands. It was time to dress for dinner then, and Gwen was glad for the distraction as her thoughts had grown far too wandering for her tastes.

As she had yet to have a tour of the manor house, Kent escorted Gwen to the dining room before retiring below stairs until Gwen would require her before bed.

The dining room was much like the rest of the house. A work of simple design with its plain wainscoting along the bottom half of the walls and unadorned cornices at the corners of the ceiling. A fireplace took up one end of the room while the center was filled with a yawning table that could certainly seat more than fifty people. The sight of it stopped her dead as she recalled her mother's second instruction that she would be expected to host a dinner party of such a size to introduce herself as the new Countess of Gracey. She would think about that tomorrow.

She turned to the head of the table, and her stomach sank. Only one place was set for dinner.

It was a moment before she realized she had been hoping her husband would join her for the evening meal, but perhaps Grandmother Bitsy was correct. Sheep farmers never did leave their flocks.

She didn't wait for a footman to pull out her chair. She was ravenous even after the small plate Mrs. Rehnquist had sent up, and she wasn't about to wait on ceremony.

She was not surprised to find dinner was a quality affair, exceeding any expectations she had for the meal but aligning with what she had come to expect from Scarcroft. Excellent management and incredible skill in the staff. There was a white soup to start followed by partridge pies, the meat so fresh it must have come from Scarcroft's reserves. There was a cheese course then and the meal was finished with a Savoy cake piled high with succulent berries. It was more of a feast than a dinner, and she had the sudden urge to meet the cook.

She made a mental note to meet with Mrs. Rehnquist in the morning. If Gwen's assistance in the running of the house could be kept to a minimum as the skill of the staff would suggest, she would be freed to dedicate more time to Felicity's care.

She left dinner feeling resolved, and she made her way up to her rooms to find Kent already turning down the bedclothes. Shedding her dinner gown, Gwen gleefully accepted her nightrail and allowed Kent to take down her hair and braid it. The maid added coal to the fire before bidding Gwen good night, and then, finally, the new Countess of Gracey was alone.

She thought she would fall asleep the moment her head struck the pillow. As her husband had not been at dinner, she no longer worried he would come to her bedchamber that night, and she wanted nothing more than to sleep. Her husband's actions had clearly indicated he intended to keep their relations at a minimum, and the worry over her wedding night slipped easily from her mind.

Sleep, however, did not come.

Her thoughts were full and myriad, and she found herself studying the canopy over the bed, wondering where she would begin with Felicity. There really was much to be done for the child, not the least of which was to replace her bassinet with a proper crib and secure a new wardrobe. While some mothers chose not to differentiate gender when it came to children's clothing, it was usually that the boys tended to wear girl's clothing. It wouldn't do for Felicity to wear boy's clothing. Something must be done about it.

The girl would need schooling, of course, but formal lessons would come later. Gwen must ascertain what developmental milestones the child was missing and work to help her achieve them. She had done much the same with Eloise and Annie before the smallpox. It would hardly be any different with Felicity.

Then why, when she thought of conducting the same work with Felicity, did Gwen feel such a warmness near her heart?

Somewhere a clock struck the hour, and Gwen realized it was midnight. She'd been lying there for hours, and sleep was nowhere to be found. Tossing back the covers, she fetched her slippers and dressing gown and made her way out into the corridor.

There was a full moon, and it lit her way along the hall through the expansive windows that marked one side. She wasn't sure why, but she made certain not to make a noise. If Scarcroft was built like other noble houses, the earl's rooms must be near the countess's, and it wouldn't do to wake the earl.

She reached the door of the nursery only to find it open. Her heart thudded once in fear, and she plunged forward only to catch herself against the jamb, abruptly stopping her forward movement.

The Earl of Gracey was asleep in the hardback wooden chair under the window, one hand resting on the carved wooden rail of his daughter's bassinet. Her breath caught in her throat at the sight of his face, relaxed in sleep and bathed in moonlight, that one protective hand reaching for his daughter even in sleep. She couldn't name the feelings that rose up in her then, the ones that congealed in her throat and threatened to choke her, but they were many and deep and painful, and she turned away, but it was too late.

The picture of father and daughter was already seared on her mind.

* * *

LOGAN MADE his way to the lambing barns the next morning confident that no one would stop him with news about Miss Haversham.

He had woken sometime in the night as he usually did, his rest interrupted by the onset of soreness sleeping in a wooden chair could cause. He was forced to walk by the countess's rooms on the way to his, and he found his feet stalling, his gaze moving to her door, wondering if his new bride slept peacefully within.

Shirking the thought, he'd made his way to his own bed to spend the remaining hours of the night in a fitful sleep. He hadn't slept well in years, and spending part of the night in the chair next to his daughter's bassinet relieved some of the pressure of wondering if sleep would come.

He'd finally given up on sleep for the night when the sky had shown its first hints of day in streaks of orange and yellow and peach. He'd left his rooms knowing a wedding would not interrupt his efforts, and he could make the day a productive one.

The fact that he was now married—*again*—kept sneaking up on him as he'd been happy to see the deed done and forget about it. But the world kept reminding him that he had a wife now. Between Hatrick and Mrs. Rehnquist, he was hardly likely to forget it.

This was perfectly fine in his mind. As with anything new, it would only require a period of adjustment, and his wife would become like any other thing. A part of his life but not something which required his attention.

A tiny whisper had passed through the far recesses of his brain at this dismissive thought, but he ignored it even as he felt the clench of urgency deep inside of him. He would spend some time in the flock. It always helped to distract him from more concerning matters when he focused on what he could control.

After dressing, he retreated through the kitchen, snatching some still warm bread and a small block of cheese as he made his way out the door.

"My lord!" Cook called after him, and he picked up his pace. "My lord, you really must eat something more nourishing."

He escaped without further interference. He knew his midnight raids of the larder were likely not to go unnoticed. The caliber of servants he hired would never allow such a thing, and this was even likelier to have reached the notice of Mrs. Rehnquist. Some day she would confront him about his habits as she could hardly be expected to run a household if he never kept to a predictable schedule. Like everything else, he'd worry about that later.

The flock was scattered on the western hills, the grassy slopes rising up to a tree-lined ridge that bordered that edge of the property before slipping onto Bartlesfield's lands. He trekked up the rocky hillside, picking his way carefully through the few scrubby trees to the plush grasses where the sheep had already taken up residence for their morning grazing.

The flock was kept in the barns at night, but the farmhands had strict orders to release the sheep at first light so they could spend much of the day partaking of the lush greens that would give them the nutrients they needed to produce fine wool. He scouted out a couple of ewes that had been of concern, one with an infection in one hoof from having stepped on a nail that had become lodged in the laminae and another who had been showing discharge from her ear, likely caused from an irritation from the environment, pollen or some kind of grass she had encountered.

The sun was just cresting, the morning rays splashing the hillside of sheep in a bath of vibrant orange when he settled down at the base of one of the scrub trees to have his breakfast. He let the cool morning breeze playing with the brim of his hat, the sounds of sheep rustling, and the still warm bread bolster him.

It was much like the mornings he had spent on the hillside with his father, and he missed the man all over again. His hand absently went to the pocket where his watch lay, but he resisted the urge to take it out and read the inscription there, the one his father had dedicated to him. The urge grew less persistent with every passing day, and he wondered if one day it would disappear entirely.

The sun had fully risen by the time he climbed down the hill and found Hatrick waiting for him. It would be another busy day of lambing, and he knew soon he would be forced to curtail his nightly visits to Felicity to sleep in the barn with the ewes. Just as it did every year since her birth, he felt the odd pang of guilt at leaving her even though he was fairly certain she didn't even know he was there. Still. The idea of not being with her for those few hours made him despair.

He finished with Hatrick and made his way across the park in the direction of the house to where a team of builders was constructing the new paddocks. After yesterday's incident with the ram, he wanted an update on their progress and to see if the building timeline could be hurried along.

Except when he rounded the rear of the house, he spotted his daughter, and fear turned his heart to ice in his chest. It was the kind of all-pervasive fear he had only felt one other time in his life and had hoped never to feel again. But in that moment, seeing Felicity, exposed and vulnerable in what used to be the gardens of the manor house, that fear came back with a swift cunning that stole his breath.

Felicity should not have been out of doors, and she most certainly should not have been attached to his new wife.

"Gwendolyn." He was surprised to find his wife's name coming out with such shock instead of the scolding he had intended. "What is the child doing out here?"

She didn't answer him immediately, her lips pursing ever so slightly, and in that hesitation, his eyes dropped without his say-so, taking in the simple gown she wore with a hideous bunch of lace at the throat.

"I'm afraid not very much," she finally muttered. She gestured behind her. "What happened to the gardens?"

He glanced in the direction of her outstretched arm only to move his gaze back to her face. "I'm having ram paddocks installed."

This was quite obvious as the builders had already laid the foundations and were even now raising the walls of the structure. Seeing the construction hardened the fear in his chest, and he found himself reaching for his daughter like he hadn't in the nearly two years since she'd been born, but a noise from his wife had him stopping.

The sound Gwendolyn released might only be described as frustration, and it was then that he took in the rest of her. Her bonnet lay against her back, the bow about her neck nearly undone, her hair frizzy and loose, several strands falling about her face. She wore a plain frock of indeterminate color, somewhere between gray and brown, and she'd unbuttoned her pelisse. He noted the slight sheen of perspiration on her forehead and wondered what kind of exercise she had been engaging in before he found her and why she should choose to wear such a ridiculous garment when such exercise would have called for a more suitable walking dress.

She had been holding Felicity by the hands as the baby wobbled on unsteady legs but now she bent and picked the girl up, placing her smoothly on her hip. He took an involuntary step back, blinking in the direction of the builders, wondering if he'd gotten something in his eye.

"It is obvious construction is taking place, my lord." He turned back at her careful tone to find her jaw nearly frozen shut. "My question is why are they building in the middle of the gardens?"

He looked again at the builders and realized what she was seeing. "Ah, I understand now." He flung a hand at the place where several earls ago a sprawling rose garden had been installed. "The land was not being used efficiently, so I had the gardeners tear up the rose gardens so ram paddocks could be built." He nodded, sure she would understand, only to find a look of horror on her features when he turned back to her.

"You had them rip out a rose garden? For ram paddocks?"

He studied her, not entirely believing her proclamation of sanity from the day before in the carriage. Had Lord Stoke Bruerne swindled him by selling him a dim-witted bride?

"Of course, I did. It's the most logical location to house the rams." He pointed back in the direction he had come where the lambing pens, barns, and gates into the pastures were at the rear of the manor house. "The rams need only be moved a handful of yards into the pasture, but they're far enough away from the lambing ewes not to disturb them. It makes perfect sense."

As his wife's expression remained unchanged, he doubted she saw as much. When she didn't reply, he found himself watching her eyes for longer than he probably should have and in them, he saw the same disbelieving wonder he had noticed when they stood in front of the vicar, and much as it had the day before, it struck a sorrowful note inside of him he didn't much care for.

He cleared his throat. "It really is the best for the operation of the flock."

"Of course," his wife said then, but her voice was so low now, he almost didn't hear it. "Excuse me." She was nearly to the stone steps, all that remained of the original design of the rose garden that led back up to the manor house before he realized she had dismissed him.

He wished to feel relief that the encounter was over, but as he watched her walk away, his daughter on her hip, her back uncomfortably straight as though she were physically trying to hold herself together, he felt the fear inside of him spar with the sense that he had disappointed her.

"Gwendolyn," he called after her. He would set this to rights. It was not he who was in the wrong here. It was her. She turned but didn't retrace her steps, and he saw Felicity toying with the bow holding his wife's bonnet in place, and he realized now why it lay against her back instead of tied neatly atop her head.

Something happened to his heart then, something irreversible. He prided himself on his logic and efficiency, but right then, standing in what used to be the rose garden, he was quite certain his heart had stopped beating.

A flush traveled through his body, starting at his neck and spreading through him until his fingertips went numb, and he forgot how to speak.

It was only when Gwendolyn raised a hand to shield her eyes from the sun that he was shaken from the momentary incapacitation.

He stepped toward her, stopping only when a shadow fell across her face, and he knew she could see him properly now as he blocked the sun from her eyes.

"The baby is not to be outside." He was pleased with how even his voice was. There was no reason to raise one's voice, nor to scold. His wife was new to Scarcroft and likely didn't know the rules. There was no reason to reprimand.

But her eyes went huge at his words, and he felt his stomach turn, sensing a confrontation.

"I'm sorry?" She pinned him with a look he'd only ever seen on a stubborn ram.

He shifted. "The baby." He nodded at Felicity who had now stuck one end of the bonnet ribbon in her mouth. "She's not to be outside."

"Why not?" His wife fired back the question so quickly he didn't have an answer ready, and he found his mouth open without sound emerging.

He couldn't tell her why. Not really. She need only know what was necessary, and what had happened that night to cause this unnamed fear inside of him was not necessary. "Because it is unsafe. As you yourself discovered yesterday, the flock—"

"She's your daughter. Is she not more important than your blasted flock?"

He retreated a step before he understood what he was doing, so surprised by his wife's outburst that his body had taken defensive measures without his mind actively thinking of it.

"You are in the wrong, Gwendolyn." He felt the anger tightening his jaw, but he knew it was directed at himself and not at her, and he hated himself all the more for it.

She stepped toward him, not allowing his retreat. "No, Lord Gracey, you are in the wrong." Her deep brown eyes flared with a heat that he'd never before witnessed. "Are you aware that your daughter cannot walk? She's nearly two years of age. She should be toddling about by now and yet she can't. Where have you been the last two years when you were not properly seeing to your daughter's upbringing? Are your blasted sheep more precious than the development of your only child?"

"You cannot possibly understand the importance of this baby, and I would suggest you not try. You are stepping outside your place, Lady Gracey, and I will not stand for it."

He watched his words register, saw the flicker of heat flare in her eyes, and then…nothing. The light went out of them entirely, replaced by something he could only think might be sad understanding.

He wished to feel satisfaction, but instead, he found himself feeling ever more the cad. What on earth was he saying? Stepping outside her place? He'd never once spoken to a woman with such condescension, not even to Catherine, and he feared his words were in response to the actions of another woman, and Gwendolyn was an innocent victim.

It was in that moment he realized what Hatrick was trying to tell him, and the last of his anger drained from him, the inevitable remorse taking its place.

"Is that so?" she said, her voice surprisingly calm, and suddenly, worry crept over him.

The worry was well placed because what she did next was utterly unexpected. She handed Felicity to him, releasing the baby so he had no choice but to take her. He hadn't held his daughter since the day she was born, and he found her an awkward, squirming bundle in his arms. There was a moment when their eyes met, daughter to father, and he knew she understood just how strange this was. But instead of bursting into tears, her little mouth split into a bubbling grin, and his heart shattered with the simple joy of it. This would not do.

Felicity had grown, a lot, and it took a great deal of strength and concentration to hold her. So much so that he lost track of his wife and found her nearly to the house by the time he came to his senses.

"Lady Gracey!" He did shout now, and he didn't miss the turned heads of the builders as he chased after his wife. "Lady Gracey, what do you think you're doing?"

Felicity screamed in delight at his charge, clapping her hands together as though she thought it a game, but when Gwendolyn turned about, her face told him this was no such game.

"I'm returning to London," she said. "It's clear I'm not needed here." And then she marched into the house.

CHAPTER 5

Of all the nerve.

The rudeness, the shortness, they were one thing. But treating her as though she were a child? That was too far. She wanted to hurl insults and accusations at him, but the truth was he was right.

You are stepping outside your place.

That was the very problem, wasn't it? Gwendolyn Bounds didn't have a place. Not since that day when she had been bundled off, outcast from society for a thing over which she'd had no control.

Had her father known there was a previous wife? That there was a child? That Lord Gracey was only looking for a mother for the baby he had ignored since birth?

She stopped short at this thought, both because she sensed that wasn't entirely true, not after what she'd accidentally witnessed the previous night in the nursery, and because she didn't quite know where she was.

That morning, after a handful of restless hours of dream-filled sleep, she had risen in search of Mrs. Rehnquist. After so much back and forth, a maid was located who could act as temporary nursemaid while the misunderstanding with Miss Haversham could be resolved.

Gwen asked the governess to join her at breakfast only to learn that it was Cook's day to go to market. Although it was abrupt, it had seemed ideal for Rachel to ride with Cook as the woman frequented the market in the next town over, a much larger town where the poor governess might have hope of locating a hiring agency that could help her with her inquiries regarding a new post.

Gwen had felt a sharp pang at the idea that things were once more changing so quickly, but really it was for the best. If she had any hope of settling into this new life and feeling once more secure in her future, it must be set to rights as soon as possible. So it was that Rachel was dispatched with Cook and the groom who would drive them into the next town.

Wishing not to wallow in maudlin thoughts, she'd finished her breakfast and taken the stairs up to the nursery to find Mary, the maid Mrs. Rehnquist had reallocated, just finishing up Felicity's bath. The little girl splashed riotously in the little tub Mary had brought up with her, and Gwen had caught them both in mid-laugh.

The maid had apologized, head down, for her enthusiasm, which had only served to stoke the niggling concerns that the household might be run *too* efficiently, but Gwen had merely raised her chin with a warm smile and assured the girl such enthusiasm for her work was to be commended.

The poor maid looked as though Gwen had accused her of stealing the silver.

Wishing to ignore it, she'd collected Felicity and dressed her for the outdoors. Though the sun was shining, it was still early March, and she'd dressed the girl carefully in what she could find amongst the garments that had been made for a child of both different size and sex. In the end, Felicity had looked unfortunately like an overstuffed pillow.

Gwen would need to make it a priority to go into the village to find a seamstress who could remedy the problem.

Mary had appeared puzzled when Gwen had asked about the gardens, and she'd soon discovered why. The nursemaid led her back down to the foyer only to weave her way back under the stairs to the rear of the house. Gwen had been correct the previous day when she thought the house must extend straight back from the front entrance as Mary took them on what felt like an endless trek away from the front door. Finally the nursemaid had gestured to a drawing room off the main corridor, and when Gwen stepped inside she saw a turret window with doors leading out into the gardens.

Only there were no gardens.

When she'd stepped outside, Felicity bouncing in her arms, she thought there had been some kind of mistake, but when she'd turned back to ask Mary, the maid was gone. Where the gardens should have been was a swarm of builders, hammering, sawing, and yelling, destroying the tranquility of what should have been a peaceful scene. A small stone terrace led from the turret to a set of steps cut into the slight slope that ran away from the house. At the bottom of the stairs, there was only cut lawn and loose stone, scattered lumber and tools.

She'd taken Felicity to a cleared part of the lawn a safe distance from the builders before setting her down and taking her hands into her own. The girl had seemed confused at first by the positioning, and instead of lifting her feet, she dragged them as Gwen urged the child forward.

She knew Felicity could pull herself up, and she was curious when it came to exploration, but Gwen feared the girl had spent an inordinate amount of time neglected in a basket and hadn't developed the muscles she would need to move her legs forward to make steps.

Gwen had been prevented from further discovery by the arrival of Lord Gracey, and now she was lost somewhere in Scarcroft Manor. She turned around and went back in the direction she'd come and instead of turning right off the drawing room door, she went the other way even though she was certain Mary had brought her from the original direction.

She stumbled from room to room—drawing, billiards, sewing—until she was so turned around she wasn't sure if she'd ever find her way back to the stairs. She had just determined to ring a bell pull and wait for a servant to assist her when a voice behind her made her jump.

"Will you please stop moving?"

She spun about, her hand going to her throat, her fingers finding the extra lace she had had added there to cover her scars. Her husband stood in the doorway behind her, Felicity swinging awkwardly from both of his hands, his arms outstretched as though she were something foul of which he meant to dispose.

"Why are you wandering around? I thought you intended to leave." He had that look in his eyes again that suggested she was missing some of her faculties.

She picked up her chin. "I haven't been given a tour of the house, and I don't know where I am. I assure you as soon as I can return to my room I shall have my things packed and be away. You mustn't worry."

"You shall not be leaving. You have a duty to care for this." He crossed the room so quickly she didn't have time to react. He shoved Felicity against her, so she had no choice but to take the child back into her arms lest the poor darling be dropped.

Gwen rocked back, adjusting the squirming child in her

arms. Felicity let out a stream of giggles as though this were the most fun she'd ever had. But Gwen never took her eyes from her husband's face. She watched him as he backed up, his expression stern and cold, but in his eyes, she saw something else. Was he uncomfortable? How could such a thing be when this little girl was his daughter? It was impossible to match this man with the tableau she had inadvertently witnessed the night before. The exhausted, devoted father, uncomfortably perched in a wooden chair beside his sleeping daughter.

She thought she had imagined how big Gracey was. That the events of the previous day had lent an added stress to the situation that had exaggerated things in her mind, but today she saw that it wasn't an affliction of her memory. Her husband was big. Tall and broad of shoulder, he had the sleeves of his shirt rolled up again, and she could see plainly the corded muscles there.

She swallowed and returned her gaze to his face, but that wasn't exactly better. He clearly hadn't attended to his toilette that morning, and a dark shadow covered his cheeks and chin lending him a compelling roughness she found entirely too appealing.

"It is my understanding that my father signed a contract for me to be wed. There was no mention of a child." This was a bald-faced lie. She had no idea what her father knew, but she was tired of this man's bullying.

A shadow passed over his face then, and she wondered if it was guilt. The emotion seemed one that would hardly be familiar to her husband, and when Felicity squirmed to be let down, she moved, ignoring the momentary sympathy she felt for the man.

She discovered a basket of rolled yarn under a small table in the corner, and setting Felicity on the rug at her feet, she pulled the basket over for the child to explore. Felicity clapped her hands together, bubbling some kind of exclamation Gwen was coming to understand meant the child was excited. The girl dug into the balls of yarn, pulling them out one at a time to press against her cheek, clearly enjoying the softness of the wool.

It was such an innocent picture Gwen almost forgot her husband loomed over her.

But then he cleared his throat, and she was jolted back to the present.

She straightened, folding her hands delicately before her. She would not give this man the pleasure of knowing just how unsettled she was.

"I believed an explanation of my circumstances were unneeded. I negotiated with your father for a wife, and it was my assumption that the requirements of a wife are universally understood."

"Liar." The word shot out of her mouth before she could think better of it.

It was as though she had slapped him, and the sight of her husband's expression coupled with the efficiency and behavior of the servants suddenly had her realizing just how long Gracey's rule at Scarcroft had gone unchallenged.

She took a step closer to him. "You knew perfectly well that the existence of a previous wife and a child were conditions of marriage my father should have been made aware of. Marriage contracts for second wives are entirely different from that of first wives, especially if an heir is already secured." Something flashed in his eyes when she spoke the word *heir*, and heat sprang up along her neck. She plowed on, hoping to distract him. "The care of a child is another matter, and my father should have been made aware when negotiating the specifics of this arrangement. I will not remain here under such falsehoods."

She picked up her skirts and even managed to turn in the

direction of the door without tripping over the balls of yarn Felicity had now scattered across the rug at her feet, but Gracey's words stopped her.

"You're right." He paused, and she could almost hear him shifting in defeat. "I should have relayed that information to your father, and I'm sorry. Will you allow me to explain?"

She turned only her head to peer at him. He looked different somehow, although he was very much the same man who had treated her so harshly the day before, and he was certainly just as tall and broad, making her feel as though she were little more than a waif.

Felicity threw a violet ball of yarn then, letting out a gargled exclamation, drawing their gazes to her. The ball bounced against Gracey's boot, sending it flying in the opposite direction. Felicity laughed.

Gwen smiled, her heart warming as it always seemed to do when she heard the child laugh. She was so caught up in the moment she almost didn't look up in time to see the soft smile on Gracey's face. The expression was so unusual it had her turning about completely, her body bracing as if she might suddenly feel something for this man.

Gracey composed himself, his stoic expression once more in place when he met her gaze again. "I was married previously, and Felicity is a result of that union. My first wife was not suitable. She did not possess the qualities a wife of such an estate as that of Scarcroft, nor the title of Gracey, required. She was willful and selfish, and her actions blemished the title."

Her heart dropped. It wasn't until the disappointment hit her that she realized she had been expecting him to speak of a love lost and the heartbreak that had driven him to such lies, but instead he spoke of his first marriage like he might review an incompetent servant. Was his first wife willful and selfish or did she simply have the nerve to state her own mind, likely in defiance of her domineering husband?

"When I approached your father, I explained that I required a strong wife. A woman who possessed the qualities fit for the title of countess and who would be intelligent and stalwart. He assured me you possessed those qualities, and I know we've only known one another for a short time, but I believe your father was correct in his assessment of your person."

Her lips parted. Was that a compliment? If it wasn't, it was at least the nicest thing he had said to her since their acquaintance.

Stalwart.

It wasn't exactly the thing young girls dreamed of when they thought of their future husbands, but it was a sight better than having him question her sanity.

"You must have known my father would see the existence of a child unfavorably, otherwise you would have told him about Felicity."

A line appeared between his brows. "Your father said he was desperate to marry you off as you were too old for a season and would accept nearly any conditions. I took that to mean the presence of a child was a moot point."

She should have been concerned at the lack of effect this revelation had on her. Her father was pragmatic. Three daughters were a lot. She understood that. Of course, he would be eager to marry any of them off.

"While that explains your actions, that still leaves me in a position for which I wasn't prepared."

"I agree."

She had meant to say more, but his admission stopped her.

"I'm looking for a partner, Gwendolyn. Not a wife exactly. I should like a woman who can care for Felicity, run a household with efficiency, and represent the title of Gracey with respect and consideration."

He had said something similar in the carriage on the way to their wedding, but today when she heard the words something shifted inside of her. It was like hope dying. When she had heard her father's announcement that she was to wed, she knew a part of her had perked up, a part she had thought she had long given up on and one which she didn't wish to admit to still having. But now she knew it was dead for good.

"A partner?" she asked, keeping her voice steady.

His eyes moved over her face, and she wondered what he was looking for. Had she let some of her inner turmoil slip to her features? She raised her chin, hoping the movement would reset her expression.

His gaze stopped its perusal, but there was something about the way he looked at her now, as if with some kind of understanding, that had her stomach tightening.

"Yes. And if you should have any question of what I expect, I ask that you speak with me."

She pointed to Felicity. "Then I would ask you to leave Felicity's care to me. I believe I am best suited to seeing to it. Fresh air and exercise are important to a child's development."

His eyes drifted down to the child before returning to her face. "Yes, but I reserve the right to ask questions of you as well."

"Agreed." It was so cold, so removed, and she mourned the loss of the thing for which she didn't even know she still hoped.

Love.

Marriage.

Family.

Connection.

A chance to make something of this life she had been given after surmounting such odds.

A partnership.

At least it would be something.

He nodded and made to move around her for the door. Felicity chose that moment to overturn the basket, sending the remainder of the balls of yarn skittering haphazardly across the rug. Gracey had already taken a step though, his foot coming down on two of the balls of yarn. She watched in horror as his foot slid, his body shifting with the sudden instability.

She reached up instinctively, making to grab for him before he could fall, but he was already reaching for her. His strong hands closed around her upper arms as her palms cupped his elbows. Dimly she was aware of Felicity shrieking in delight, but everything else had fallen away except for her husband. He was so close, bent against her as he stumbled to regain his footing and stalled before straightening as if captured by her sudden nearness.

The thought was a ridiculous one, but then she was ridiculous, the way she stared into his eyes, memorized his scent—pine and earth—fought the urge to touch his cheek, feel the stubble beneath her fingertips.

And worst of all, hope that he might kiss her.

She held his gaze, and she watched as a spectrum of emotions ran through them, surprise, frustration, annoyance, and then finally—

Desire.

It was so unexpected it stole her breath, but then he moved, let go of her, and walked away, and she was left wondering if it had happened at all.

* * *

GWEN WAS STILL WONDERING if she had imagined the look in her husband's eyes when Rachel returned that afternoon. Mary had just taken Felicity up to the nursery for her afternoon nap, and Gwen found herself in the foyer with a perhaps unwise determination to ascertain the layout of Scarcroft Manor. It was humiliating to have her husband find her wandering about like that, and she wouldn't let it happen again.

Rachel appeared in the foyer, still in pelisse and bonnet from her excursion with Cook when Gwen came to the realization that her endeavors really would be aided by someone who knew the house.

Rachel paused, one hand on the bow at her throat. "Are you lost or are you avoiding someone?" Her smile was softly knowing, and Gwen couldn't help but smile in return.

"I suppose a little of both," she admitted. "I should like to figure out the layout of my new home, but I'm finding the task rather overwhelming." She thought it would be best to leave out the fact that her husband had found her wandering around like the child he had treated her as.

Rachel tugged the bow at her throat loose and removing her bonnet and pelisse, set them aside on the front table. "I should be happy to take you about. Although I can't say how much good it will do. I'm afraid the manor house has been the victim of many spontaneous additions, and it can be rather vexing to reach your intended destination. Let's start with the drawing rooms, shall we? There are seven of them," Rachel said with a small laugh.

They proceeded to the corridor behind the stairs and began the trek through the seven drawing rooms. They were named by color, which made it easier to remember them, although Gwen thought the peach color chosen for one of the rooms was a rather unfortunate decision and one she might remedy in future.

They had reached a gallery off an awkward corridor that ran between the billiards and sewing rooms when Gwen felt the rainbow of colors she was attempting to remember turn to molten wax in her mind. As Rachel pointed out the third Earl of Gracey's portrait along the gallery, Gwen decided she'd had enough.

"Rachel, where is your family from?"

Rachel dropped her hand from where she'd been indicating the third earl's first wife and turned, mild surprise on her features. "Sussex," she said simply. "My father was a baron. Unfortunately he passed away before I had a season, and his debts took the remainder of his estate." The corners of her lips turned up self-deprecatingly, and Gwen had that odd sense that once again she might have been Rachel if her father hadn't signed the contract for her marriage to Gracey.

"I'm so very sorry," Gwen said. "I've never had a season either. They do seem like a terrible amount of work, don't they?" She wrinkled her nose to emphasize her point.

Rachel's smile warmed. "They do seem that way, yes. I do like the gowns though."

Gwen nodded as they continued down the gallery. "My sister had the loveliest gown made. It's of pale pink with tiny rosebuds along the cuffs. It makes her look like something from a confectionery's case."

Rachel made the appropriate noises of interest. "I've always wanted to look like something from a confectionary's case."

Gwen laughed, feeling the tension of the morning begin to ease. It was unusual for her to find someone with whom she shared a similar wit, and she wondered if she weren't just finding friends in a sea of opposition. But when she glanced at Rachel from the corner of her eye, Gwen found Rachel's expression had turned.

"What is it?" Gwen asked, her footsteps stalling on the carpet.

Rachel took two steps before stopping and turning back to her. "I've been thinking about what you said yesterday. About knowing the facts so you can properly manage this household." Rachel worried her lower lip with her teeth, and Gwen felt a distinct sinking feeling in her gut.

"The servants…they sometimes whisper about the earl's first wife, Lady Catherine."

Catherine.

Hearing a name for the woman who had taken up residence in Gwen's mind as a phantom was unsettling.

"What is it that they say?"

Rachel swallowed, her teeth worrying her lip again. "They say she was unkind. That she…" Rachel's eyes darted about them as if they worried they might be overheard. She took a step closer, pitching her voice lower. "They say she deserved what happened to her."

Gwen's heart rate kicked up. "You mean that she died in childbirth?"

Rachel shook her head. "She died after childbirth but… I'm not certain of the circumstances. They never say outright. Only that it was terrible, and that—"

Here the poor woman's voice cut off entirely, and Gwen felt almost guilty for making the woman go on, but she sensed there was something here. Something that Gwen needed to know if she were to have a chance at making something of this new life she'd been given.

"That what?" she pressed.

If the servants believed Catherine had deserved her end, then perhaps Gracey's words earlier that day weren't tainted by his own prospective. Perhaps his wife *was* selfish and willful. With what little she knew of her husband, she couldn't imagine such a woman being a good fit for him. The word he had used was partner. Such a woman could never be a partner if he were telling the truth of the matter.

"That she must have suffered gravely," Rachel finished, her voice all but gone.

Gwen stood very still for several seconds, absorbing Rachel's words, trying to assemble all the pieces of her new life she had discovered so far. Her husband's brusqueness, the things he said he required of a new wife, Felicity, and now...Catherine.

Gwen took Rachel's hands into her own and squeezed. "Thank you, Rachel. You were right in telling me this. I appreciate your thoughtfulness."

Rachel's expression lifted somewhat. "You've been so understanding, especially allowing me to go with Cook this morning. I wanted to repay you in some way."

Gwen took the opportunity to change the subject and hopefully clear away the dread that seemed to have descended on their afternoon. "And how did this morning go?"

Rachel's expression gave Gwen her answer before she spoke as the woman's features had turned crestfallen. "I'm afraid Glendale is no better than Maywoods. There was nothing there to offer me hope of a new posting."

Gwen squeezed the woman's hands once more before letting them go and resuming their walk down the corridor. "I'm very sorry to hear that. I'm afraid you might need to travel to London if you're to find a hiring agency that could help."

"I was wondering if Leeds might have something for me. What with all the new building and industry there. There might be new families in the city who require a governess."

"That's a splendid idea, Rachel. We must look into it."

Rachel seemed to hesitate at this. "Although I had hoped to stay as long as the church spring fair."

Gwen glanced sideways at the other woman. In the two days since she had known Rachel, she'd never heard that tone of voice from her. It was almost as if she were embarrassed to mention it.

"The spring fair? Is it a big to do in the village then?"

Rachel shrugged, but the movement looked awkward and forced. "I'm not sure really. I have only the word of Reverend Simons to go on." Rachel looked away then, taking an inordinate amount of interest in the portrait of what Gwen assumed was another one of the Gracey earls.

"Reverend Simons?"

Rachel looked back, and there was a definite pink to her cheeks now. "Yes, you must have met him yesterday." Her words stopped so quickly it was as though they had backed up in her throat and might choke her.

Gwen laughed. There was nothing else for it really. "You must mean the poor vicar who was forced to conduct my wedding ceremony." Gwen took a few more steps down the gallery. "Please be honest with me, Rachel. Does the earl always expect to get what he wants?"

Gwen was surprised when Rachel hesitated, her face folding into something akin to sadness.

"I think the earl gets what he wants, yes, but I'm not sure it's always what he needs," she said.

CHAPTER 6

For the first time since his daughter was born, Logan was glad to spend every night possible in the barn with the ewes.

He only entered the manor house when he spotted Gwendolyn in the park with Felicity and Miss Haversham. He would not admit how he looked for her in the fortnight after their disastrous encounter when he'd almost kissed her, how his eyes involuntarily searched for her in the park, on the terrace, under the giant oak that stood in the middle of the lawn and whose ample branches provided much desired shade in the middle of a sunny afternoon.

It had been so close. When he'd tripped over that blasted yarn, all he could think was this was it. He could kiss her and claim it an accident. Say he was overcome by the moment. What codswallop and yet he would have done it if only to discover the taste of her lips.

It was best that he stay in the lambing barn.

He managed a fortnight like that although it felt like an eternity. He in the pasture, taking surreptitious glances toward the house to see if it was safe to enter his own home and really hoping he might catch a glimpse of her. He had spent all of two days in the company of his new bride, and now he squatted in the pastures like a ruffian, more at ease with the sheep than his wife.

His solicitors had written to say the funds for Gwendolyn's dowry had been transferred, and with such a cash influx, he immersed himself in the work of the farm. His plans for the expanded paddocks were moving swiftly along, and he focused on the lambing. That had been his intent, after all. Find a bride that would be a suitable mother to Felicity and a respectable representative of the title and leave it at that, so he was free to focus on the health of the herd.

He was never meant to find his wife desirable.

Every time the thought entered his mind his throat began to close, memories of his first marriage parading through his mind like a runaway carriage on the verge of catastrophe followed closely by Hatrick's warning.

No, it was best he stay with the sheep.

The lambing was proving bountiful, exceeding their expectations, and even the steward was showing signs of satisfaction. At this rate, the flock would double before his projections. He would need to adjust his plans for expansion. Perhaps even take in more land for pasturing or broker a deal with the Bartlesfield estate.

But the flourishing of the flock came with a price, and as he surveyed the lambing barns near the end of March, he felt the twisting in his gut. The key to a successful flock was not in the management of its day-to-day needs but rather in the care and planning of generation upon generation. It was this part that would prove cumbersome.

For at some point, he would need to get his wife with child, sire an heir that could inherit Scarcroft and the flock his father had worked so hard to build and a responsibility Logan now carried forward. Every time he thought of it his hand strayed to his waistcoat pocket where the watch his father had given him lay safely tucked away.

Catherine's betrayal always burned hotter when Logan thought of his father. The devastation the man had overcome to bring Scarcroft back from the brink, the challenges he had entrusted to Logan upon his deathbed, the promises Logan would die trying to keep, the ones Catherine had so easily ignored.

He would carry on his father's legacy and build something worthy of Logan's own heir, and he wouldn't let another damn wife endanger this pursuit.

Using the sleeve of his shirt, he wiped sweat from his brow as he made his way up the hill of the western pasture. It was unusually hot for the second half of March, but the sky threatened rain, clouds building up in the distance. He worried it would let loose a spring storm in the coming hours, and he and Hatrick had set about locating the entirety of the flock, ensuring they would be safe if the storm, indeed, developed.

He could see Hatrick disappearing through the grove that led to the south pasture, but something out of the corner of his eye caught his attention. He turned fully, a shock of concern traveling through him that it might be an animal in distress only to find his wife clambering over the fence along the bottom edge of the pasture.

He was man enough to admit that for a split second he wondered if he could run. Had she spotted him? She must have if she was coming into the pasture to find him.

But then he registered the stern look on her face and knew she must be seeking him out for something important.

He resolutely turned his back on her and continued his climb up the hill. Let her catch up if it was so important. He must tend to the flock before the storm moved in.

He made it all of three steps before he stopped, scratching

at his forehead under the brim of his hat. That day in the drawing room they seemed to have reached an understanding. Partners. She had stuck to this bargain because in all of two weeks she had not once sought him out, and what he had seen for himself in her exercises with Felicity and the reports from Mrs. Rehnquist, she was more than adequately fulfilling her side of the arrangement.

It wasn't necessary to recount the number of times he had inadvertently stumbled upon her in that time. Inadvertently being when his feet carried him in her direction, knowing perfectly well she exercised Felicity under the oak tree at half eleven every morning and also knowing he shouldn't return to his office in the barn at that time simply because his path would run directly parallel to where she worked with the child. Not once had she looked up from her work, and he wondered if he had chosen too well in selecting a mother for Felicity.

He shook his head at the thought and turned about, bracing to speak with his wife only to have sheer terror course through him. He stumbled the last few steps down the hill to where she stood. Her face was scarlet, and perspiration beaded along her forehead under the rim of her bonnet. Her lips were parted as he saw her struggling to gain air.

At first he thought her in some sort of distress, but then he took in the anatomy of her garments. She wore a walking dress of heavy wool with a neckline that traveled clear up her throat. On top of this she wore a jacket following the same contour as the gown below with a smart collar ending just below the fringe of lace at her throat.

Without speaking, he seized her arm and dragged her the last few steps up the hillside to the scrub trees where he preferred to break his fast. The sun at this hour was angled just so as to create a pool of shadow on one side of the trees, and he shoved her into it, not releasing his grip until she had safely settled onto the boulder he often used as a back rest.

"Thank you, my lord," she gasped, her chest still heaving with exertion. "I hadn't realized quite how warm it had grown."

He eyed her gown. "Do you have no other garments? This is hardly suited to a country summer day."

She returned his glare. "It's hardly summer, my lord, and this gown is perfectly reasonable when it's not so hot." She peered around them as if taking in the landscape, but one hand still tugged at the lace at her throat as if she were struggling for air. "My lord, I hope I'm not interrupting your work, but I had a pressing matter to address with you. I know the lambing keeps you with the flock, and I didn't know of a better time to discuss this."

Her chest rose and fell with her deep breaths, and he found his eyes falling of their own accord. The smart jacket, he realized, was only clipped at her throat, allowing the rest of it to lay open. Sweat had dampened the line where the lace at her throat met the bodice of the wool gown, and the fabric clung to her. He wrenched his gaze away.

This was why he had stayed in the barn.

"What matter is this?" Thankfully she hadn't been looking at him to see his wandering gaze, but she looked at him now, a line appearing between her brows as she tugged at the lace of her collar once more.

"It's about Miss Haversham, I'm afraid."

He blinked. "Who?"

Her expression turned icy. "The governess." She closed her eyes and shook her head. "I'm sorry. I believe you hired her as a nanny."

He shifted his feet along the hillside. "Oh right, the nanny. What about her?"

"She isn't suited to the position of nanny. She simply isn't trained for it. I had hoped to help her find a new position that was better fitted to her strengths, but I'm afraid she hasn't found much luck here. We're too removed from the places where well-to-do families would be seeking such a person." She had three fingers down the lace collar now as if creating a channel for air to find its way against her likely warm throat.

He pictured her throat then, completely unbidden, and wondered what it would be like to run his tongue down it.

He turned away entirely and sucked in a breath. It was only his self-inflicted celibacy that was getting to him. Catherine had been dead for two years, but they had stopped any suggestion of marital intimacy when she'd become pregnant with Felicity. It was only the length of time that was making him weak and not the feelings Gwendolyn stirred in him.

"And what is it you need from me?" He cleared his throat as the words seemed to struggle making their way to his mouth.

She tugged at the lace now, the three fingers alone apparently not enough. Moisture beaded along her brow. It almost hurt to look at her. Why was she dressed so? And that damn jacket with the collar.

"I should like to take her into Leeds to inquire at a hiring agency. She can't go alone as a single woman, and I should like to borrow a footman to travel with us. We'll need use of the carriage, of course—"

"I can't spare anyone right now during the lambing." He was appalled by his own rudeness, but if she tugged on her collar one more time, he might very well rip her clothes from her body. "I should be happy to lend you the resources you need once all the ewes have delivered."

Several emotions passed over her face then, and he braced himself for the kind of tirade at which Catherine had excelled. But instead, Gwendolyn's features settled into something akin to resigned acceptance, and she pushed to her feet.

"I suppose you're right. We shall wait for the lambing to be done." She swayed slightly, her hand going up ineffectually as if she meant to press the back of it to her forehead, but she missed, swaying backward.

It was enough.

He seized her. The jacket came undone in one simple flick of his thumb, the garment held together by nothing more than a clasp. He wrenched it down her shoulders until it fell to the ground. And then, with both hands, he gripped that damn lace at her throat and pulled.

She made a noise then, a sound between alarm and protest, but it was too late. The fragile lace came loose with little effort, and her neck and chest were exposed above the bodice of the wool gown.

Her neck and chest which were covered in smallpox scars.

He felt every inch a bastard. By her wide eyes and parted lips, by the way her shoulders froze into place, her body held so carefully, he realized why she would wear such things in such extreme heat, and suddenly he was angry. Angry that she felt the need to cover herself so, angry that there was likely someone or perhaps someones in her past that had taught her to cover up, even at the expense of her own health.

"Why would you wear such ridiculous garments in this weather? Have you no care for your wellbeing?"

Her hand finally moved in an aborted gesture toward her throat as if to cover up her scars, but it shook too much to make the motion, and he hated himself even more.

"My scars make people uncomfortable." Her voice was soft and faraway, and a different kind of anger seized him.

"You would suffer heat exhaustion to avoid making someone else *uncomfortable*?" The word was jagged in his throat, and the need to hit something—*hard*—washed over him.

She only blinked as she tried again to raise her hand, and there was something about that weak and, God, *frightened* gesture that had him catching her hand in his own.

He regretted it immediately. He was back in the drawing room, so close to her that stealing a kiss seemed inevitable, but he couldn't do it. Because as he'd reached out to grab her hand, it brought his gaze to her neck once more, capturing his attention.

The scars swept in waves up one side of her neck and down across her chest as if beckoning his eye to her collarbones. She was slender but not overly thin, and her collarbones were well defined, as if acting as a frame for the rest of her compelling face. He hated it at the same time he couldn't look away. And then horribly he was touching them, a single finger tracing the delicate bone there as if he couldn't be sure they were real unless he felt them.

It wasn't until he'd reached the other side of her chest from where he had started that he realized she was breathing more heavily now, and then that funny little sound escaped her again, but this time the sound was recognizable. It was a sound of pleasure.

He snatched his hand back. Bending, he retrieved her jacket and upon straightening, shoved both the jacket and the lace into her hands, and without another word, stomped off up the hill, hoping the storm would unleash above him.

* * *

Gwen sat at her dressing table, contemplating the lapels of her dressing gown.

She hadn't known to be ashamed of her scars, not at first. She'd been a child after all, and it wasn't until she had noticed how people looked away, their expressions tight, that she realized they made others uncomfortable.

It had been easier to learn how to dress so the majority of her scars were covered rather than face the looks of disdain and disgust. Gwen knew her mother saw the looks too, and there had always been a part of Gwen that wondered if her mother hadn't suggested Gwen refrain from having a season because of those looks.

She sat at her dressing table now though, her eyes unable to move from the place where he had touched her, battling the urge to push aside her dressing gown to see what he had seen that day on the hill.

It had taken nearly a week to convince herself that she'd been mistaken in what she'd observed that day in the drawing room. She was unfamiliar with such intimate relations between a man and wife, and it was easy to conclude that she had incorrectly surmised what had happened between them. That her husband hadn't gazed down at her with desire in his eyes.

But the incident on the hill had eradicated any such notion.

Her husband wanted her. As impossible as that was to believe, it was the truth.

The savagery with which he'd torn the lace collar from her gown had been thrilling. It felt wrong, but her body burned with the simple memory of it. The way he had touched her, bare skin to bare skin. No one had ever touched her like that, and she had made a noise, as if her body wept with the relief of it.

She reached up and shoved away her dressing gown, letting it drop against her shoulders as she took in her neck and upper chest.

What had he seen?

What had caused that flash of heat in his eyes?

The scars marred the skin along one side of her neck, puckering the paleness into small craters. The mottled tapestry spread down along one collarbone until meeting up with a splash of marked skin across the tops of her breasts. Absently she traced her collarbones the way he had. She watched her finger in the mirror, hypnotized as she tried to recall his face that day.

She had caught sight of his expression the moment he realized she had entered the pasture. While it had tightened in what might have been displeasure, he hadn't retreated. He'd waited patiently for her to climb up to him, and their conversation had been more civil than the one they'd had in the drawing room. It wasn't until he'd exposed her neck and the upper part of her torso that something had come over him, something base and carnal.

She'd watched it happen. It was like a spark at first, small and bright, until something had caught inside of him, and fire roared. It had taken her breath.

And then he'd touched her.

She'd never danced with a gentleman. She'd never promenaded. She'd never so much as brushed the fingers of a footman passing her her bonnet.

It was only Logan who touched her, even since that first day she'd arrived. She closed her eyes at the memory of his body pressed against her. She'd gone from nothing to so much in so little time, and her body ached.

And yet he hadn't kissed her.

She snatched her hand away and pulled up the shoulders of her dressing gown. There was no time for such nonsense. They were due in the village for a morning appointment with the seamstress, and they mustn't be late.

She had thought to take Felicity to the seamstress when

she'd first arrived at Scarcroft, but upon informing Mrs. Rehnquist of her intent, the housekeeper had advised Gwen to inventory the dining room linens before placing her order with the seamstress. Mrs. Rehnquist had been correct in her suggestion. The linens were unacceptable.

She hadn't forgotten her mother's instructions and knew soon she must host a dinner to introduce herself to the local gentry, and the dining linens would be the first thing she as the countess would show off to her guests. Logan had asked for a partner that would represent the title well, and if she should host the dinner with the current linens, it would be a disgrace. There had been nothing for it.

She'd gone herself to the first appointment to select suitable fabrics for a new wardrobe for Felicity and to request Mrs. Blankenship, the seamstress, order appropriate fabric for dining linens as the woman had none on hand as an outfit of such refined linens was not in demand in the village. Mrs. Blankenship had only sent word the previous day that Felicity's wardrobe was ready for a fitting and that the fabrics Gwen had requested had arrived for her inspection.

It likely would have been better and faster to have sent to London for what she required, but part of being a good countess was supporting the local tradespeople. She had been more than happy to wait as it only pushed off the inevitable.

Her introduction to society as the wife of Lord Gracey.

She found herself tugging at the high collar of her gown an hour later at the thought as she pushed into Mrs. Blankenship's shop, Felicity on her hip, gurgling happily at the tinkling of the bell above the door. Gwen was pleased to find the shop rather busy for such an early hour, hoping this meant the seamstress had ample business to support her trade. Mrs. Blankenship looked up from where she was sorting through fabric swatches with another patron and smiled in greeting.

"I'll be right with you, your ladyship," she said in her high, clear tone. "My girl, Bethany, will fetch the dining linens you requested, and you can have a look-see while I finish up here."

Gwen smiled in return. "That would be lovely, Mrs. Blankenship. Thank you."

She moved away from the door to allow a couple of women to leave. Even as she shifted Felicity on her hip, she didn't miss the way the women glanced in her direction only to look quickly away, hurrying through the door.

She ignored the women and set Felicity down, pleased to see the child automatically reaching for Gwen's hands in order to walk over to the display in the window. She easily forgot about the women as she watched Felicity's strong legs and easy movements, her heart warming at how much progress the girl had made in so little time but also delighting in her eagerness at reaching the waterfalls of silk and gossamer that trailed from the window display.

Gwen crouched and helped Felicity gently touch the luxurious fabric and smiled as the child squealed in delight.

"Skirt," Gwen intoned carefully when Felicity looked back at her.

After improving the child's ability to walk, it soon became apparent that there were other developments the child had not made. Speech being the one with the greatest deficit. She now spoke the name of any object Felicity showed interest in to reaffirm the word and its meaning in the little girl's mind in hopes that she would begin to communicate more clearly.

Keeping her hands on either side of the child so she wouldn't fall, she watched as Felicity pulled a fold of deep emerald velvet forward to rub along her cheek, cooing in surprise as her eyes widened. Before Gwen knew what the girl was about, Felicity pulled the fabric around and rubbed it gently along Gwen's cheek.

Just as it did that day on the drive when she took Felicity from Rachel, Gwen's heart broke a little. Here it was. Her second chance. Her second chance to live and yet it was just the tiniest bit off the mark. Did it matter though? Did it matter when a child that was not of her blood looked at her like this? As if Gwen could possibly be the most precious thing in the world to her?

She scooped Felicity up, pressing her in a hug, unable to bear it any longer as the overwhelming need to hold the child overcame her.

"Lady Gracey?"

Gwen turned to find a young woman, arms filled with folds of fabric. The woman's blond hair was twisted up in an overly complicated style adorned with flowers that had already gone limp. Along the bodice of the woman's gown were sprays of glass beads, mismatched and bright as though the woman had selected them from discards to attach to the garish pink of her gown.

But it was the woman's expression that immediately put Gwen on guard. The young woman didn't look away when Gwen turned. If anything her eyes devoured Gwen's face, following the line of scars from forehead to cheek and down, only to be thwarted by the high neck of Gwen's gown. It didn't dim the mischievous gleam of the woman's eye as she looked up.

Gwen moved Felicity instinctively to her other hip, away from the woman.

"Yes?" she asked, keeping her voice even.

"I'm Mrs. Blankenship's assistant, Bethany. I have the fabrics you requested for your linen order if you'd like to review them. I can make note of the ones you'd like for the tablecloths and which you'd like for napkins while Mrs. Blankenship finishes up with Lady Kendall."

There was something predatory about the young woman's smile, and Gwen held Felicity a little closer. She glanced in the seamstress's direction only to find her deep in discussion with the woman Gwen assumed was Lady Kendall. It was nearing the lunch hour, and Felicity would be hungry. A hungry toddler would not be the most agreeable in a fitting. It was best to get moving with their appointment.

"That will be fine," she said and followed Bethany to a large mahogany table set into an alcove to the side.

The space was small but surrounded on three sides by tall windows that provided excellent light for reviewing fabrics. Bethany gestured for Gwen to take a seat by the window while she laid out the fabrics on the table. Gwen found herself reaching for a cream organza that would do nicely for family dinners while her eyes drifted to a variety of brighter shades of cotton that would be more fitting for formal gatherings.

"Is it true you married Logan Bender?"

Gwen looked up, startled to hear her husband's given name spoken so casually by the seamstress's assistant, but when she met the woman's eyes, she saw that same mischievous gleam there, but now her mouth tilted up on one side as though anticipating some kind of response she could share with the patrons she would see that afternoon.

Gwen looked to find Mrs. Blankenship, but the woman was gone, likely having taken Lady Kendall into one of the fitting rooms. Gwen returned her gaze to Bethany.

"My husband is the fifth Earl of Gracey, addressed formally as Lord Gracey." She put enough ice into her tone to have quelled the sullied interest of any gossipmonger, but the woman didn't back down.

Instead she pulled out a chair close to Gwen and leaned across the table, dropping her voice to a whisper. "Is it true what they say about his late wife, Catherine? That she died when she broke her neck falling from her horse? I heard it was because she was running away from him to be with her lover." Bethany leaned even closer, pulling against the mahogany table with flattened hands, her palms leaving sweaty streaks on the polished wood. "I heard it was him what killed her. Chasing after her like that. He scared her stupid, and she fell."

Gwen had developed a skill for keeping her feelings from showing on her face after countless encounters with people like Bethany. The ones who looked furtively in her direction only to whisper with their heads bent together, or the ones who openly stared or the ones who were bold enough to tell her she was ugly because of her scars. But hearing this woman, this stranger really, speak ill of her husband stretched her abilities to the brink.

She drew a deep, steadying breath and smiled sweetly. "I wouldn't know, I'm afraid." The woman sat back, letting out a breath heavy with disappointment. Gwen only smiled more sweetly. "I wouldn't know because real ladies don't gossip."

Bethany clearly did not possess the same skill as Gwen for hiding her emotions for when Gwen's remark landed, Bethany's lips parted, and her eyes narrowed in anger.

Before the woman could utter a retort, Gwen stood. "I'll give my order to Mrs. Blankenship then, shall I?"

She left the assistant floundering at the table as she went in search of the seamstress.

CHAPTER 7

Much later that night, she studied the play of shadows across the canopy of her bed as she tried to determine whether or not her husband was a murderer.

Her instincts told her he wasn't. That the seamstress's assistant had just been trying to stoke a fire that wasn't there, but that still didn't stop Gwen from trying to piece together what she knew of Logan's wife.

She could remember that day in the drawing room so clearly when Logan had explained why it was he had sought out a wife and what he expected of her. His words were easy to recall, but it was the emotion behind them that flittered at the edges of her mind. If only she had paid better attention. But then, in those very first days of her marriage, her mind had been too cluttered with her own emotions to catalog the emotions of another.

When he had spoken of his late wife, Logan had sounded as though he were reciting a list. Willful and selfish.

But now the words of the seamstress's assistant muddled Gwen's memory of the encounter, leaving her wondering.

Had there been derision in his voice when he spoke of how his wife had blemished the title? Or was it simple disappointment?

Had Logan called Catherine selfish because she'd taken a lover, abandoning her marriage vows to seek her own pleasure? Or was that mere gossip, made more salacious each time the story was told?

Rachel had said Catherine had died after Felicity's birth, but if the woman had been dead for nearly two years, had she returned so soon to her lover?

Gwen sat up in bed, clutching the bedclothes to her chest.

Was Felicity even Logan's daughter? Or was she the offspring of her mother's selfish and hedonistic ways? Was that why Logan was so clearly uncomfortable around his daughter?

Gwen's heart cracked just a little more, but then an entirely different idea flooded her.

Was his first wife's behavior the reason Logan held her, Gwen, at bay? Was that the reason he treated her with such erratic behavior? She knew he wanted her, and yet...he'd never even tried to kiss her.

The very idea was too perilous to consider any longer, and she pushed off the bedclothes and stood, the floor cold but solid beneath her bare feet. She found her slippers and donned her dressing gown. There was no point in lying there having such ridiculous thoughts. The seamstress's assistant only enjoyed telling tales, and there was no reason for Gwen to lose sight of her intentions.

Felicity's new wardrobe had been a success, and Gwen tried to focus on that, knowing she was making progress at Scarcroft. Her favorite of the child's new dresses was of a soft blue with yellow flowers embroidered along the collar. Felicity seemed to sense the difference too. It was like watching the child find the sunshine for the first time as she toddled happily about in proper fitting clothes, allowing her greater movement and freedom.

Just that afternoon when they'd returned to the manor to exercise in the park, Felicity had moved with greater confidence, no longer restricted by the clothing she had long outgrown, and she nearly ran to poor Hatrick who had been passing under the oak just as they'd arrived.

The steward had introduced himself one afternoon weeks ago now when Gwen had first taken Felicity into the park, and she'd learned that Hatrick was not only a proud papa but a proud grandpapa as well. He'd scooped Felicity into his arms without hesitation and twirled her above his head until Felicity crumpled in laughter and delight.

It was like that wherever Gwen took Felicity on the estate. Cook and Mrs. Rehnquist cut dainty sandwiches and petit fours and placed them on delicate teacup saucers, and they'd have tea with Felicity in Mrs. Rehnquist's office with a teapot filled with water and the tiny sandwiches they'd made.

The warmth and surprise on everyone's face suggested just what a rarity it was to see Felicity outside the nursery, and Gwen's resolve wobbled just a little. She wanted to hate Logan for what he'd done to his daughter, but she couldn't. She couldn't because she didn't know the reasons for his intentions, and she was coming to understand Logan Bender did nothing without reason.

And until she could get him to open up to her, she would refrain from casting blame.

She avoided the nursery in the late hours of the night, knowing better now than to tread there. The image of Logan asleep in the hardback chair next to his slumbering daughter was one that refused to leave her memory. It only served to reinforce what she was already coming to suspect. That beneath that crusty exterior her husband was a kind man whose only fault was having had his heart broken once.

She had spent the past few weeks following Mrs. Rehn-quist about the manor, inventorying room after room, enough so that she walked the halls in the near darkness without much effort, her mind continuing to wallow in her tumultuous thoughts. It was a far cry from her wandering trek through the manor when she'd had every intention of returning to London. Now there was no rush. She simply let her feet carry her through her new home.

She wasn't surprised to find herself in the kitchen minutes later, the room dark and cool and silent around her with only the glow from a single sconce to light her way. Cook was like the rest of the Scarcroft servants, efficient and meticulous in her work. The kitchen was one of Gwen's favorite places to retreat to when sleep evaded her. There was something about the orderliness of the room when Cook left it for the night that was like a balm to Gwen's spin-ning thoughts.

It was no different now. As soon as she stepped into the room, the clean surfaces, the still warm stove, and the tidied bundles of food stuffs soothed her. She had only taken a couple of steps when she became aware of something different about the room that night, a lingering scent that was hardly more than a ghost on the air.

Pie.

Apple pie.

Her eyes swept the scarred worktable in the center of the room, but she knew she would find it scrubbed cleaned. The benches along the wall showed much the same, and seeing the empty surfaces only made Gwen's stomach growl. She was certain apple pie was somewhere, and she would find it.

She'd taken two more steps when the sound of the door to the kitchen garden closing stopped her cold. It was a strange thing that happened then. Both fear and elation swept through her, an intoxicating and heady mix of emotion as her heart began to race in anticipation. Because there was only one other person that she knew might walk the halls of Scarcroft Manor in the dead of night.

Logan.

She didn't know why she was so certain it was him. Maybe she had become used to the sound of his footsteps. Or maybe it was just in the change in the air his very presence wrought. Whatever it was, she knew it could only be he who had come through the door.

She was frozen in the middle of the kitchen, that same strange mix of fear and elation coursing through her, and suddenly she didn't wish for him to find her there. Between that day on the hill and the rumors still filtering through her mind, she couldn't possibly face him. How could she ask him what had happened to his wife when she'd just gotten him to agree to help Rachel? To allow her to exercise Felicity in the park?

What if she were to let something slip in his presence? Something she had no right to know. There was nothing for it. Without further thought, she slipped into the larder, closing the door softly behind her.

She heard his footsteps come into the kitchen, their gait soft but certain, and she slowed her breath, waiting for the sound of his footsteps to retreat to the stairs. He was probably on his way to see Felicity. Surely that must be it. She must only remain very still for a little while longer, and then he would be gone.

But his footsteps didn't retreat.

They only grew louder. Louder and louder until—

She didn't scream when he opened the door. That was at least something. But she did throw out her arms, latching on to a shelf on either side of her as if bracing herself for a coming storm.

And the sight of her husband in the shadows, his eyes

hard, his jaw unforgiving—it might very well have been a storm.

"Gwendolyn." Only her name and then a curious pause. "What are you doing?"

"I'm—" *Hiding? Running away from you?* Neither of those were good options. She forced her gaze away from his, afraid the accusation there would force a confession she didn't intend to make when her eyes found the very thing she'd been looking for. She dropped her arms and stepped forward to snatch it from the shelf. "I was looking for pie," she said, holding the pie aloft in both hands as if she'd just discovered fire. "Would you like some?"

His eyes didn't change, and his expression didn't soften. He watched her, and she couldn't help but feel as though his scrutiny had turned from one of suspicion to one of unwilling warmth. She swallowed, focusing her attention on the buttery, golden crust of the pie, the way the tin was still slightly warm in her palms.

"How did you know there was pie?" No, it was still suspicion then. She must gain control of her wayward thoughts.

She lowered her prize but raised her chin. "The smell," she said.

He raised an eyebrow in challenge, but she merely pushed past him, keeping her hands steady on the pie and her chin raised. He needn't know how she wished to linger there under his hard gaze, how she wished to step just a little closer to see if he still smelled of pine and earth. She set the pie on the worktable in the middle of the kitchen and went in search of plates.

"Didn't you smell it when you came in?" she asked over her shoulder as she retrieved the plates and forks and a knife with which to cut the pie.

"It's the middle of the night."

"Yes, it is," she said, concentrating on cutting a generous

slice and ignoring the way her face flamed under his gaze. "I couldn't sleep." She offered him a plate. "What is your excuse for wandering about in the night?" She meant to smile, but it faltered when she met his eyes.

There was kindness there, and for a moment, she wondered if he cared about what might have kept her from her bed that night.

"Lambing," he said finally, brusquely, but took the plate she offered. He set it down on the worktable untouched, and she felt momentarily disappointed. But then he simply turned about, drawing two wooden stools away from the wall and pushing one into position beside her.

She stared at the two stools, hating the way her heart thrilled at the sight of them. They were to have pie then, here in the nearly dark kitchen in the middle of the night. It would be the first time they had ever taken a meal together. Or at least, something resembling a meal. She cut herself her own slice and gathering her nightrail and dressing gown in one hand, clambered atop the stool as gracefully as possible.

It wasn't until her dressing gown was in her hand that she remembered what she was wearing, her hand going to her throat. Her nightrail's collar was modest, but it didn't cover her neck the way her modified gowns did. She glanced at Logan to find he'd picked up his fork but sat unmoving, his eyes on her. She dropped her hand and straightened, picking up her own fork.

"Are the ewes always lambing? It feels as though you've been in the barn for weeks." She stuffed a bite of pie into her mouth, concentrating on her plate until she was certain the redness of embarrassment had left her cheeks. It was one thing to think of Grandmother Bitsy's words. It was another to say them out loud.

And worse, would he think she had been keeping track of him? That she was aware of his absence? Bethany's tale chose that moment to rear up in her mind, and Gwen suddenly wondered if Logan spent so much time with the flock because his first wife had broken him in some way.

"It's the size of the flock," he said, his voice much the same as though nothing at all had happened, as if thoughts of his first wife being indecent weren't parading through her mind. "It's grown to where the lambing takes some time in the spring. It wasn't always like this, but we've been fortunate to have several years of growth behind us."

His words brought her thoughts under a semblance of control. "The flock here hasn't always been this large?"

He swallowed a bite of pie as he shook his head. "It was once larger than this actually, but it suffered some loss in the floods of '46."

Her fork stilled, and she watched him eat. He attacked the pie much like he attacked anything, methodically and with a degree of calculation.

"I'm so sorry," she said, unsure if that was the correct thing to say. "I'm not familiar with the methods of sheep farming. How exactly did the flock suffer in the floods?"

"They drowned." He said the words as though they were little more than a comment on the weather.

She set down her fork, the pie turning to dust in her mouth. "They drowned?"

He must have heard something in her voice because he finally looked up from his plate. Much like that day in the drawing room she watched as his face transformed from question to decision. He too set down his fork.

"The pastures used to be situated at the southeastern end of the estate along the border with the Kendall land. Do you recall a river crossing when you came from London?"

"Yes, I do." It occurred to her that this was the most normal interaction they had ever had.

Since the moment they were married—no, before then

really—their encounters either involved some degree of confrontation, outright yelling, or the most unsettling of all, her attempt to deduce whether or not he was trying to keep himself from ravishing her. But right there in the stillness of the kitchen, everything felt so…normal.

It struck her then how good it felt. Sitting there with him. Discussing the flock. Suddenly she wanted a lifetime of this. These midnight chats in the near dark. Just the two of them as if the entire world stood aside just for them.

She was so absorbed in her reverie it took a moment to return to what he was saying.

"The pastures abutted the river, and the waters rose so quickly, my father and his men couldn't save the flock. More than half of it was lost in a single afternoon." His voice held the most emotion she had ever heard in it, and she curled her hands in her lap as he went on. "My father was inconsolable. A loss like that was devastating to the estate."

"Devastating how?"

Something flickered over his face then as if she had surprised him. "The flock is the life blood of the estate. Without it there are no funds to maintain the land, make improvements, and ensure the livelihood of all who rely on the estate to make a profit."

"The servants?"

"The servants," he confirmed with a nod of his head. "And the village that does business with the estate and the tenants who live off the land. The economy of all that surrounds us depends on the health of the flock here. When it was lost in the floods, my father felt as though he had let down all of Yorkshire."

She recalled with sudden clarity their conversation that day in the drawing room like she hadn't been able to only an hour before. Logan had said he wanted a wife to represent the title of Gracey the way it deserved to be represented. His first wife had *blemished* the title. That was the word he had used, and her throat suddenly closed.

She picked up her fork if only to do something with her hands as she tried to block the sound of Bethany's voice from her head. "But the flock is growing again?"

"Yes."

There was the slightest hesitation in his voice that drew her attention. "Yes?"

He considered her, but his gaze was different now than it had been when he'd found her in the larder. It was softer, curious, and dare she say trusting?

"A healthy, flourishing flock takes generations. I'm only continuing what my father had started. For the herd to be truly successful, I must have an heir to pass it onto one day."

She tried to look away or at least blink, anything to break the sudden tension that vibrated between them.

Heir.

Felicity was his child, but as a girl, she could not inherit. In order for Logan to pass on the estate to a rightful heir, he would need to have a legitimate boy child. With his wife.

But Gwen was his wife.

Everything became clear so quickly, she thought she might have lost the ability to breathe. She should say something. Anything. The trust she had seen in his eyes had seemed so precious, so rare, and she thought if she didn't say exactly the right thing in that moment that little spark of trust would be snuffed out.

But she was prevented from saying anything at all when the garden door opened again, the sound of hurried footsteps carrying down the corridor. A groom she recognized from their walks in the park appeared in the doorway, his hat pushed back on his head as if in excitement.

"Another lamb's coming, my lord. Mr. Hatrick wanted me to tell ye."

"Thank you, Ian. I'll be along shortly."

The lad disappeared without further comment, and Gwen stood, gathering their dishes when he surprised her yet again by laying a hand on her arm, stilling her movements.

She looked up, hoping her features were calm or at least neutral.

"Would you like to see a lamb be born?" he asked.

Something had shifted between them. She wasn't sure how it had happened or when, but it had. He had asked for a partner, but until that moment, he had not truly treated her as one. His question now was about more than seeing the birth of a lamb. So much more, and yet she couldn't have said specifically what. They existed in some sort of in between place. Not husband and wife and yet no longer careful strangers.

She answered the only way she could. "Yes."

* * *

HE REGRETTED ASKING her to come with him the moment the words were out.

There was a strange keening sound in his ears as memories of Catherine and her myriad betrayals raced through his mind like an unstoppable locomotive. Gwendolyn was not Catherine. He had been plain when speaking of his requirements for a wife, and she had accepted them with surprising understanding.

She had asked after the flock. Catherine had never expressed interest in the estate, and perhaps it was this that had caused him to drop his guard momentarily.

Or maybe it was the quiet of the kitchen, the soft glow the single sconce cast about the room, or the glimpse of bare ankle he had seen when she'd pulled herself atop her stool. The intimacy of it had drugged him after being so careful to keep himself apart. He had been weak when something so dangerous as a bare ankle had arisen, and he'd fallen victim to it.

For who could resist the hope of a newborn lamb?

He stopped at the garden door and rummaged amongst the boots there, finding something suitable for Gwendolyn. He presented an old pair of tall brown boots to her, marked with wear and caked with yesterday's mud now dried into pale flakes. Catherine would have been appalled. Gwendolyn simply took them and exchanged her slippers for them without comment. He turned his back lest he catch another glimpse of that damnable ankle.

The night was warm except for the wind, which held the last bite of spring, but the lambing barns were sheltered enough although he wondered if he should go back and fetch a coat for Gwendolyn for the walk there. Too late he realized she had moved ahead of him, her arms swinging as she made her way to the barns, her head up as if she were surveying the sky. He followed her gaze, surprised to find the blanket of stars there.

"Do you ever get used to it? This many stars?" Her voice carried in the stillness, and he caught himself watching her for overlong before he could reply.

"I suppose I don't often have the time to observe them."

She faltered but only for a moment, and in the dim light, he wondered if that was pity on her features. "That's too bad," she said and returned to her quick pace in the direction of the barns. "My sisters and I often watch the stars."

He nearly tripped. "Sisters?"

She turned her head. "Yes, sisters."

"How many sisters?"

Her pace slowed, and her tone was guarded as she said, "Two. Annie and Eloise."

He didn't know what else to say, already so damn uncomfortable with the closeness he didn't know what else to do.

As soon as they stepped into the shelter of the lambing barn, he could feel the change in temperature. It was warmer, both from the heat of the sheep scattered about in their pens, the mothers and their new lambs, and the ewes still preparing to birth their babies, but also because the barn had been specifically built so the wind was blocked coming off the hill, leaving the space inside warm and comfortable.

Lanterns hung from nails along several of the posts that spanned the space, and finally he got a good look at his wife, concern and embarrassment flashing through him. He reached out a hand to stop her, but she'd already lifted her dressing gown into one hand to step into the straw and mud that had become the aisles between the pens.

"Hello, Mr. Hatrick," she called, and Logan could do nothing but watch.

His wife was in the lambing barn in nothing but her dressing gown, her hair in a wild braid down her back.

He had never seen anything more beautiful, and something warm began to spread through his chest.

Dear God, he was dying.

That could be the only explanation for the lightness that spread through him then, at the rightness that tingled through his extremities. Death was the only possible answer to why everything seemed brighter, and the air was suddenly easier to breathe.

Hatrick looked up from the pen over which he had been crouched, a smile springing to his lips as he scratched at his forehead with one hand, his fingers adorned in knotted red strings. "Your ladyship," he gasped, his eyes wide with surprise—and delight? "I hope the lad didn't wake you."

Gwendolyn shook her head and stepped around the post

to get closer to the pen Hatrick had been inspecting. "Not at all. Am I to understand she is to have her lamb this night?"

Logan watched as his wife bent over the railing to see into the enclosure where the ewe was even now keening in one corner, listing to one side as she prepared to give birth.

"Right she is, my lady," Hatrick said.

When had Hatrick been introduced to his wife? Why hadn't Logan been informed of such?

Logan reached the pen and stood purposefully between his steward and his wife. "How far along is she?" he asked even though he could see perfectly well for himself. The curve of one small hoof appeared beneath the bovid's tail along with the very tip of the nose. To his wife he said, "I wasn't aware you had been introduced to Mr. Hatrick." Even he could hear the jealousy in his voice, and the unfamiliar feeling of shame washed over him at his wife's sideways glance.

"Mr. Hatrick was kind enough to introduce himself when he came across us in the park a few weeks ago." His wife kept her gaze on the ewe, her voice neutral.

The wonderment he had seen in her face not minutes before was replaced by a guarded carefulness, and the shame grew more persistent.

"I'm glad to hear as much," he said, the words bursting forth much too loudly.

He felt her gaze on him, but he didn't look away from the ewe. Not when he felt Hatrick's stare or the many curious glances of the farm hands tending to the other ewes.

"What happens now?" Gwendolyn asked, saving him from further embarrassment.

"The ewe knows what to do, and we'll leave her to it unless she needs our help," he said.

The ewe glanced over as though sensing he spoke of her and gave him a withering look before she began to push.

"What is her name?"

This drew his attention away from the ewe. "Her name?"

Gwendolyn looked up, the question in her eyes. "Her name. The ewe. What do you call her?"

"Sheep Forty-seven."

She laughed, a small snort of a sound, and he wondered if that was happiness he felt at having made her laugh.

She sobered though when she looked at him. "You must be joking. You can't call her Sheep Forty-seven."

"Why not? That's which number she is."

Gwendolyn looked back at the sheep. "She isn't a Forty-seven. She should be a Mildred or a Maeve or a Lily or something."

"We can't name her."

"Why ever not?" Now she cast him a challenging look.

"Because we might eat her later."

Her expression evaporated. "Oh, I suppose you're right," she mumbled and went back to watching the sheep.

He had to shake himself from staring at his wife and remember he should be watching the ewe.

The suggestion of nose he had seen before surged forward until almost all of the tip of it was visible before the ewe relaxed again against the straw. In the contraction more of the one visible hoof had slipped free, and Logan was over the side of the enclosure before he remembered the others gathered there.

"The leg is stuck," he said, wrestling the ewe to her side so he could reach into her to find the other leg. "Gwendolyn, would you like to help me?"

Was he attempting to hasten his own death? Or had the sight of her wonderment at the stars somehow enraptured him? Was this the effect intimacy had on him now? It addled his wits?

He certainly should not have asked about her sisters.

Gwendolyn hiked up her dressing gown and followed him over the enclosure without comment. He stared, momentarily struck dumb by the sight of his wife climbing the enclosure as if she were doing little more than sidestepping a wicket on a croquet pitch. Her boots sank in the straw on the other side, and she waded through it, her dressing gown tangling about her legs.

"What do I do?" she asked, kneeling in the straw beside the struggling ewe.

"I'm going to free its leg, and then we'll need to pull together to help her birth the lamb. Take hold of its leg there. Be sure to get a firm grip, and don't pull until I tell you."

Gwendolyn reached forward without hesitation, her delicate fingers closing around the one hoof that had slipped free, heedless of the amniotic fluid that encrusted the animal.

"I'm going to push the lamb back so we can free the leg, and then we'll pull. Are you ready?"

The ewe chose that moment to rear up, bleating loudly in protest. The animal was huge with pregnancy and the movement so sudden it knocked him off his feet. He slipped through the straw, blood and fluid soaking his pants as he struggled to maintain his grip on the lamb. He couldn't let the ewe push again or the lamb would become further stuck.

So focused on the struggling sheep, he didn't notice his wife until she'd scrambled back up on her knees beside him, having been knocked into the straw as well. Her eyes were bright with excitement, a small smile of determination on her lips as she swiped at a curl of hair that had come loose in the commotion. Mud streaked her cheek where she'd pushed the hair away with the back of her hand, but she didn't seem to care. The little bit of mud hardly seemed to matter when her dressing gown was now soaked in blood.

An apology sprang to his lips, but she said, "Go on then," with laughter and joy in her voice before he could speak.

She regained a hold of the lamb's one hoof, and he went to work, easing the lamb backward so he could bring the trapped leg forward inside the birth canal. As if sensing a change in the lamb's position, the ewe pushed, grunting and panting. Logan eased his arm free, catching the lamb's hoof as it emerged.

As soon as he felt the ewe stop pushing, he shouted above the din, "Pull!"

Together they pulled the lamb forward in one smooth motion until the small animal dropped to the straw. The lamb tumbled out in a surge of fluid and blood. With a quick motion, he jerked the fluid from around its nose and mouth until the lamb let out a gurgled cry, and then he sat back, scooting along his knees.

Gwendolyn knelt where he had left her, her gaze transfixed by the tiny lamb lying on the straw. He seized her shoulders, bringing her back to his chest as he scooted them both away until he had placed a good distance now between them and mother and babe.

The ewe swung around as soon as he had removed his hand from the lamb's mouth, and she licked at the animal furiously.

He wasn't sure what had happened, but slowly he became aware of his own positioning, half kneeling, half sitting in the straw, his wife pinned against his chest as he had one hand at her collarbone, one along her shoulder. But she didn't struggle against the positioning. She was still mesmerized by the scene before her and him by her.

She was supposed to mean nothing to him. He hadn't wanted a wife at all. But kneeling there, holding her against him, her wild hair tickling his cheek, her face a study in joy, he knew with sudden dread that she meant something to him now.

"What is she doing?" she whispered, and it was a moment

before he could break his gaze away from her face to look back at the ewe.

Mother continued to lick furiously at her babe, and the lamb had picked up its head from the straw, baaing softly as its mother tended to it.

"She's learning her baby's scent and trying to hide its birth from predators by eating the birthing fluid."

"That's so beautiful," she breathed, and he watched, both fear and happiness filling his belly as her hand rose up to twine her fingers through his against her chest.

They sat like that for some time, she watching mother and babe, he watching her as she held his hand pressed to her heart, and in that moment, he knew one thing above all else.

By morning, that damn sheep would have a name.

CHAPTER 8

In the end, Logan let Gwendolyn pick the name.
Or rather names.

She named the ewe Daffodil and the lamb Buttercup, and Logan went for a very long walk that ended in a very cold swim in the stream at the southeastern edge of the property.

He returned to avoiding her. It was the only thing he could do really. He had already gotten too close to her.

Even days later, he still thought of their conversation in the kitchen that night. The normality of it, the way she truly seemed to care. He spent hours picking apart their words, looking for the traps.

Catherine had been skilled at laying traps.

He would think they had had a perfectly reasonable conversation only to find out later that she had been laying the groundwork to ask for something for which the estate had no money or something entirely unreasonable. When he denied her request, she'd run to her father and cry cruelty.

But no matter how he poked at it, he couldn't find anything devious about the conversation he'd had with Gwendolyn. In fact, she'd gone straight back to her routines as far as he could tell. Every morning he found her under the oak with Felicity, usually with Miss Haversham in attendance, and every evening, he received the inquiry from Mrs. Rehnquist asking if he would be dining with his wife that evening. The answer always being in the negative, of course.

But no matter how easy and normal everything seemed, he couldn't shake the feeling that she was trying to penetrate his defenses.

There was something in the way her hand had felt against his. He wasn't sure if it was because it felt as though she trusted him or that he felt he could trust her. The way she had vaulted over that enclosure, blood soaking her dressing gown instantly, and yet she hadn't hesitated. When he'd told her to pull, she had.

Catherine had never entered the barns.

Shame burned through him at the thought. By even thinking of comparing Catherine to Gwendolyn so directly, it felt like a betrayal and a disservice to Gwendolyn.

Something had changed between him and his wife, and as long as he remained outside, he wouldn't be forced to admit it.

But he knew the truth even if he wouldn't face it.

She was no longer a lady he contracted to be his wife. She was no longer a pretty stranger over whom he felt a silly, boyish surge of lust. It was much worse than that.

He was beginning to *like* her.

He scrubbed a hand over his face as he tried to concentrate on what Hatrick was saying to him. This was the very reason he had been so careful in selecting a second wife. He hadn't wanted all of these complications. There was the herd to see to, the future of the estate, and the title of Gracey. He didn't have time to think about naming bloody sheep.

"Thirty-eight," he heard himself say even as his thoughts remained scattered.

"We already have a thirty-eight," Hatrick said from beside him, his pencil scratching at the ledger he'd braced against the roundness of his belly.

"We do?" Logan leaned over to scan the neat column of numbers Hatrick had penciled into the book.

They were tagging the lambs. So many had been born in the past week that there was quite a lot to do. To make matters worse, two ewes had rejected their lambs, and the lads were still trying to get one of the other mothers to take them. Logan feared if one of the other ewes didn't take the lambs, he would find Gwendolyn in the barn giving the lambs a bottle.

There were still twenty ewes ready to give birth, and he was torn between watching each birth carefully for any signs of distress from the mother and ensuring the lambs were properly tagged to their mother that by the end of the day, he felt as though he were actually being split in two. No wonder he couldn't remember which number they were on.

He hadn't slept more than a handful of hours each day of the past week, and then it had been on the cot in the barn office. He was tired, he was sore, and worst of all, he smelled.

Hatrick pointed at the row of figures they were on with an index finger, knotted red string snug against its base. "Thirty-eight. This one must be thirty-nine."

Logan watched as the man penciled in the number along with his mother's corresponding figure. Logan scrubbed a hand over his face again, and when he blinked his gaze back into focus, he found Hatrick watching him carefully.

"Do you think you might like a break, my lord? We can finish this tomorrow."

Logan shook his head. "I'm fine. Let's continue."

But he'd only made it through the next enclosure when he found himself transposing the numbers entirely. He made lamb forty-two, twenty-four, and Hatrick insisted they call it a day.

Logan knew the steward was right, but he didn't like admitting defeat. Except as he made his way back to his office, he caught a whiff of his odor, and he knew he must return to the manor house at least long enough to see to a bath and change of clothes.

He found the day's post on his desk when he returned, and he picked it up, happy for the distraction, only to have Hatrick sail into the office behind him.

"My lord, truly. You must rest. Even I leave the barn from time to time." The steward replaced the lambing ledger on the stack on his table along with the others.

Logan sorted through the post, muttering, "Yes, yes, of course. Just one more minute."

The post was snatched from his hands before he knew what was happening. He looked up, surprised to find his steward on the other side of his desk, the post tucked carefully under one arm.

"Not another minute, my lord. Right now. You need a bath and a hot meal. That's what my Sue would say." The steward gave a firm nod and tapped on Logan's desk with a single finger. "Your father wouldn't want you working yourself to death, and you know as much."

Guilt flashed through him then at the invocation of his father. Because it wasn't only fatigue that had his mind wandering.

He sank into the chair behind his desk and put his face in his hands. "Hatrick, I think I have a problem."

He wasn't one to voice his problems, and really, he didn't like to admit he had a problem. But Hatrick had known him since he was a lad, and there was something about the longevity of their relationship that splintered the dam Logan liked to keep around his feelings.

The scraping of a chair against the concrete floor had Logan dropping his hands to see Hatrick pulling his chair closer to the desk before settling into it, elbows to knees.

"You'd best better tell me, my lord," Hatrick said gravely, his beard scratching at his worn scarf as he spoke.

"I think you might have been right about my wife," he said, and then changed his mind. "Or at least, how it is that I treat her."

Hatrick's frown was swift. "I thought as much, my lord. But you mustn't blame yourself. Your first wife taught you a nasty lesson. One no one should ever learn."

Hearing Hatrick speak of his first wife felt odd, almost as if Logan were removed entirely from the situation and hadn't taken the brunt of Catherine's wrath. It was disconcerting to hear from someone who had witnessed Catherine's destruction, and he remembered just how much his first wife's selfish decisions had affected everyone at Scarcroft.

Logan shifted in his seat. "I meant what you said about treating the current countess as though she were Catherine."

Hatrick sat back, blinking. "You mean how you distrust her?"

"How do you know that?" The words came too quickly from his lips to explain them away.

"I see the way you watch her when she's not looking." Hatrick shrugged. "We all do. Mrs. Rehnquist is concerned you're going to have a stroke."

Logan sat up. "You all are talking about me."

Hatrick shrugged again. "We always talk about you. That's what the servants do, my lord." Hatrick smiled broad enough to reveal his missing left incisor.

"Certainly you do not."

Hatrick did not have the decency to look ashamed. "Of course, we do. We wouldn't talk about you if we didn't care about you."

Logan had had a reprimand on his tongue, but the words vanished at this statement. He slid back in his chair, suddenly very uncomfortable.

It was a beat before he said rather quietly, "I'm not going to have a stroke."

Hatrick gave a snort of laughter. "If you don't have a stroke, you'll take a pitchfork through the heart for not paying attention to where you're going."

Logan looked away, picturing such a fate, and realized Hatrick might be right.

"Be that as it may, I'm still left…" His mind went blank. How could he put into words what it was he was feeling?

That he *liked* Gwendolyn. That he thought her a fit mother for Felicity. Hell, that he'd never before seen a better mother. That she was like sunshine enveloped in a body, spreading hope wherever she went. She'd named the damn sheep, for heaven's sake.

And yet, the specter of his dead wife continued to haunt him, standing between him and Gwendolyn until he couldn't see one for the other.

"With fear," Hatrick finished for him.

Logan looked up at this. Of all the things swirling inside of him, he didn't think fear was one of them, but Hatrick had spoken the word with such conviction.

Hatrick nodded at Logan's look. "You're afraid if you trust her she'll turn out to be just like Catherine. That's a perfectly normal human condition, my lord."

"What do I do about it?" He swallowed, hard. Why was he asking such a question? He had no desire to conquer the distrust he felt for his wife. Distrust was what was going to keep him safe, keep the estate safe, keep everyone *safe*.

Hatrick shook his head, his expression suddenly heavy. "There's nothing that can be done about it, I'm afraid. The only thing to dispel distrust is faith, and sometimes this world has a way of destroying our faith."

Catherine had certainly destroyed his. "I'm afraid I don't have any faith left."

Hatrick laughed now, his smile even broader. "We all have faith, my lord. It's all around us if we know where to look." He snapped his fingers and pointed at him. "Why just the other night I witnessed faith with my own two eyes and so did you."

Logan frowned. "And when was that?"

"When that ewe let you help her birth that lamb. The one her ladyship helped you with." There was a strange gleam in Hatrick's eye, and Logan couldn't be sure the man hadn't brought up that night on purpose.

"That's not faith. That's an animal in distress."

Hatrick's lips thinned. "That's Catherine what's taught you that. That more than anything that woman did is a travesty." Hatrick pushed at his thighs and stood. "You need to find your way between the distrust and your lady wife, or your thoughts will wear a path round your mind."

Hatrick was almost to the door when Logan said, "And how do I go about getting those thoughts lined up enough to make sense of them?"

Hatrick paused and looked back at him. "The only thing for that is exercise."

* * *

Gwen encountered no further issues with sleeping.

She wondered if she should be concerned about how well she slept, in fact, after that night in the lambing barn. Both what Rachel and the seamstress's assistant had told her traveled through her mind periodically, but now instead of worrying her husband might be a murderer, she could only reflect on his past with curiosity and a bit of sadness.

Who was Catherine? What had she done to him?

She knew there must be some validity in the things she had heard about the woman. After all, she saw the evidence of it on her husband's face every time he thought about kissing her.

For now she *knew* he was thinking about kissing her.

It was no longer a doubt in her mind. Not after that night in the kitchen when he had told her he needed an heir. In the six weeks since she had come to Scarcroft Manor, their relationship had never progressed physically, not beyond the odd moments of tension between them, and at first she had thought it was her scars to blame.

But it wasn't.

There was something in Logan's past that held him back, that chained him to a lonely life.

But what was it?

What had Catherine done?

The only person to ask was Logan as she would never place a servant in a position that required them to tattle on their master. But she couldn't ask Logan. Their partnership had shifted that night in the barn, and she didn't wish to jeopardize the progress they had made. While he still held himself back, he no longer made a point to observe her with Felicity when they took their daily exercise in the park.

She had noticed that, of course. The way he always seemed to be walking across the front lawn at the same time she would be taking Felicity out for a walk. Perhaps it was just the daily sequence of responsibility that had him crossing the lawn at the same time she was outside with his daughter, but she thought not.

Only now she didn't see him, and she wondered if she'd

passed some kind of test the night she'd help him deliver the lamb.

She shouldn't be required to pass a test though, and that was what was so troubling about it.

But it seemed enough had settled within her to end the fitful nights of sleep she'd endured upon her first arrival. Which was probably for the best as she did not wish to encounter her husband in the darkest hours of the night. It always seemed to cause trouble when she did, and she was just starting to find her way in her new life, and she didn't wish for anything to put that in danger.

Even Rachel had grown more confident with Felicity. Once she was no longer required to see to the child's every need, she had relaxed. When Felicity began to toddle across the park on her own, Rachel had chased after the girl like a mother hen after her chick. Gwen had assured her Felicity would do no more than tumble into the grass should she fall, but that hadn't reassured the woman. Yet with each passing day, governess and child grew more confident. They spent wonderful lazy hours out of doors, exploring every sign of spring they could find.

Felicity's favorite were the deep purple irises at the front gate. Gwen took her to them every day so she could trace a delicate finger along their soft petals. The child was proving surprisingly tactile, preferring things with texture and shape. Gwen worried this was because she had been deprived of other means of sensory development such as speech and music.

The girl did seem to enjoy the hymns at Sunday service. At first Gwen thought it unwise to take Felicity, but Rachel had insisted Reverend Simons would welcome her. Gwen was surprised to discover Reverend Simons had a way with children. They clambered atop him like some sort of gymnasium, and Gwen struggled with matching this warm, laughing man with the man who had wed her, but she suddenly better understood the cause for Rachel's pink cheeks whenever she spoke of the vicar.

So it was that Gwen no longer felt the squeeze of time and the things Felicity should be doing at her age. There was plenty of time to focus on the child, and once the lambing was done for the year and Logan had more flexibility to his time, Gwen would think about the dinner she knew she must plan.

But with the pressure of said dinner far from her mind, Gwen slept soundly.

Until the pounding began.

She woke with a suddenness that had her sitting motionless in her bed until her mind could connect what she had heard in her sleep with the reality around her. A flash of light at the windows had a gasp catching in her throat, but the fright was momentary as her brain connected with the sound.

Thunder.

A storm had come up in the night after she'd fallen asleep. That was all. Heart still racing, she lay back against her pillows, her eyes almost closed as the sound of rain striking the windows lulled her back to sleep until—

Thump. Thump.

She bolted upright. That was not thunder. That was coming from inside the house.

Her feet struck the cold floor before her mind could think what to do, her instincts telling her to get to Felicity. She threw open the door to her room, not stopping to find her slippers or dressing gown. The thumping grew louder in the corridor. Her feet padded noiselessly across the carpet, down the hallway to the center staircase that led up to the nursery. Her foot was on the first step when she stopped, her ears ringing as she tried to listen.

The noise was not coming from the floor above. It was coming from the other corridor across the landing.

She paused, turning her head as if it would help her better hear, but her racing heart thrummed in her ears, making it impossible to tell what was happening. Her hand slid from the railing as she turned. She took a tentative step across the landing, pitching her head forward toward the noise.

Thump. Thump. Thump.

She glanced back at the stairs and then again in the direction of her room. She should return to her bedchamber. Hadn't she just resolved not to wander about at night?

But that noise…

What if it was something that could hurt Felicity? What if it was the start of a fire? A window left open? A window left open by some intruder?

She shook her head and marched down the corridor in the direction of the noise. She was being silly. There must be a perfectly reasonable explanation for what was happening. She would see to the matter and return to bed before anything else could happen.

She passed several closed doors, her eyes searching through the dimness. It was darker in this corridor as it didn't have the benefit of a bank of windows to let in the moonlight, but she'd traveled this way enough times with Mrs. Rehnquist. This corridor housed the guest rooms, rooms that had gone unused for years according to the housekeeper.

Had one of the windows come unlatched from disuse? Was it just a tree branch that had been allowed to grow and it now knocked into the side of the house?

She was halfway down the corridor when she saw it. One of the doors was open, a small sliver of light escaping into the hallway.

When her eyes lit upon it, she knew she should turn

around. She should go—no, run—back to her room, close the door, and bury herself under the covers.

But if she did that, she'd never discover what was behind that door. Part of her knew it was Logan. She didn't how she knew it, but she knew it, and her heart started pounding again, but this time in anticipation, not fear.

If she stepped through that door something would happen. She knew it. It made her palms tingle and her toes curl into the carpet. If she didn't force something to happen, they would continue to exist like they had been for the past month and a half. A careful distance maintained between them like two countries at war calling a detente.

She stepped forward and slipped through the door before she could think of it further.

And regretted it immediately.

It was her husband. She had been right. But what she hadn't expected was that her husband was naked to the waist, the light of the lanterns lit about the room highlighting every curve of muscle so she would not be mistaken about one thing.

Her husband was magnificent.

She swallowed, startled, and backed into the door only to send it closed with a bang.

"Sorry," she mumbled, her hand reaching for the collar of her nightrail because she didn't know what to do with it, but worse, she couldn't pry her eyes from Logan. From every delicious muscle that glistened with a sheen of sweat.

"Gwendolyn." Of God, his voice. It was rough, terribly so, and she wanted to curl against him and listen to the purr of it in his chest.

She forced her eyes away, taking in the rest of the room. Furniture covered in dust cloths was scattered about, a table here and there uncovered enough to set a lamp upon it. That was all rather normal but as her eyes swept to the other side of the room, she saw the cause of the thumping noise that had awakened her.

The opposite wall was a mirror, floor to ceiling, and in front of it hung a punching bag suspended from the ceiling by a thick cable. The mirror afforded the user an excellent view of one's progress at the sport, but it only gave Gwen a fine view of her husband's defined butt in his tight trousers.

She pried her eyes away and looked up to meet Logan's furious gaze.

"What are you doing here?" His voice was no longer rough. It was deathly quiet and even, sinfully so, as he unspooled yards of wrapping from his fists.

She pointed at the bag. "I heard a noise. I thought Felicity might be in danger."

"She's not the one in danger."

Her eyes flew back to his face, her heart catapulting into her throat as she took in the darkness of his eyes, the steeliness of his jaw. She backed up, forgetting she'd already done that and encountered the wall behind her. She pressed her palms to the paneling, willing her heart to slow.

"You should go back to bed," Logan said now, dropping the wrapping on a table behind him.

He was right. She should go back to bed, but her feet wouldn't move. Her body tingled at the sight of him, and wild ideas raced through her mind. What it would feel like to run her fingers through the mat of hair on his chest, to trace every muscle there, to discover every curve. To press her mouth against his hot skin.

She didn't want to leave. If she left, nothing would change, and they would go on living a life carefully removed from one another, and her heart couldn't bear the thought. So instead she stepped away from the wall, planting her feet on the floor.

She knew what she looked like. She wore only her thin

nightrail, and there were two lamps along the wall at her back, the light striking her from behind. If she were brave enough, she could look at the mirror for confirmation, but she knew. He could see all of her through the nightrail. Every part of her that he was trying so very hard to ignore.

"I don't want to go back to bed." The words tumbled from her lips effortlessly even though her heart raced, and her body trembled.

He didn't move, only his gaze narrowed as if trying to determine how serious she was, how courageous she was.

She swallowed, the words she knew would push him over the edge coming to her lips. "I want you to see me."

CHAPTER 9

She shouldn't be here.

This was what she thought she had wanted, but years of being an outcast couldn't be overcome in a single night, no matter her bravado, and she shook with the unfairness of it, her courage having abruptly fled the moment he stepped toward her. Suddenly she realized the power he held over her because in that moment, he could reject her, and everything she had thought, believed, *hoped for* could be proven a lie, only the wishful thinking of a woman who just wanted to be loved.

She should have run when she had the chance, but it was too late now. He was advancing on her, one agonizingly slow step at a time. She wanted to look away, but she couldn't. The candlelight glinted off his sweat-dampened chest, defining every impossible muscle as though she might have somehow managed to miss the exquisiteness of her husband's body, and it must call her attention to it once more.

But she didn't need reminding.

Her heart pounded as she willed herself to draw a steady

breath. He mustn't see the reaction he stirred in her. She couldn't possibly let him know because then…then…

Then he could hurt her.

If he knew how very much she wanted him to touch her, he could use it against her. Ridicule her for wanting things she didn't deserve and shouldn't have. Scold her for thinking someone as beautiful as him could want someone like her.

She ducked her chin, the humiliation too great, the only thing that could force her eyes from the lure of his naked chest, but it didn't matter. He had already reached her, and there was nowhere for her to hide unless she shut her eyes. And she couldn't shut her eyes. Because just then he placed a bent finger under her chin, forcing her head up, forcing her to meet his gaze.

His finger hardly touched her, yet it felt like a thousand pinpricks at once, lighting her body with a fire that was more electricity than heat. Like a warning, the charge spread through her, and she quivered, but he had already let go of her. There was a space between them. She knew that, and yet it didn't matter because the heat of him still reached her, the allure of him still suffocated her, and the hope of him still drowned her.

And then he said the thing she knew he would say, but somehow it hurt so much more to hear it in his voice.

"I don't want to see you. I don't want to even think about you." The words were the ones she'd feared, but his voice—his voice was gravelly and strained, and her heart beat faster in response to it, her mind awash with confusion until she had only her senses left to rely on, and they told her a story much different than the lies she told herself. "I don't want to think about you when I first wake up in the morning," he went on, his voice rough and so close. "I don't want to think about you when I'm trying to work. I don't want to think about you when I come into the house. I don't want to think about you at all."

With each word, he held her gaze. With each sentence, he came closer without moving until she felt the wall at her back, the heat of her husband holding her there even as he didn't touch her. Dimly she became aware of the rain slashing at the windows, pounding the roof, and she wondered if the storm had picked up or if that roaring was only in her ears.

He did move finally, and she licked her lips, her stomach tightening in anticipation, but he moved only his head, bringing his lips to her ear but not quite.

He went on with his torment. "I don't like how my eyes search a room for you when I've barely entered it. I don't like how my feet carry me out of my way in hopes of stealing a glimpse of you. I don't like how my ears listen for the sound of your laugh."

Was that the brush of his lips against her skin? She closed her eyes, unable to bear it. Her heart would surely burst now. Her stomach already tied in too many knots. How much more of this would he force on her? How much more could she endure?

The tears leaked from the corners of her eyes, and she once more pressed her palms into the paneling at her back, her fingernails digging into the wood to stop herself from reaching for him.

"Ah, Gwendolyn," he said as if he had discovered something, as if he had conjured something from her, and she nearly whimpered at the knowing sound of his voice. "Gwendolyn, my darling, none of that is what plagues me now. Those things are but the symptoms of a lovesick lad, and I stopped being a lad a long time ago." His lips did brush her ear then, she was sure of it, and the shiver it sent down her body echoed long after he stopped touching her. "Do you know what it is that plagues me, Gwendolyn love?"

No. Anything but that. She squeezed her eyes shut tight, willing the hope in her chest to disappear like a shadow in the sun, but it took root, holding firm to that one, perilous word.

Love.

He didn't keep speaking though. In fact, the silence stretched and stretched and finally she couldn't bear it anymore. She opened her eyes to find him in front of her, his body completely separate from hers when she had been certain he had become a part of her.

His eyes were clear and certain, a dusky green in the candlelight, and she envied the certainty she saw there.

"Do you know what plagues me, Gwendolyn?" His voice had lost its gravelly tone, and his words were strong and sure, compelling an answer she didn't have to give.

Her lips parted without sound, and her eyes implored him to go on, to end this torment and let her be, but he didn't stop. He continued to hold her gaze with his own, continued to hold her without so much as a single finger pressed to her skin.

Finally he leaned forward—or maybe not, maybe that was just a trick of the light—but suddenly he took up the whole of her vision and there was nothing but him when he said, "I hate to see the hunger I feel reflected back at me in your eyes, Gwendolyn."

A sound escaped her lips then, a damning sound that spoke more than any words could, and she knew then that it was too late. She couldn't deny it for there was nothing to deny, and there was nothing to say for he had already said it all. Accused and condemned in the same moment, and she could do nothing but stand there, her palms pressed into the wall behind her, forcing back her shoulders as if she meant to spread herself before him like an offering. Perhaps she did. Perhaps her body had taken over when her mind had likely fled.

When he stepped forward, it was swift and complete, both of his hands coming up to cup her face with impossible gentleness as she sucked in a shocked breath.

He held her face in his hands, and she tried so very hard not to feel anything that could later hurt her as he said, "If the desire was only one-sided I could ignore it. But I can't ignore the way you look at me." His lips hovered just out of reach, toying with hers as they whispered back and forth. "Deny it, Gwendolyn. Tell me I'm wrong, and I'll leave you be. Tell me you don't want me."

Her eyes flew open at the pain she heard in his voice, and she wondered for an impossible second if he were frightened too. Frightened of this enormous thing that had erupted between them so unexpectedly. And in his gaze, she saw it.

Searching.

Longing.

Hoping.

"I want you," she said because it was the only thing to say.

He studied her face, and she couldn't help but feel that he was looking for a lie, but she wasn't lying. She couldn't lie. Not about this. Peeling her fingers from the paneling, she reached up and put her hands over his, holding his gaze as much as she held his body.

When he kissed her it was like an explosion, like the force of a waterfall hitting her body, power and lust exploding against her, heat and torment swarming her body. But no. The breaking wasn't against her. It was coming from inside of her like a dam finally giving way under the pressure.

Finally.

But kissing wasn't enough anymore. She let go of his hands to wrap her arms around his torso, to pull him firmly against her, her aching breasts flattening against his chest, her leg coming up to wrap around him, to hold him snugly against the part of her that ached with passion.

Her hips moved of their own volition, and she ground against him. She moaned, deep in her throat, right before he tore his mouth from hers, his hands going to her traitorous hips.

His eyes were huge and not a little startled as he whispered a single word. "Minx." He kneaded her hips, his big hands spanning her body, and she was suddenly glad she hadn't taken the time to retrieve her dressing gown. The thin gauze of her nightrail was no barrier, and the heat of his touch seared her skin. But he held her *just* far enough away, and she whimpered, arching her back as if to regain sensual contact with his body. Her breasts ached, and she wanted him to touch her there, but he didn't. He only dropped his gaze.

When the heat flared in his eyes, she realized what he saw, and the part of her that ached most for him tightened until she thought she couldn't bear it.

She couldn't help it. She looked down too and saw her tightened nipples outlined by the thin fabric of her nightrail, their stiff peaks practically begging for attention.

He didn't make a sound and neither did she. It was as though even the rain had stopped as they hung there suspended, evidence of her desire clear for him to see. He couldn't doubt her now. Her fingers curled into the coiling muscles of his back, encouraging him to touch her even when she couldn't do more.

Slowly, so painfully slowly, his hands slid from her hips, up her torso to cup her full breasts. His fingers toyed with her, circling her erect nipples, circling and circling, but never touching her. She arched again, a mewl caught in her throat, but he pulled his hands away. She whimpered now, but he only returned his hands to their sensual torture when she relaxed against the wall once more.

He traced the curve of one breast and then the other, pulling her nightrail taut against her until her dusky nipples were visible through the fabric. She couldn't help but look, mesmerized by the way he seemed so entranced by her body. No one had ever looked at her like that, like she was someone who *could* be desired. But when he looked at her, like this, she wondered how she thought anything else was possible.

He bent his head, and she stared, transfixed, as his tongue darted out, licking one aching nipple through the rough fabric. She jerked against the wall, her fingers digging into his back as pure pleasure shot through her.

"Logan." His name was both plea and permission, but he heeded neither.

His tongue continued its sensual assault, scraping against her sensitive peak until she thought she could bear it no more, but then he only switched his attention to the other nipple. She gripped his head now, one hand going into his hair to hold him against her or maybe push him away, she couldn't tell any longer.

She only knew the part of her that ached most for him was wet now, the dampness spreading between her thighs, and embarrassment flooded her. How could her body be so weak? This man who had tormented her since the moment she arrived could spark such passion inside of her, could beckon such a carnal response from her.

She hated it and wanted more of it. She wanted all of it.

He released her nipple only to put his hot lips against her collarbone, and then the column of her neck, and the line of her jaw.

"Ah God," he murmured against her neck. "I've been wanting to do that for so long."

Shock overwhelmed her pleasure for but a moment as his words struck bone. He *had* wanted this. She thought he would kiss her again, but he didn't. Instead he did something terrible.

He leaned back, and without warning drove one hand between her legs, finding that part of her that was so embarrassingly wet. She clung to his shoulders as if she could stop him, but suddenly pleasure so vibrant flooded through her at the very spot he touched her that she didn't want him to stop. Her legs buckled, and she fell harder against his roaming hand, her body pulsing where he explored her, and she cried out, burying her face against his neck in humiliation.

"Oh, minx," he murmured against her ear. "You don't know what's happening do you. You don't know why your body cries for mine."

His words confused her, but their tone told her not to be embarrassed about the wetness between her legs, that something about it was natural and right, and heart thumping, she lifted her head to meet his gaze. Surprise registered in his eyes, and she reveled in it. He might think her unschooled, but she wasn't weak, and she would prove it.

She held his gaze as she moved her hips, driving her body against his wandering fingers. The pleasure was just as intense, but this time it held an edge, a blissful edge because she had pleasured herself. Heat flared in his eyes, and she realized he was enjoying this, watching her take her pleasure.

A single finger prodded at her opening, and she widened her stance, giving him access to her. He pushed inside of her, his finger covered in her nightrail so the fabric scraped against her most sensitive parts.

"Logan," she whimpered, her head falling back against the wall, unable to hold it up any longer.

The pleasure was too great, too acute, too much. It had to end.

But then he pulled his hand away, and suddenly he gripped her shoulders, tugging her from the wall until she fell against him.

His lips touched her ear as he growled, "I want you to see what I see."

He spun her about as his words echoed inside of her, and then she saw it. They faced the mirrored wall, and a gasp stuck in her throat as her gaze found them.

The woman in the mirror could not be her. Dowdy, scarred Gwendolyn. The woman in the mirror was a vixen with her long, dark hair wild about her shoulders, her eyes bright with anticipation. The small buttons at the neck of her nightrail had come undone, the fabric parting to reveal the shadowy valley between her breasts, and—Oh God, *Logan*.

He stood behind her, his arms wrapped around her so as to accentuate the bulge of his biceps, and his hands—his hands were too big, spread like that over the flatness of her belly and lower...lower...where a damp mark on her nightrail spoke of what he had done to her.

She shivered at the sight of her, of *them*, and she shut her eyes, unable to look any longer.

He made a scolding noise in her ear, and his hand pressed into her belly, driving up beneath her breasts, until her eyes flew open, impatient to see if he would finally touch her, if he would finally rub her nipples the way they ached to be rubbed.

"Watch, Gwendolyn," he whispered against her ear. "Watch what your body can do."

With that it wasn't about him. It was about *her*, and a new kind of pleasure roared through her until she gripped the arm he had pinned to her chest as if to hold on.

And she watched—she must watch—as his other hand

began to pull up her nightrail, inch by painful inch. She wasn't sure which was worse—watching as each bit of her pale legs was exposed or realizing how deftly his fingers moved and wondering what it would feel like to have his hands on her bare skin.

She didn't have long to wait to find out. As he tugged up the last of her nightrail, she saw the small triangle of hair he exposed and what it meant, and her fingers curled into his arm.

"Logan, what…"

But she didn't have the breath to finish the sentence because finally—*finally*—he touched her. A single finger, blunt and hard, moving against her intimate folds. She shifted ever so much, her leg pivoting to give him greater access, and then—

She knew she was supposed to watch, but the ecstasy of his touch had her head falling back against his shoulder, her mouth opening without sound.

"Logan, you…you need to hold me." She didn't know why she said it or how she knew something bigger, something greater was coming, but she knew she couldn't hold on much longer. The pleasure was too great, too focused, and it had to stop. It must or else—

"Watch me, minx. Watch me give you pleasure." His words once more had the power to open her eyes, had her gaze flying back to the mirror, and the erotic image they presented. Once more he growled as he said, "I want you to see what it looks like when I make you come."

Again, his words confused her, but it didn't matter because at that moment it happened. Her body splintered, and a pleasure so pure washed over her, she could do nothing but cling to him. It took all she had to keep her eyes open as the sensual pulse traveled through her, as he gave her a pleasure she could never have imagined.

But as she did as he bade her, even as she kept her eyes on their reflection, she didn't watch herself. She watched him, her husband, as if maybe, for a moment, she might see someone else. The someone he'd been before he'd been hurt.

* * *

He eased her away from him slowly, even as the urgency of his own release threatened the fly of his trousers. He'd send her back to bed and then take care of himself. There was nothing else to be done. He couldn't...he couldn't...he swallowed away the taste of despair.

"Gwendolyn." His voice sounded scratchy, and he swallowed again. "Gwendolyn, you must return to your room now."

She had been steady beneath his palms, but at his words, she swayed, turning to face him, confusion and, hell, hurt on her features.

"My...room? But..." Her eyes fell to his trousers, and he wondered just how much she knew about the love act.

He turned away before she could see the truth of his desire, pacing to the other side of the room until a smattering of discarded chairs stood between them. "Go to bed, Gwendolyn. You must be tired." He kept his back to her as he sucked in a steadying breath, blowing it out slowly between his lips as he willed himself to calm.

She would be gone soon, and he could finish what her tempting body had started. He would think of her when he took himself in his hand. He couldn't stop himself from remembering how she had ground her hips against him, how her fingers had dug into him, of the pleading, whimpering sounds she made when he—

"No." The word was so soft he almost missed it, but then she spoke again, firmer this time. "No."

133

He spun about when the sound of footsteps reached him, her bare feet slapping madly against the floor as she strode over to him, her long hair flying behind her, and her face—damn if he didn't harden even more at the determination he saw there.

For a moment, he pictured her hand wrapped around him, her slim, pale fingers stroking him from hilt to tip until she gained the courage to put her lips—

He grabbed the chair nearest him, pulling it directly in front of his body like a shield. "Gwendolyn, what are you—"

She bent and before he realized what she was about, she yanked the chair he'd been holding out from his grasp by tugging on the legs beneath the dust cloth. He was standing with said dust cloth in both of his hands, the chair tossed aside as his wife advanced. He wrapped the cloth around his fists several times, determined to hold on to the last remnants of his defense.

"Don't you dare hide from me," she said. Her hair tangled about her shoulders, a reminder of what they had done, of the way he had pressed her against the wall, her body arching into his—

With a slap of her hand, the dust cloth was gone, and he tumbled backward in surprise, landing in a chair behind him. She was on him in an instant, the skirts of her nightrail snatched up into one hand as she launched herself atop him, straddling him as her free hand braced herself against the back of the chair.

He had no choice but to grip the armrests to keep from touching her as his heart thudded and his cock strained as every erotic dream that had tormented him for the past month and a half rocketed through him.

She let go of her skirts, but it did nothing to cover her warm body as the fabric did little more than fall taut against her spread thighs. Leaning in, she grabbed his chin, forcing him to look at her.

"Don't hide from me, Logan. I'm not a ghost. I'm real, I'm here, and I want you." She pried his hand from the armrest and with no inhibition, brought it between her legs. He watched her carefully, registering the small flinch as she tried to contain her own desire as she turned his hand and placed his palm against her.

She was so wet, and once again, the very idea that he had done this made his own desire swell.

But she wasn't done. She traced the back of his hand until her fingers encircled one of his, drawing it down the line of her intimate folds until she applied just enough pressure to separate her for him, to push him deeper until the tip of his finger pressed against her sensitive nub.

It was harder now for her to control her desire. He knew that, and the fingers of his other hand nearly ripped the armrest from the chair as he struggled to hold himself back, to see how far she would go.

And damn her if she didn't go much farther than he ever dreamt she would.

She moved his finger against her, circling her nub, her hips gyrating as if of their own accord. The damn minx was using his hand to bring herself to climax.

He let go of the armrest as he slipped his hand under her nightrail. Unchecked desire made his movements hasty, and he heard the rip of fabric, but he had to touch her. He found one breast, and then the other, kneading them, rolling the nipple between his fingers. He studied her face as it transformed at his touch, as her mouth opened on a silent scream even as her head went back in relief as though she had been waiting for him to touch her.

The thought was too much.

He ripped his hand from her grip, leaving her reeling and

bereft, a protest dying on her lips as he grabbed the front of her nightrail and tore it asunder, splitting the thin fabric directly down the middle until her heaving breasts spilled out.

And then he plundered.

"Logan." Her cry of surprise urged him on, and he sucked her nipple into his mouth, flicking his tongue against the stiff peak before doing the same to the other one.

She was wild against him, her hips rocking for a completion he had stolen from her, her fingers digging into his shoulders as he continued his torment against her breasts.

He needed her. His hand would no longer be enough. If he didn't take her now, the image of her like this, straddling him, her nightrail ripped from her lithe body, her breasts so heavy and full, on display for him, offered for him—it would haunt him.

He let go of her, wanting two hands to free himself from his trousers. Fabric ripped once more in his impatience, but he didn't care.

"Logan." The wonder in her voice startled him, and he looked up to find her watching him, her lips parted ever so slightly, her eyes steady on his hands.

His cock twitched in response, and he suddenly wished for more time. More time like this. More time with her. Just…more.

He could have more. Hell, he had forever. She was his wife. This could be every night for the rest of his life if he just had the courage to take it.

But the fear was there. It was always there. Mocking him. Reminding him.

So he didn't think any more. He didn't think about this night or any of the other nights of the rest of his life. He only thought of this moment. Right now. With his wife atop him, ready for him, *wanting* him.

He drove inside of her. He should have been careful, gentle. He should have eased into her, allowed her the time to get used to him, but he couldn't hold on. He couldn't hold back.

His head slammed back against the chair as the intensity of it nearly broke him in half. She was too tight, far too tight, and he couldn't last. It had been too long since he'd been with a woman, and he should never have broken his celibacy with a virgin. But he knew then that he would never do this again with another woman.

It would only be her. Gwendolyn. His wife.

And this realization was what finally broke him.

He pounded into her, lifting his hips to drive himself deeper inside of her as though he could never be deep enough. She met him, thrust for thrust, her hips coming down to take him deeper, but no. It was more than that. With each thrust, she rubbed herself against him, her hips circling just so much. His hands shot out as if by touching her he could stop the inevitable, but it was too late.

She was too much. It was too much.

When his orgasm hit, he very much thought it would kill him.

A sound erupted from him, a sound so raw and guttural, he thought it might frighten her, but when he dared to look at her, he found her head thrown back, a smile on her lips as she…as she…climaxed *again*.

The sight of her in that moment, claiming her desire, finding her pleasure, it was a sight that he added to all the rest he had collected over the past month. The ones he sometimes took out in the dark when the past threatened to consume him, and the only thing that kept him from letting the dark have him was the images of her he held in his mind.

Finally she collapsed against his chest, her head falling to his shoulder, and his arms came around her, holding her to him. She was so close, and for a minute, he didn't know whose orgasm still echoed through him, hers or his, but he knew he'd never felt anything like it before.

It was too much.

He knew it was, and yet he had denied it for weeks. But now with his heart still racing, with his wife's warm body in his arms, he wondered if it was finally enough to chase away his demons.

CHAPTER 10

She didn't know how long she lay there, crumpled against his chest.

But his arms were secure around her, one hand pressed into her back, the other cupping the back of her head as though she were something precious. And right then, she almost believed she was something precious.

It felt as though her limbs were no longer connected. She didn't know one could *ache* from so much pleasure, but she did. If he asked her to leave now, she simply couldn't. She hadn't the strength for it.

But he didn't ask, and she didn't wish to, so time passed, and they stayed where they were, entwined and silent.

She must have fallen asleep because the next she was aware of anything, he was carrying her. In a flash, she realized he must be taking her back to her bed, the lonely bed in which she had tossed and turned, tormented by the near touches, the heated glances of her husband for the past several weeks, and she suddenly wished to protest.

Except she didn't.

Something had shifted. For a moment there in that room,

she had held the power. Finally, after so many weeks of whatever tense game they had played, she had had the upper hand, and she had used it to her advantage. But she knew that wasn't true anymore. She had broken through a barrier her husband did not want breached, and she knew she treaded on dangerous ground.

For now, she would let him have his way, let him think he could repair the defenses she had knocked down, and later, she would show him there was no pushing her away once she broke through.

His steps were sure, and his arms never quivered as he held her against his chest. They were in the corridor of the countess's rooms, and her heart squeezed at the understanding that soon she would be alone again. After all they had done that night, she didn't want to face it, so she closed her eyes and buried her face against his neck.

He shifted her against his chest, and she knew he must have been opening a door. She squeezed her eyes more tightly shut, whether to keep out what he was doing or to keep the tears in she didn't know. Perhaps a bit of both.

The softness of the bed didn't surprise her, nor its clean, freshly laundered scent. She had grown used to finding herself in a cold bed every night, and she instinctively curled in on herself as he lay her down. But the moment his arms slipped away it was all she could do to stifle the cry that had become lodged in her throat.

Each of his retreating footsteps was a blow to her heart, and when the sound of the door shutting rent the air, it was like a bullet directly to her chest. She turned her head into the pillow, ready to give in to her tears when she heard another noise.

Footsteps. Coming back to her.

She couldn't help it. She rolled onto her back, lifting her head just enough to see what was happening.

There was a single lamp lit somewhere on the other side of the room, but she didn't know where because this wasn't the countess's room. Her heart beat once, loudly, before beginning to gallop in her chest.

He'd brought her to his room.

She didn't have time to gather her surroundings because then she caught sight of him. He retrieved a shirt discarded on a chair by the bed, the shirt he must have taken off earlier before going into that room, and turned backed to her. She wished she could see his face, but the light of the lamp didn't reach this side of the room, and his features were in shadows.

He didn't speak until he sat on the bed beside her, his shirt in both of his hands.

"Sit up, darling." His voice was low and soft, the tension from earlier having fled. "I've ruined your nightrail, and you'll need to put this on. I don't want you getting cold in the night."

She was sitting up before he had finished, his words confusing her into action. He had not offered her such plain kindness since she had arrived, and yet it seemed only natural that he should offer her his shirt. It was easy to get out of her nightrail as there wasn't much left of it, but she felt a moment of shyness when she was naked, sitting in his bed. It was only a moment though before he helped her slip his shirt over her head. It was far too big for her, but it smelled of him, and she wrapped her arms about herself as if she were holding him to her heart.

She watched as he rose from the bed, her stomach twisting in apprehension or anticipation. She didn't know anymore. The night was entirely too confusing, too raw, too...new. He walked to the other side of the room and snuffed out the lamp. Moonlight came through a crack in the curtains somewhere, but it was hardly enough to lift the darkness from the space around them. She heard him retrace his steps toward the bed, but he paused somewhere. A rustling noise she could only assume was the sound of him shedding his trousers reached her, and she fell back against the pillows, pulling at the bedclothes as if to shield her from her own dangerous thoughts.

Somewhere in the darkness he was naked, and by the sound of his footsteps, he was coming toward her.

The bed dipped, and then his arms were around her. He tucked her against him, her back to his chest, one solid arm wrapped about her belly. His muscular thighs pressed against the back of her legs as he slipped one foot over hers, drawing her feet into his warmth. Her toes were like ice. She only realized it when they met the heat of his body, and she wondered how he knew.

He settled on the pillow behind her, his breath warm against her neck as he said, "Now go to sleep, minx. I can't take any more of you today."

She smiled. It was impossible not to. And then, even more impossibly, she fell asleep in his arms.

* * *

She woke with a start.

Sunlight.

That was the first thing she noticed. The second thing being that the bed was empty beside her.

The events of the previous night came flooding back to her, tumbling over one another until they were out of order, a kaleidoscope of sensations and feelings coursing through her body. She went hot at the memories and then cold as she realized her husband had left the bed.

Her hand skimmed the mattress behind her where he had pulled her against him and found the sheets cool. He had left some time ago.

A sharp stab of pain split her chest, but she ignored it. He was often up early to tend to the flock, and just because he wasn't there when she woke didn't mean he had left *her*. It just meant he had gotten up before her.

She scrambled from the bed, his shirt tangling in her legs as she gained her feet, and she paused long enough to inhale the scent of him that still lingered on the fabric. Wrapping the copious folds of the garment about herself, she went to the window, pulling back one side of the curtain to peer out.

The sun was high in the sky, bathing the pastures that spread up the hill in warm yellow light, and she knew she had slept late. Too late.

She dropped the curtain to scrub a hand over her face and made to retreat to her room only to stop at the foot of the bed, her gaze wandering about her.

She didn't know how to get to her room.

The earl's chamber was appointed in the same style as the countess's. The walls were dark, intricate wood paneling accented with brass wall sconces and a single painting of hounds in hunt above an empty fireplace. The carpets were forest green and gold, soft and compelling yet refined. The few pieces of furniture, a dressing table, a pair of chairs by the fireplace with a small table, and another chair by a door on the opposite side of the bed were understated and simple. Her eyes lingered on the chair by the door in the opposite wall, her hand idly fingering his shirt she still wore, and she wondered if that were the chair where he'd discarded his trousers.

It was empty now, and she felt the pang of loss that seemed so ridiculous. He was only tending to his duties. It wasn't like he had run away from her.

As the thought entered her mind, her heart skipped a little in her chest, and she looked away. There was another door beside her, and she went to it, testing the knob. It turned easily in her hand, and she poked her head through the door cautiously to find Kent on the other side holding up the remnants of Gwen's nightrail.

The two women froze when they spotted each other, and for a moment, Gwen wanted nothing more than to retreat back into Logan's bedchamber, but then something happened.

Kent smiled softly and dropped the nightrail into the basket at her feet that looked to contain garments to be laundered. "Good morning, my lady. I hope I didn't disturb you. His lordship wished for you to get your rest." She retrieved the basket at her feet with an efficiency that somehow forgave Gwen for the momentary awkwardness. "Should you like a bath this morning, my lady? I can have one brought up at once."

A bath sounded delightful, and after last night, she thought she could do with a good soak, and perhaps a long, hot bath would dispel the unsettled feeling roiling in her stomach.

She would let Logan return to the flock. Just as she had decided in the middle of the night, she would allow him to think he could rebuild his defenses. A long bath was just the thing.

She stepped fully through the door, shutting it resolutely behind her. "A bath would be lovely, Kent. Thank you."

It was only when Kent's eyes dropped ever so slightly that Gwen remembered she still wore Logan's shirt.

She raised her chin, forcing her voice to sound casual. "I take it Mary is tending to Felicity."

Kent's eyes returned to Gwen's face. "Yes, of course, my lady. The girl has had a bath herself and is now taking some breakfast in the nursery with Miss Haversham."

Gwen raised an eyebrow at this. "Miss Haversham?" It seemed the governess *was* growing fond of the babe.

Kent nodded. "Oh, aye. She's been in the nursery most of the morning." The maid settled the basket on her hip. "I'll see to your bath now, my lady."

It arrived much more quickly than Gwen had anticipated, and she wondered if Mrs. Rehnquist had anticipated the need for a bath that morning and had had the water at the ready. As it was, Gwen barely had time to don her dressing gown to conceal her husband's shirt before the servants started filing in with the water, towels, soap, and hip bath.

While she spent a focused amount of time on her toilette, she did not tarry. The events of the night had given her a surge of new hope, the tethers holding her to Scarcroft that had felt settled if tenuous now felt solid and real, and climbing from the tub several minutes later, she thought she might even feel a bit of confidence.

She dressed with efficiency, and in no time Kent was placing the last pin in her hair.

"I should like to check in on Felicity before I go down to break my fast," she announced as she stood from the dressing table.

Kent turned from where she gathered the towels beside the tub. "Lady Felicity is no longer in the nursery. His lordship wished to see her before he departed. I believe Miss Haversham took her for a stroll in the park afterward, and she is likely still out of doors."

Gwen froze. The niggling dread she had been feeling since finding herself alone in bed that morning now gripped the back of her neck with a deathly cold hand, any semblance of confidence evaporating.

"His lordship departed?" She spoke the words carefully as if by speaking too quickly one of them might catch fire and burn her.

Kent folded the soiled towels over her arm. "Oh yes, my

lady. I am not certain as to why he departed so hastily, but I saw him speaking with Mrs. Rehnquist. She's likely to know."

"Yes, I'll just go down then." She might have smiled, but the blood had rushed to her face, and she could no longer feel it.

Logan had departed hastily. Her mind wished to conjure any number of things right then, most of them casting her in a negative light, and she refused to allow it.

She kept her pace sedate as she made her way below stairs. She mustn't let the servants know something had disturbed her no matter how her own thoughts tortured her.

Mrs. Rehnquist was in her rooms behind the kitchen, and she clattered to a standing position behind her desk as Gwen entered.

"My lady," Mrs. Rehnquist breathed. "You need only ring if you wish to see me." The housekeeper's eyes were round with guilt.

Gwen smiled to reassure the woman. "I wanted to stretch my legs, Mrs. Rehnquist. It's nothing at all."

The servant's features softened as if she accepted this, but her expression remained wary. "Then how may I help you, my lady?"

"I understand his lordship departed this morning. I wasn't aware he had plans to leave."

Mrs. Rehnquist's face transformed then as if finding comfort in the familiarity of dealing with household business. "Yes, he did, my lady. It was quite sudden. He received word of a new array of rams that were available. He's gone to Nottingham, I believe. He said he would be gone for several days, I'm afraid." She had the foresight to look dismal at this proclamation. Gwen would give her that. But then the housekeeper brightened as if suddenly recalling something. She dug about in the pocket of her starched white apron, withdrawing a folded slip of paper. "He did leave this for you, my lady. He asked me to give it to you when you came down this morning." Her smile was not unlike that of a proud child bestowing a parent with a messy drawing.

Gwen took the folded piece of paper carefully between two fingers. "Thank you, Mrs. Rehnquist."

She turned mechanically toward the door and only heard Mrs. Rehnquist call out after her when she reached the corridor.

"My lady," Mrs. Rehnquist said, her voice sounding as though she'd called out the address several times. "Should I have breakfast laid out for you?"

Gwen shook her head. "No, thank you. I should like some fresh air first."

She didn't remember leaving the house or walking through the kitchen gardens to reach the park. Logan's note burned the ungloved palm of her hand as she pressed it against her stomach. Only when she reached the towering oak at the corner of the house did she stop.

She didn't bother taking a seat on the bench beneath the oak's spreading limbs. She simply unfolded the piece of paper and read. Logan's note was short, but then it would have been. Her husband was never one for lengthy explanations.

It merely read:

I CAN'T.

AND THEN BELOW THAT, in a far less steady hand were the words that brought tears to her eyes.

I'M SORRY.

. . .

SHE DASHED the tears away with one hand, her gaze flying to the horizon as if there could possibly be something there that could stop her heart from breaking. Refolding the note, she pressed it once more to her stomach and drew a calming breath. While the tears remained in her eyes, she wouldn't let them fall. She kept her gaze to the horizon and made herself think.

She hadn't wanted this. She hadn't wanted any of this. Only months ago, her future was determined, set. She would be a spinster. She would look after her mother in her doddering years. It was all so simple and safe and boring. When she'd dreamed of her second chance, she'd never imagined this kind of heartbreak.

This wasn't how she wanted her second chance to be.

How many times had he upset her in the past several weeks?

How many times had he made her yearn?

How many times had Felicity made her laugh?

How many times had she risen from bed with a purpose?

Damn him.

No, not him. Damn Catherine. It was her fault. It must be. If only Gwen knew why. Surely there lay the answer. What had Catherine done that even now drove a wedge between Gwen and the man she feared she was coming to love?

But now Logan had run away. When she'd finally cracked through some of his defenses, he'd retreated. And quite frankly, she couldn't blame him. When she'd learned of her father's plans, she too had wanted to retreat. It was instinctual to do what was needed to protect one's self, and she wouldn't fault her husband for the same action she had wished to commit herself.

It could have been so easy to blame herself. The flash of

confidence she had felt that morning seemed so far away now, and she could so easily let years of scorn bring her down, but she wouldn't do it. There was a moment last night when nothing stood between them, and she knew the truth for the first time. She had to hold on to that.

She wiped her eyes once more, ready to banish any thought of him from her mind. There were other things that required her attention. Other places where she was needed.

She would just…wait. Wait for him to come home. And then she would demand an explanation. She bloody well deserved one.

It was then something in the distance caught her eye, and she saw Rachel along the hill, Felicity in hand. The little girl toddled about the park, her pudgy legs moving madly as Rachel held her hands aloft. The girl's steps were confident if not always steady, and Gwen smiled through her tears. At least something had come of her weeks at Scarcroft Manor.

Gwen stopped smiling.

If Logan was no longer in residence, there was no reason for her to stay there. She couldn't very well plan a dinner if the host himself would be absent. He had asked her to wait until the lambing was completed to take Rachel to Leeds, but he'd harried off on his own, leaving them without his very self as a resource. Surely he could spare the carriage and a footman or two. And Leeds wouldn't really do, would it?

She would take Rachel and Felicity to London. Rachel could inquire at hiring agencies while Gwen acquired the remaining items she would need to play the proper hostess.

It was time Logan got what he needed instead of what he wanted.

CHAPTER 11

The Countess Stoke Bruerne held Felicity in front of her with both hands. "He had a child?" Her icy glare turned to her husband. "Henry, did you know about this?"

They were seated in the drawing room of Gwen's child-hood home, the remains of tea scattered on the low table before them. Grandmother Bitsy pretended to nap in her usual chair before the fire while Henry sat in the opposite chair, one leg crossed over his knee, newspaper held between his hands like a shield. Annie sat beside her on the sofa while their mother sat opposite, inspecting Felicity as a commander might inspect one of his sailors.

Gwen had wanted Rachel to come to tea with her, but the governess had wanted to visit as many hiring agencies as possible that day to make the most of her time in London. Oddly Rachel had seemed almost melancholy about the prospect, and Gwen couldn't help but wonder if it had anything to do with Reverend Simons.

They had arrived in London only the previous day and found the Gracey townhome run just as efficiently as Scarcroft Manor. Mrs. Rehnquist had sent word ahead to have the house opened, and Gwen was pleased to find the home staffed with remarkable servants so like those at Scarcroft. Perhaps it was the familiarities to Yorkshire and what she'd left there that had sent Rachel off in a hurry that morning.

Henry made a noise behind his newspaper that was indecipherable. This seemed to make little impression on Nancy who turned her gaze back to Gwen.

"When exactly did he inform you of the presence of this child?"

"Directly after the wedding ceremony." Gwen had already written to Eloise of all this, but Eloise was mysteriously absent.

Her youngest sister's letters of late had been spotty and disjointed, and Gwen had been hoping to see for herself how Eloise was faring. She had tried asking Annie, but as usual, Annie was rather silent on the topic.

Nancy's expression remained unchanged. "But look at her. How could something so precious not be mentioned at all?" Nancy moved the child back to her lap where Felicity had been sitting for much of the afternoon, Gwen's mother unwilling to relinquish the child. She touched the sleeve of the girl's gown. It was the palest lavender and embroidered with white daisies. "I remember selecting dresses for the three of you. Oh what a delight that was." Nancy looked up. "Well, for the two of you at least. Eloise could never seem to keep her dresses very clean, to say nothing of how much mending they required."

"Where is Eloise?" Gwen took the opportunity to ask her mother.

From the moment Gwen had arrived, her mother's attention had been centered on Felicity, and trying to get her to speak of anything but the child had proven difficult. Gwen hadn't realized how much her mother had wanted grandchildren until she'd witnessed the woman's face transform at the sight of the girl. She glanced at Annie to find her sister sipping her tea, her eyes downcast.

"She's out with that Rosemoran girl, you know the one. Something about needing new ribbons. Or perhaps gloves?" Nancy shook her head as she twirled a lock of Felicity's fine hair around her finger until it made a perfect curl. "I haven't the foggiest what that girl is up to. It's been weeks now, and she continues to flit around at every ball and soiree and garden party. It's as though she is deliberately preventing Ardley from courting her."

"Ardley?"

"The Duke of Ardley," Annie said. "He's one of the dukes looking for a wife this season."

Gwen turned to her mother. "The Duke of Ardley is seeking a wife?"

Nancy booped Felicity's nose, which sent the child into a fit of giggles. "Yes, he is, and your sister is doing nothing to recommend herself to him. I don't even know why I bother."

"Who is the other duke?" Gwen asked, inquiring about the second duke that was on the Marriage Mart that season.

"Grimsby," Henry said with a gruff clearing of his throat.

Gwen couldn't stop her gaze from flying to Annie who studied her teacup as if it were a piece in the British Museum. Gabriel Phelps, the Duke of Grimsby, had been Annie's husband's greatest confidante and lifelong friend. Before she could think otherwise, Gwen reached out and placed her hand on Annie's wrist. Her sister flinched, and Gwen's heart squeezed for her and the obvious pain she was attempting to hide.

Gwen looked up, wondering if she might implore her mother not to pressure Annie into finding another husband this season, so soon after the end of her mourning, but she found Nancy watching Annie as well, a look of heart-breaking understanding on her face.

The silence in the room was near to buzzing when Grandmother Bitsy said, "Gwennie, darling, where is that sheep farmer of yours?"

Gwen had already answered this same question twice, but she said, "He's in Nottingham, Grandmother."

"Nottingham? How unusual. And he's let you come to London all by yourself? What kind of husband is that?"

The words stung, and she couldn't help but think of the brief note Logan had left her. She had felt mildly childish for leaving him a similar note, but he deserved as much, running away like he did.

"A hardworking one, Grandmother," she heard herself say. She couldn't very well tell her family Logan was a coward, but then she didn't think he was one either.

If only he would talk to her about his first wife, tell her what had happened, then maybe she could understand why he was so afraid, why he wouldn't let her get close to him. She reached up to tug at the high collar of her gown when she recalled it wasn't there. She'd foregone the usual addition of lace to her gowns that morning they'd left Scarcroft, and she hadn't felt the need to resume them.

She stuck her hand in her lap, pressing into the palm of the opposite one. "He's seeing to a stock of rams he's thinking of adding to the herd. He has ambitious plans for the estate, and a healthy herd is needed to see those plans through."

Her father lowered the newspaper at this. "See, Nancy. I said the man was financially sound. He obviously gives the attention to his affairs that are required to see them profitable. He will take good care of Gwennie."

Nancy gestured with her hand flat, palm up, to Felicity who now sat on the sofa beside her gleefully turning the pages of a watercolor book. "He failed to mention the existence of a child, Henry. No amount of financial prowess can forgive that." Her mother turned in Gwen's direction. "But Grandmother Bitsy is correct. A woman traveling alone to London. It is rather unusual."

Gwen shook her head and reached for a biscuit. "Not when it's lambing season." She gestured to Bitsy. "Grandmother was correct. Sheep farmers take the wellbeing of their herd very seriously. I even got to help birth a lamb." She took a bite of her biscuit as her mother's mouth opened, eyes going round.

"Gwendolyn, you didn't."

Gwen's smile was genuine as she recalled that night in the barn. She wiped her hands on her napkin. "I did. It was the most glorious thing really. The lamb was stuck, you see. It had one foreleg pinned behind it, and the poor mother was in distress. His lordship let me help deliver it."

Her father had returned to hiding behind his newspaper, but he peered around the edge of it at this. It was only because she happened to be looking in his direction that she caught the curious expression on Annie's face. It took a moment for Gwen to realize the look wasn't a curious one but one of disbelief.

Gwen hurried on. "The mother took to the lamb immediately, thank heavens. If a mother rejects her lamb, you must hope one of the other ewes will take it in. His lordship truly cares for the flock and has done a remarkable job of hiring a qualified staff to care for them."

Something flashed over Annie's features then, and now Gwen was certain the emotion she saw there was indeed disbelief, but Felicity chose that moment to let up a cry of discomfort Gwen had come to recognize.

She made to stand, but Nancy was already on her feet, lifting the child into her arms. "It's a full nappy we have here.

Isn't that right, wee Felicity?" Nancy gestured to the bag Gwen had brought with her. "I assume a clean nappy can be found in there."

Gwen stood, fetching the bag at the same time she reached for Felicity. "I've brought her nursemaid with me. We can see to—"

Nancy was already moving around the sitting arrangement to the Queen Anne table that sat under the portrait of the second Earl Stoke Bruerne. "Nonsense. With the number of nappies I've dealt with, it would be a crime to make the poor nurse come all the way up here from the servant's hall for that. Just ring for a ewer of water, and we'll get her cleaned up."

Gwen watched as her mother used one hand to pluck a small quilt from the bag Gwen had brought while still juggling Felicity with the other. With a dexterity Gwen envied, her mother maneuvered Felicity and the quilt onto the table at the same time all while entertaining the child by blowing softly in her face, turning her cries of discomfort into confused giggles of glee.

After ringing for the water, Gwen stood where she was and crossed her arms over her chest, feeling rather useless.

"I hope you brought a suitable gown for tonight with you, Gwennie," her mother said as she unclasped and unbuttoned and unraveled poor Felicity.

"Suitable gown for what?" As they'd only just arrived in town the previous day, she hadn't received any invitations yet. As it was she wasn't sure there would be time to attend any gatherings unless, of course, it would help the title for her to do so. She had planned to see to the things she needed from London and after a visit with her family return to Yorkshire.

"Lady Fenhorn's ball. I'd like to show you off to Viscountess Bowes."

Gwen raised her eyebrows, shock echoing through her bones. Her mother had never shown her off to anyone. "Excuse me?"

With only a single hand, Nancy pulled up Felicity by the legs, the girl's ankles carefully trapped in one hand as Nancy tugged the soiled nappy free. "Viscountess Bowes debuted her youngest daughter this season." Nancy glanced in Gwen's direction, her face hard. "The girl is only seven and ten. It's despicable. But that means Rosemary has four daughters vying for the dukes this season. I want her to see I've already managed to get an earl for one of my daughters."

Gwen licked her lips, feeling as though she were on the deck of a ship in a stormy sea. "But you didn't even wish for me to have a season."

Nancy stopped so abruptly Felicity let out a startled cry. "What are you talking about? Of course, I wanted you to have a season."

Gwen blinked. "No, you didn't. That's why I never debuted—"

"That's not from lack of trying."

Gwen turned to her father to find him hiding behind his newspaper, but Grandmother Bitsy appeared very awake all of a sudden. "Your father didn't wish to debut you, shortcake. He didn't want those cruel people of the *ton* to hurt you." She pointed a shaking hand at Nancy. "It was the one thing your dear mother has ever given in on."

Her father moved his paper only enough to say, "I swore to your mother I would find you a husband in a different fashion. I wouldn't let those terrible people be cruel to you, and I followed through on my promise." He gave a perfunctory nod and went back to his paper.

Gwen returned her gaze to her mother, feeling as though everything she had thought was true was suddenly something else, and for a moment, her heart squeezed with what might have happened. She couldn't deny her family's love for her, but she wondered if perhaps they loved her too much. Her father's insistence on keeping her safe, and her family's understanding that she be a companion to her mother so she would always have a place. If Logan hadn't offered for her, she might never have found love and her second chance. Her mother's fierce expression then had her springing back to the matter at hand.

"If I couldn't give you a season, I shall damn well show you off now," she said and yanked the dirty nappy straight out from under Felicity.

Gwen glanced back at Annie who shrugged before saying, "It's practically a duel, I'm afraid." She gestured in their mother's direction. "She's been like this all season. The matrons are at war, and they'll use anything to get the advantage."

Gwen frowned. "I must say I'm glad Father married me off then. This sounds rather uncomfortable."

Annie grimaced. "Just wait for tonight."

* * *

"What do you mean she's gone?"

Mrs. Rehnquist blinked like a frightened owl, and he regretted his harsh tone. He closed his eyes and focused on slowing his heartbeat. After all, it wasn't the housekeeper with whom he was angry.

He opened his eyes and tried again. "What do you mean my wife is no longer in residence?"

He had returned to Scarcroft Manor only an hour ago, determined to speak with Gwendolyn. The journey to Nottingham had been fortuitous, and he was bolstered by this success. The urge to run away had been strong after what had happened that night more than a week ago. He had sworn never to allow himself to care for another person, and with Gwendolyn heavy in his arms, he knew he had violated his own vow. The only cure for it was distance, but then, when he had carried her to bed, had watched her curl so innocently against his pillow, the urge to protect her had burst suddenly inside of him, overpowering the need to run away.

For a few, blissful hours, he had slept with her in his arms, and it was only with the morning sun that he felt the need for distance creep over him again. He couldn't let the false comfort of the dark undo years of vigilance. The opportunity to inspect possible rams for the flock had seemed foolish to pass up.

But now, with time, he thought he might strike a happy medium.

After all, a pleasant relationship with his wife would aid him in his goals, and what was there to say there couldn't be an amicable understanding between them. Only every time he thought of it he remembered the passion that had roared between them, and the word *amicable* tasted like watered-down tea.

He could do it though. He could keep her close but not too close, secure an heir, and carry on with his plans. He would see the flock at Scarcroft thrive, see the heritage of the Gracey title restored, and his wife would be happy.

He felt the sting of the lie in the thought. Gwendolyn wouldn't be satisfied with such an arrangement, but perhaps she might settle for it. It was all he could give her.

Upon reaching the manor house, he'd gone straight to her rooms, not at all surprised to find them empty. In the few weeks she'd been at Scarcroft, she had proven an ambitious sort, and her rooms often were empty, but it had been a place to start. When the nursery, sewing room, drawing room, and even the damn kitchen had proven to not contain his wife as well, he'd sought out Mrs. Rehnquist in, of all places, the larder. If he had had the presence of mind, he would have let the poor woman come out of the small space before thundering into it, demanding to know where his wife was.

Only belatedly did he realize he might have looked in the larder to begin with.

Mrs. Rehnquist blinked owlishly again, pressing her back against the sacks of flour balanced in one corner. "She's gone to London, my lord. She said she would inform you of her plans."

So Gwendolyn had finally made good on her threat to return to her family. He straightened, the muscles at his neck coiling in defense.

The housekeeper must have sensed a change in him because she quickly held up her hands. "I assure you, my lord, Felicity is quite safe. Miss Haversham went with them as well as Mr. Piven." She looked about as if searching for answers among the canned beets. "Mr. Piven seemed the best choice at the time, my lord, to accompany them. What with you being gone and Mr. Hatrick attending the lambing, Mr. Piven was the only other choice."

"It is not her ladyship's choice of companions that concerns me, Mrs. Rehnquist."

The housekeeper put her head to one side. "Then what is it, my lord? I should think you would be pleased with her ladyship's insight and willingness to take advantage of your absence to have everything ready for her introduction when you returned."

Mrs. Rehnquist's words were so confusing *he* looked to the canned beets for help. He rubbed a hand over his face. "I am afraid I am not following."

When he returned his gaze to the housekeeper's face, he took a step back. Her features had hardened in a way he had never seen before, and he wondered for a moment if this was what it felt like to be one of her maids, facing such a steely expression.

"Lady Gracey has gone to London to secure the last of the things necessary for the formal dinner she will host to introduce herself to the local gentry as is required of the title. She wishes to have only the best linens, cutlery, and china for the evening. The current inventories of such things are either of worn quality or out of style, and the offerings of the village are limited. She cannot possibly hold the dinner without you in attendance and took advantage of your absence to see to the matters. She had the presence of mind to take Miss Haversham with her so the woman could inquire at hiring agencies in town." Mrs. Rehnquist's gaze narrowed even further if it were possible. "If I may speak frankly, my lord, your wife possesses an incredible degree of intellect, strength, and sense." The housekeeper tugged on the chatelaine of keys at her waist as if to emphasize her point.

"Yes, she does," he heard himself say even as he moved for the door. "Thank you, Mrs. Rehnquist."

He made his way to his study in almost a daze, his thoughts muddied with what his housekeeper had relayed. Gwendolyn had taken advantage of his absence to go to London. Taken advantage. More like run away when the opportunity had presented itself.

Just as he had done.

He collapsed in his chair behind his desk just as the thought entered his mind. It was true. She'd done the same as he had, and he wondered if they were not like a dog chasing its tail except he couldn't work out which of one of them was the tail and which the dog.

It was while he was trying to figure this out that he spotted the folded note in the center of his desk. He stared at it, remembering a similar note he had left for her.

When he could bear it no longer, he snatched it up and unfolded it, revealing two lines of text.

I AM NOT CATHERINE.

WHEN YOU WISH to stop treating me as though I am, you can find me in London.

HIS HAND SHOOK as he refolded the note and placed it carefully on his desk. He watched it as one might watch an adder.

Catherine.

How had Gwendolyn learned his first wife's name? Surely the servants wouldn't have spoken of her. They were too loyal for that. Gwendolyn must have encountered someone in the village who had spoken of Catherine.

What had Gwendolyn been told? Worse, what had she surmised from the information?

It didn't matter really because the most important part of the entire thing was that Gwendolyn was correct. He was treating her as though she were Catherine just as Hatrick had predicted. By keeping her just that much apart from himself, he was shielding Felicity and the title from any damage Gwendolyn may wrought. But in doing so, he was also protecting himself.

From what?

Gwendolyn was not Catherine. He knew that now. He'd suspected it from the first he'd laid eyes on her, but that night in the lambing barn when she'd vaulted over the enclosure in her dressing gown, knelt in the straw beside him to bring the lamb into the world, he had known.

Gwendolyn wasn't Catherine. His brain knew it, but how could he convince his heart of it?

He found Hatrick with the builders at the ram enclosures. The structure was up, posts and beams installed, and Hatrick was going over the final details of where the individual enclosures should go. He looked up at Logan's approach, one thumb unconsciously going to the scarlet knot on his index finger.

"My lord, Smithers and his men should be finished here by the end of the week. How was the trip to Nottingham?" He gestured with a nod of his head to the work continuing behind him. "Will we have these pens full by the end of the month?"

Logan peered over Hatrick's shoulder as a crew of men carried planks to the opposite end of the structure, fitting them for the first row of enclosures.

"Nottingham proved a success. I should like you to arrange for the purchase and transport. What is the status on the lambing?"

Hatrick shifted the building plans in his hands. "Four more lambs delivered while you were gone, my lord. Cottontail delivered a pair herself."

Logan blinked, moving his gaze to his steward. "Cottontail?"

Hatrick shifted the building plans again, licking his lips. "Sorry, my lord. Twenty-eight delivered a set of lambs."

Logan crossed his arms over his chest. "Has my wife been in the lambing barns again?"

Hatrick shook his head, but Logan could see the flare of loyalty in the man's eyes. "Wasn't in the barns, my lord. She was walking the little one past the pastures and Cottontail— er, Twenty-eight—was standing by the fence, you see. The little one took a liking to her, and her ladyship dubbed her Cottontail."

"Hatrick." Logan kept his tone neutral. "Do you feel as though you can manage things here for the next few weeks?"

If Hatrick were nervous before, he was damn near rattled now, nearly dropping the building plans to the ground. "Few weeks? My lord, the lambing is in full swing. There will be—"

"It looks as though you've managed things quite well this past week while I was in Nottingham. There's nothing to say you cannot continue to do so."

"But my lord, you never leave during the lambing." Hatrick bundled the building plans together until they were a folded mess clutched in both arms.

Logan couldn't stop his gaze from traveling back toward the house, to the spot on the knoll where he'd first spotted Gwendolyn helping Felicity to walk, and he let the memory squeeze his heart.

"It seems I'm needed in London," he said.

CHAPTER 12

Gwen soon discovered exactly what Annie had meant. She'd been in London a week now and having not expected to attend a single ball was now standing in the middle of her fourth. This time it was to allow her mother to show her off to the Baroness Mattersly. Gwen didn't even know who that was, but according to Annie, it was a bold strategic move.

Gwen only continued to agree to come to these things because it gave her the best chance of seeing Eloise. Gwen couldn't stop the suspicion that her youngest sister was hiding something from her, but she couldn't fathom what it might be or why she felt the need for secrecy.

She had attended any number of these things as her mother's companion, and she had to admit Annie was right. There was something different about this season, probably because of the presence of two dukes on the Marriage Mart, and she was suddenly glad she hadn't been there for it.

Her heart clenched thinking of Logan, and she resolutely pushed all thoughts of him away.

At least Gwen had been able to order suitable crystal and had placed an inquiry at various agencies for a proper nanny. She was to meet several candidates the next day, and if all went according to plan, she would be home to Scarcroft at the end of the following week.

Her stomach flipped when she realized she thought of Scarcroft as home, but it was the truth. Somehow in the past two months it had become home.

But would Logan be there when she returned?

She shook herself from her thoughts when she realized Grandmother Bitsy was speaking beside her.

"Oh, the child could wear a flour sack and still be the cutest thing I have seen all season," Grandmother Bitsy intoned.

Gwen fully turned her attention to the diminutive woman to find her dunking a biscuit in her lemonade. Her kid gloves spotted dark splotches which could only have come from the lemonade, but the woman seemed not to care as she continued to dunk the confection in it, her various beaded bracelets bouncing along her arm as she did so. The light caught the cut crystals of her dangling earrings as she munched on her treat.

"I'm glad you think so, Bitsy." Gwen meant it. She hadn't realized how important it was to her that her mother and grandmother take to the child, and she was glad she hadn't realized it until Felicity had become a part of the family. "I quite like the gowns you and Mother chose for her today."

Nancy had insisted on taking her new granddaughter to the modiste to select a special gown for her. One gown had turned into five as Nancy and Grandmother Bitsy fought over which were the prettiest. Felicity, meanwhile, had sorted through the various velvets on display, cooing ever louder at each one.

Gwen turned back to her mother. "Is there any progress on the ducal front?"

Her mother looked quickly away as though her gaze had been caught by a rival. At the same moment, Grandmother Bitsy made a grunting noise in her lemonade. Gwen glanced swiftly at the woman, afraid she might be choking, but she was only grumbling into her drink. Something about dukes and duels.

"Mother?" Gwen prompted when the woman was silent for too long.

"Eloise swears she's making progress with the Duke of Ardley," Nancy finally said.

Gwen nodded. "That's encouraging."

Gwen tried to follow her mother's gaze across the room only to find Rosemary Hayes-Martin, Viscountess Bowes. It was then that Gwen became aware of Nancy muttering much like Grandmother Bitsy.

"I'm afraid she's going to turn out much the same as Grandmother."

Gwen jumped and spun around. "Eloise," she breathed.

Eloise's smile was bright, but her eyes remained far away even as she pulled her sister into a hug.

"Have you been avoiding me?" Gwen asked.

Eloise's expression blanked, her eyes widening like that of a child caught doing something naughty before her features settled into a bland look of politeness. "Of course not. Why would you think that?" She gestured about them. "There's just so much that requires my attention this season."

Gwen opened her mouth to reply, but then Eloise's eyes skated away from her face, and Gwen turned once more, attempting to see what had caught Eloise's attention. She saw a tall man coming through the crowd, his hair almost the same color as Eloise's, his gait lively, and his eyes sweeping the crowd as if searching for—

"Eloise," Gwen said, but by the time she turned around again Eloise was gone. "Mother," Gwen said now. "Is Eloise avoiding me?"

Grandmother Bitsy let out a crack of a laugh while Nancy harrumphed.

"I haven't the slightest idea what your sisters are about, Gwen. I have three daughters and likely the least chance of becoming the mother to a duchess in all of the marrying mamas this season." She took a sip of her champagne and stared resolutely away.

Gwen frowned, but it wasn't as though she could do anything about it. Her father had seen to that when he'd signed the marriage contract with Logan so many weeks ago. Besides, she didn't wish to be married to anyone else.

Her stomach gave a jolt at the thought, and she pressed a hand there as if to stop herself from somersaulting to the floor. It was true though. She couldn't imagine her life in any other fashion now. There was only Logan.

And Felicity and Mrs. Rehnquist and Kent and Scarcroft Manor.

Was it only several weeks ago that she had left London in a turmoil of uncertainty? How could everything have changed so quickly?

Would it be enough though? If Logan continued to run from her? If he continued to keep a part of himself separate from her?

She didn't know. But the alternative of not having him at all seemed unacceptable so maybe it was.

"I think I'll find some refreshment." She made to move toward the refreshment table, but her mother's hand shot out and grabbed her arm.

"Gwen, why is that man staring at you?"

Gwen stilled, her eyes following the direction of her

mother's gaze, but she somehow already knew what she would find even if the idea itself were impossible.

Logan.

Her body tightened at the mere sight of him. He was there. With only a ballroom separating them. He wasn't moving toward her. He merely watched her, and in his gaze she saw everything.

He'd come after her.

She swallowed, heat climbing her neck. "That's Lord Gracey, Mother," she heard herself say, but the mechanics of speech had left her conscious mind.

"Oh my," Grandmother Bitsy said.

"I thought you said he was inspecting rams in Nottingham?" her mother questioned.

"He was," Gwen replied, her gaze still on her husband.

Finally he began to move, his movements sure and precise, and she wondered how he had found her.

Rachel.

Rachel was at Gracey House with Felicity. He'd probably gone there first and learned where she was to be that night. More heat flooded her body, and she wondered if she'd faint before he reached her.

"Oh, I see what you mean, shortcake," Grandmother Bitsy cooed. "He does look like a man who likes a good ram."

"Mother," Nancy scolded.

"Oh hush, Nancy," Grandmother Bitsy returned. "You should be proud of your daughter." Grandmother Bitsy had Gwen's attention now. Gwen's and Nancy's, it seemed. Grandmother Bitsy smiled, her eyebrows raised with obvious pride. "It seems Gwen has the power to get the sheep farmer out of the barn."

Gwen did not know what to say to that, but she didn't need to say anything. Grandmother Bitsy took Nancy's arm, mumbled something about needing air, and quite simply disappeared into the crowd, leaving Gwen alone the moment her husband reached her.

"Gwendolyn."

How had she missed the sound of his voice so much? It had hardly been a fortnight since she'd last seen him, and it was as though she had imagined never hearing his voice again. So when the deep, gravelly tones reached her, her knees nearly buckled.

"Logan." Her voice was none too steady.

She hadn't thought about what she'd do when she saw him next. She had been so focused on getting to London and seeing to necessities that she had forgotten to think about their next encounter.

It left her standing there, motionless, unprepared, and hurting.

"I would like to have a private word with you."

She remembered the last time they had had a private word, and the heat returned to the back of her neck.

"We can take a turn in the garden if you'd like—"

"I'm taking you home."

She had turned in the direction of the terrace doors but snapped back at his words, her eyes locking on his.

"I just got here."

"Make your excuses to your host. Our carriage is waiting."

She wouldn't allow him to speak to her like this, and yet part of her thrilled at the way he commanded her. Suddenly she *wanted* to have a private word with him, more than anything, but she worried she had a very different idea of what they might do once they were alone.

She looked about her, but her mother, grandmother, and sister had all vanished. What else was there for her to do?

Logan surprised her by offering her his arm as he led her from the room. She made her excuses to their hosts, claiming a headache, and soon Logan bundled her into their carriage.

"I thought you were in Nottingham," she said as soon as they were underway.

He did little more than grunt, and her mind went back to the first day she had met him and the terrible carriage ride to the vicar.

So that was how this was to go then. She would receive her tongue lashing once they returned home, she was sure of it.

She settled into the bench, pulling her wrap tightly about her and trying as best she could to keep her shoulder from touching his as they bounced along.

When they reached Gracey House, she didn't wait for him in the foyer. She heard Logan speaking to the butler behind her, but she went directly to her room and dismissed Kent for the night. She had removed her wrap and gloves by the time her husband flung open the door and marched inside.

She turned, chin up, but she faltered at the sight of him locking the door. Her stomach clenched, and she wondered for a moment if she hadn't been wrong in her wandering thoughts.

He was dressed for the road, and she felt a flash of guilt at having driven him to search for her in London after a long day of travel, but she dismissed it at the hard look in his eyes. He had run away from her. She wouldn't let him forget that.

He strode over to her, and she readied her retaliation, but when he grabbed her upper arms, bending her over so she was forced to grip the lapels of his coat to stay upright, all reasonable thought fled.

"Let me make one thing perfectly clear," he growled right before his mouth came down on hers.

Yes.

The singular thought traveled through her body on a wave of sudden desire, and she clung to him, this man who infuriated her at the same time he made her weak. His hand moved, plunging into her hair, sending pins flying as he took claim of her. For that was what he was doing.

Claiming her.

She had dared to defy him, and this was the consequence. He was reminding her who she was. His wife. And suddenly she didn't want to be anything else and nothing more. She only wanted to be this infuriating man's wife.

* * *

HE'D MISSED HER.

He hadn't realized until the moment his lips had touched hers. He'd been too consumed by his anger to think of anything else, to understand how much that one night with her had penetrated his every fiber, but as soon as her mouth moved under his, as soon as she grabbed hold of him, he remembered.

He wanted her.

He bent her back, reveling in the way she clung to him, feeling the power and passion flow through him. But it wasn't enough. He pushed her toward the bed, and they fell on it, arms and legs entwined, the kiss never breaking.

He rolled until she was on top of him, her thick, wild hair falling about them like a curtain. The weight of her sprawled across him was like a balm, anchoring him to the present and holding the past at bay. He couldn't get enough of her kiss, and he held her there as he took, his lips greedy and eager, but she was an equal match, taking as much as he did.

Her fingers were busy on the buttons of his coat while he clawed at her skirts, dragging them up her legs until they pooled at her waist. That night at Scarcroft her legs had been bared to him, and at the first touch of silk stockings, he jerked his hand back, the pleasure so acute it was like touching fire.

"Gwen," he moaned against her mouth.

She stilled, her lips pausing against his, but it was so quick it might have been his imagination.

"I need to see you," he murmured against her mouth before he flipped them.

He eased above her, arrested by the sight of her splayed across the bed. Her skirts were around her waist, her legs spread, and—Hell's teeth, the silk stockings seemed to go on forever. He reached out with one tentative finger and stroked the curve of her knee, up her inner thigh until he reached the lace at the top. He brushed his thumb over the small bow of ribbon that held the stocking in place, something so delicate standing between him and her virtue.

He flicked his thumb harder over the bow, watching it unravel. Slowly he tugged the ribbon loose, felt his satisfaction grow as the stocking gave way, pooling along her thigh now. He had only to ease it down.

He sat back, falling against the pillows stacked at the headboard. "Take it off."

He hadn't realized she had been watching him as he undid her stocking, and the intensity of her gaze on him had him hardening.

"What?" she whispered.

It was difficult to remember she was unschooled in this. Her courage and determination made him forget things like that. That she was young. That she was innocent.

He swallowed. "I want to watch you take off your stockings."

She had managed to get his coat off, and he tugged at his cravat now, waiting to see if she would comply. There was a flash of hesitation in her eyes, but then she sat up and faced him, pulling her knees up and wrapping her arms around them.

"No," she said.

He blinked, insecurity roaring up in his stomach. "No?"

"How do I know you won't run away again?"

Her words hurt because they were the truth, and he shoved off the bed, pacing away from her as he threw his cravat to the floor. "I didn't run away."

She stood too, not allowing him to retreat. "Yes, you did. You went to another *county*."

He faced her, startled by her sudden anger. What had he been expecting? He *had* run away. He had taken her virtue and left her, and now he expected…what exactly? That she should fall into his arms? Forgive him? He closed his eyes at this thought and turned away, pushing his hand through his hair. He didn't deserve forgiveness.

"Gwendolyn—"

She snorted, bringing his attention back to her. She stood by the bed now, arms crossed, hair loose over her shoulders.

"Sorry," she muttered. "Please do go on."

He crossed his arms, matching her stance. "No," he said. "I should like to know what that was about."

She took a very deep breath and dropped her arms. "It's nothing. Please go on."

He dropped his arms too and took a step toward her. "It was not nothing. Explain yourself."

Her eyes flew to his, and he realized his mistake when he saw the anger there. "Isn't that what you were doing?" Her voice was colder than ice.

"I'm not the one who—"

She held up a hand so quickly he nearly bit it off. She closed her eyes when he stepped away from said hand, and it was like watching a wave take apart a sandcastle, in slow, inevitable destruction. She just…deflated. When she opened her eyes again, they were soft with exhaustion.

"I don't want to fight with you." He didn't know how her voice could change so quickly like that. Hot and furious one moment and soft and compelling the next. "All we've done since we wed is fight, and I've grown weary of it."

"That's not all we've done." The words escaped him before he could stop them, and she threw him a withering glance. "I'm sorry," he said quickly and then, "I don't wish to fight either."

This seemed to please her. Her eyes brightened, and he thought maybe her lips lifted the smallest of degrees. And then, strangest of all, she took his hand, pulling him in the direction of the...windows.

"What are you doing?"

He'd never been in the countess's rooms in Gracey House. Catherine had always come to him when duty required it, and he'd always assumed their rooms were the same. But he saw now there was a bench seat carved out beneath the window, and it was stacked with plush pillows and a thick quilt. She led him over to it and pushed him down on one end. He reclined into the stack of pillows there and found it unusually comfortable.

But she wasn't through with him.

Bending, she pulled up one of his booted feet and wrestling it between her hands, yanked the boot off.

He stared, enraptured.

"Careful," he whispered. "My valet might think you're trying to steal his job."

She paused before picking up the next one and pinned him with a glare. "Depending on how this countess assignment works out, I just might be."

He didn't like how the thought of her not being his countess sliced through his chest like a dagger and forced his gaze away. She applied the same ministrations to the other foot, and then, scooping up both of his feet, she tucked them onto the window seat, covering them with a quilt as though he were a child.

He didn't have time to think further about this because then she pulled up her skirts and stepped fully up onto the bench at the opposite end and like a dog making its bed, turned about and flopped against the pillows stacked there.

"What's happening?"

"We're having a conversation," she said. "It goes like this. How was your trip to Nottingham, my lord?" She affected a refined, nasally tone for her question, and a laugh slipped through his lips. Her face fell instantly, and he regretted it. But then she said, "You laughed," as though she had just discovered St. Nicholas was real.

"I sometimes do," he whispered, afraid to break the moment.

She shook her head, her wild hair crackling against the pillows. "No, you don't." She drew her legs up again and wrapped her arms around them, and he hated how it felt like she was protecting herself from him. "How was Nottingham, my lord?"

"It went well." He fingered the quilt she put across his legs. "The stock there was fine, and I think it will make a good addition to the flock."

Her smile was soft and real when she said, "That's wonderful," and then they fell silent.

He feared there was nothing more to say between them when she spoke again.

"Why did you leave without telling me?"

"Because every time I'm near you I want to make love to you, and that was the very thing I was trying to avoid."

He disliked the fact that shock registered on her features first, as if it were impossible to believe he couldn't keep control of himself around her, but then her face turned pink, and he wondered if he had embarrassed her.

But she said, "I suppose you're right," and he realized she

might have been embarrassed by the fact that she felt the same about him.

He leaned forward and caught her hands in his. "But that doesn't excuse what I did. I'm sorry, Gwendolyn. I should have spoken with you. I—" But the words crammed up in his throat. His mouth opened once, twice, but nothing would come.

She tugged her hands free. "Here. Let's try this."

She reached up and pushed against his shoulder, shoving him back into the pillows. He let her do it as she turned about, sliding along the bench seat toward him.

"I thought we just agreed to have a conversation. Surely this won't help."

She shoved aside his arm and slipped against him, nestling into the crook of his shoulder as she lay her head against his chest, her arms coming around him. His own arms closed immediately about her, and he remembered that night she had collapsed against him. She was so small, so fragile, so precious in his arms, and he was so frightened of hurting her. Of not being able to protect her.

"Now you don't have to look at me while you talk. Sometimes that can help." Her words vibrated against his chest as she tucked her head under his chin.

God, this woman was going to be the death of him.

He closed his eyes and leaned his head back, taking just a few seconds to enjoy simply holding her.

"My first wife was not a kind person," he heard himself say, but it was like someone else was speaking. "And I never did learn how to..." The words tangled again, but he fought through them this time. "I never learned how to be with her. Not properly. Nothing ever pleased her, and she spent most of her days being disappointed or worse, *finding* ways to be disappointed. I never understood why."

"That's terrible," Gwendolyn whispered, her hair scratching the underside of his chin.

"It was," he said, brushing her hair away from his face and letting his fingers linger in the long strands. "But because of her demeanor our marriage was not a happy one, and I...I'm afraid it's caused me to tread carefully now." He paused, trying to think of how to tell her just enough. Just enough so she would understand but not so much as to tell a secret he hadn't told anyone. A secret so terrible he never wished to speak of it again. "It's left me afraid of finding myself in the same situation," he decided to say.

As if sensing his hesitation, she sat up, one hand against his chest now, and he took it in his own hand as if he needed the connection for what she was about to say.

She studied his face, and he wondered for a moment what she was looking for. Finally she said, "Your past is not mine to keep, Logan. I only ask that you give me a chance with your future and not behave with me as you did with her."

He waited, the feeling of her hand in his as he held it against his chest like a comforting weight, a reassurance that no matter what happened, this beautiful woman couldn't possibly hurt him. Not like Catherine had.

"I want to give you that chance." The words were hardly a whisper as they left his lips, but somehow they had the power to transform her face.

She smiled, fully now, and her eyes widened with a hope that had his stomach twisting. What if he couldn't do it? What if he couldn't give her just that much of himself?

She touched his face then, just a brush of her fingers against his cheek, her expression now tinged with concern. "Don't do that," she said. "Don't doubt yourself."

"It's hard not to."

She dropped her hand, an honesty taking over her features. "I know."

He found this difficult to believe. "How could you ever doubt yourself?" He hadn't meant to ask the question. In fact, it went against precisely the thing he wished to avoid. He didn't want to get to know his wife in that way. Asking a question like that was getting dangerously close to letting her in, and he would do well to remember what had happened the last time he had let a woman in.

She surprised him by pulling away. In the short time he had known her, he had grown to understand she was fierce, almost defiant, and to watch her crumble at his question had his heart quickening. He caught her arm before she could escape.

"I'm sorry," he said. "I've said something to upset you."

She shook her head. "No, it's nothing like that. It's just…"

He tugged on her arm when she looked away. "Would it be better if you didn't have to look at me?" He smiled softly, coaxing.

She returned his smile and let him drag her back into his arms. He felt that same perilous rush of contentment holding her, but he pushed away the lick of fear. He had promised to give her a chance, and he would.

"What is it, Gwendolyn?" he prompted after several seconds of silence.

She tensed ever so much, but then said, "I had smallpox as a child."

He stroked her hair. "I surmised as much."

She leaned back far enough for him to see her face, and he didn't like the uncertainty he saw there. He couldn't help but lean down and kiss her, softly, deeply. When he pulled away, her lips followed him, trying to continue the kiss, and he laid a single finger against them.

He shook his head. "I think not, my lady. We're having a conversation, remember?"

She smiled against his finger before settling back into his

arms. There was another pause before she said, "I was eight, and we're still not certain how it was I came to have it as no one else in the household ever fell ill. But I—" Her voice caught, and something protective lurched inside of him at the sound of the masked hurt in her voice.

He tightened his arms around her. "You mustn't speak of this if you don't wish to."

She shook her head against his chest. "No, it isn't that. It's just…it's just I'm always surprised how strong the memory still is. I thought I would have let it go by now."

Unbidden an image flashed in his mind. The storm. The panting horse. His wife unconscious in his arms.

He drew a steadying breath. "Some memories are like that."

There was another small silence, and he wondered if he had said too much, but she went on. "I was sent to the game-keeper's cottage. My mother was afraid I would pass the illness to my sisters, and she wished to protect them. The gamekeeper's wife cared for me until I was well. She was a kind woman, but…" Her voice trailed off, and he eased her back in his arms so he could see her face.

"You were a child. You must have been frightened." He thought of Felicity, and he knew he could never send her away if she were ill. The very idea sent ice through his veins.

The corners of her mouth lifted even as her eyes remained sad. "I was. I thought I had been banished for good. I thought—" Again her voice caught, but he only held her while she seemed to sort through her memories. "My sisters are a great deal younger than me. Eloise by six years and Annie by five. I would care for them when they were only babes, but when I took ill, my mother told me I wasn't to touch them. I thought she meant forever, and nothing could have been more terrible."

His mind went back to that day he had first seen her with

Felicity. He had been so struck with fear for his child and wariness for the woman he had chosen to be his wife that he hadn't realized what a heartwarming picture the two of them had made. Not until now. And even then, he couldn't have known how much his wife likely yearned for a babe to care for after she was banished from her sisters.

Suddenly he very much wished to see her pregnant, wished to see her arms full with a babe they had made together. The thought was terrifying, the repercussions of such a thing dangerous.

"Did your mother ever apologize for the way she treated you?"

She was quiet as if taken aback by his question. "My mother made the right, if difficult, choice. She was trying to protect her babies, and I can't fault her."

"You were her baby."

She smiled softly. "I'm not sure I was ever a baby."

He smiled too. "I believe that."

She returned his smile, but it was weak. "It wasn't being sent away that still haunts me. Not in that way. It's what came later." She met his gaze then with a ferocity he was coming to understand made up her core. "It was when society made me an outcast for something I had no control over. Those are the scars that still plague me." She touched his face. "Sometimes it makes me doubt myself. Even now."

He wanted to kiss her. He wanted to kiss her more than he'd ever wanted anything. He wanted to kiss her for her bravery and her courage. He wanted to kiss her for her forgiving nature and her determination.

He leaned forward, but she was already pulling out of his arms, and he felt oddly bereft when she slipped from the bench to stand.

She shook her finger at him, a tsking sound spilling from her lips. "What did I say? We are having a conversation." Her words were spoken matter-of-factly, but the curve of her lips suggested something else entirely. "Wasn't there something you asked of me earlier?"

He couldn't have recalled his own name just then with the way her hips swayed as she backed away. He swallowed. "I can't recall just now."

"Mmm," she nearly purred. "Pity. I'm feeling rather… agreeable."

"You are?" His throat might have collapsed entirely.

"I am," she said, her smile turning sultry as she lifted a single foot, placing it carefully on the bench just out of his reach. She settled both of her hands at her bent knee. "If I remember correctly, I think it had something to do with my…" Her fingers began to move, but only her fingers, walking her skirts up her knee.

His heart would collapse next. He was sure of it.

"Stockings," she finished as the hem of her skirt reached her knee, and the stocking in question was bared to him.

She really was going to be the death of him.

She pivoted then, spreading her leg open so he could see the paleness at the inside of her thigh, forcing her skirts to fall back against her hip until he saw—

The bow he had undone earlier.

"Gwen," he breathed, coming up off the bench only for her to push him back down.

"We're back to Gwen, I see," she said, a warmth and playfulness in her voice, but he couldn't have said what in heaven's name she was talking about. He could only see that length of ribbon, lying uselessly against the creaminess of her thigh.

"Good," she said as she took hold of the lace edge of the stocking and began to slide it along her thigh, inch by excruciating inch.

"Stop." The word tore from his beleaguered throat. "I don't trust myself if you keep going."

She rolled the stocking over her knee before complying. Keeping one hand on the stocking, she leaned toward him until he was forced to look at her. She was so close. All he had to do was lean forward and his lips would be on her, but the look on her face kept him back.

What he saw there was nothing but pure confidence, and it rocked him.

"Promise?" she whispered, her smile lifting into a wicked grin.

"Promise," he growled and grabbed her.

CHAPTER 13

*H*e couldn't stop himself from thinking how impossible it was that this was his wife, that he should kiss her like this, with so much passion and heat. That she should curve her body into his as if he could never hold her close enough. He groaned, deepening the kiss even as he backed her toward the bed.

His fingers worked the tiny buttons running along her back, but there were far too many of them, and he was too impatient. He heard fabric ripping, the startled cry from his wife, but soon his hands found the thin linen of her chemise, and he couldn't really care about anything else. He'd buy her a hundred—a thousand new gowns to replace this one. It didn't matter. He just needed to touch her, to feel her heat, to know she was real, and she was there…with him.

Her gown fell away, tumbling down her shoulders just before they reached the bed, pooling on the floor in a forgotten heap of silk and crinoline. He meant to lay her on the bed, carefully, seductively, but she had her hands fisted in his waistcoat and pulled him down with her.

It was not graceful. It was not beautiful. It was hard and

lustful and heated, and he couldn't get enough of her. She wrapped one leg around his, holding him against her as he devoured her, his lips moving from her mouth to her jaw to her neck to her collarbone—oh God, those damn collarbones that had tormented him for so long.

He wanted her naked. He wanted to see all of her at once and for as long as he pleased. He wanted slowness, but his heart raced, and his hands shook, and he found he hadn't the focus to get the strings of her corset undone.

She laughed softly and pushed his hands away—pushed *him* away, forcing him to kneel as he straddled her on the bed. Her face was magnificent, her smile sinful and her eyes bright with confidence.

"Allow me, my lord," she said, her voice thick as she plucked one string from the knot he had made of her corset ties. She tugged the string once, twice, thrice until the knot unraveled, but she didn't pull the string loose. She held it and his gaze, and it was as though she challenged him to stop her, to pull her hand away so he could be done with the task and bare her to him.

But he didn't give in to her taunts. Instead he peeled off his waistcoat and with one hand at his back, pulled his shirt over his head, tossing it aside.

When next he looked at her, the glinting confidence in her eyes was gone, replaced by naked appreciation. Her fingers had dropped the string she'd held, and carefully he pulled her hand away, picking up the tie she had discarded.

"Do you require assistance, my lady?" It was his turn to grin, and he was rewarded with a strangled, incoherent murmur in reply.

He tugged the string and watched the bow at the top of her corset come completely undone. One by one he loosened the ties until the garment parted along her torso, revealing every exquisite inch of her thin chemise. He knew he had only to push away her corset, and he would find her dusty nipples poking through the flimsy material of her chemise, but he didn't. Instead he placed a single finger in the hollow at the base of her throat, and holding her gaze with his own, ran that finger down her chest, through the valley of her breast, along her rib cage, and lower...lower...

She made a noise then, a noise so beautiful and vulnerable that he forgot what he was doing, and she was able to sit up, pressing herself against him, her hands against his back as she captured his mouth in a slow, long, hot kiss.

"Logan," she breathed. "I want to see you." Her hands slid down his back, and he couldn't stop the quiver of muscle as her touch burned him, as it sent him closer and closer to an edge he wanted nothing more than to hold at bay.

Not yet. Not yet. Not yet.

He wanted more of this. He wanted it forever.

But her fingers reached the waistband of his trousers, and he knew he wouldn't be able to resist her.

He got off the bed, nearly tumbling in his haste to escape her dangerous touch.

But the damn minx followed him, swinging her feet to the floor until he raised a hand. "Stop."

She did, surprising him. She stilled, perched on the edge of the bed in only her chemise, the corset left on the bed behind her. The angle forced the edge of her chemise taut against her thighs, and he had to look away.

He had almost gotten his trousers undone when she suddenly appeared before him, her hands reaching for him. He tried to stop her, but she swatted away his hands, and then horribly—*terrifyingly*—she sank to her knees in front of him, her hands finding the buttons of his trousers.

"I want to touch you," she said, and he wanted to object, but she wasn't looking at him. She was already undoing the remainder of the buttons, and then, without warning, he recalled that night at Scarcroft when he had thought about her hand on him, stroking him in long languid measures, and suddenly his hands fell limp at his sides.

He watched, mesmerized, as her slim fingers slipped each button free until she could push away the fabric. Without hesitation, she took him into her hand. He couldn't see her face at this angle, and he wanted to. Was she repulsed? Was she disgusted?

Her manner didn't suggest it. Her hands moved carefully, delicately, and he wished she would warp her hand around him, but she couldn't possibly know—

She looked up, her eyes steady. "Can you tell me what feels good?" She turned her hand then, cupping him. "Show me what to do."

He couldn't. She couldn't. This couldn't be happening. But then she said, "Please," and he was lost.

He swallowed. "Like this."

He adjusted her grip on him, moving her palm around him, placing each finger delicately around his shaft, and then holding on to her hand, he said, "Like this."

He used his hand to move hers, and he thought he might die from the pain of it. It was one thing to feel her small hand wrapped around him. It was another entirely to watch it, to watch his hand guiding hers, to see the way she studied him, her gaze rapt, her focus unwavering until her lips parted, and the smallest sound of pleasure escaped her.

He dropped his hand and tried to pull out of her touch, afraid he couldn't take any more, but she wouldn't let go. She stroked him, from base to tip, in long, torturous measures. He wanted to look away. He wanted to close his eyes against it, but it was—

She put her mouth on him, and he thought he'd died his heart pounded so furiously.

"Gwen." Her name barely registered, his hands tangling in her hair as he tried to hold on.

Her lips were tentative at first, as if she were trying to decide how it was done. He wanted to tell her it wasn't necessary. Hell, that she probably shouldn't if she wished to continue what they had started, but he couldn't. He wanted it. So he watched as she took him into her mouth, as she sucked, and he nearly came undone.

"Gwen," he tried again, but it came out as more of a moan, and it was all he could do to remain upright as she took him into her mouth, sliding down his length as she stroked him at the same time.

He did retreat then, pulling himself away. She looked up, startled, hurt visible in her eyes.

He cupped her face reassuringly. "No, darling. It's just that it's too good, and I can't—"

"Too good?" she said, her voice steady, curious, but it was her eyes that undid him. They had turned molten and wicked.

He lifted her, making it only as far as the edge of the bed before he dropped her, parting her legs with his hands so he could drive into her. The pleasure bordered on pain, but he couldn't stop.

"Logan." His name was a plea on her lips, her head going back as she arched into him, as her legs wrapped around his waist, urging him forward.

He reached between them, flicking his thumb over her sensitive nub, and her eyes flew open, dark, fathomless pools of passion. She reached up, cupping his face in her hand, wrapping it around his neck to pull him closer until she captured his mouth in a scorching kiss.

When she finally pulled away, it was only to whisper, "Touch me again. Please."

His cock twitched inside of her, his hips moving now of

their own accord as he felt the edge of his orgasm grow sharper. He stroked her with his thumb, watched as her eyes slid shut, as her lips parted in pleasure, as her hands slid down his chest around to his back to dig in, hold on.

When her muscles contracted around him, her cry of pleasure splitting the air as her body rocked with orgasm, only then did he let himself go, let himself fall over the edge. He tried to hold himself there as her orgasm echoed around him, but his legs shook with the effort, with the intensity of his own climax, and it wasn't long before he slipped onto the bed and pulled her into his arms, and with his body still echoing with their shared orgasm, he let sleep claim him.

It wouldn't be until he woke sometime in the night to pull the quilts more snugly around them, to slip his arm around his wife and hold her close, that he would realize how easily sleep came when he was with her.

* * *

GWEN WAS at Hammersmith's the following day making the final selections for the place settings she had been working on with the proprietor, a Mr. John H. Hammersmith, and that would be sent on to Scarcroft once she had finished her choice of pattern. She'd brought Annie with her, hoping that between the two of them a pattern may finally be chosen. The poor man, Mr. Hammersmith, had already spent two appointments with Gwen, and she had only been successful at ruling out a garish pineapple pattern and a maudlin gray. She and Logan had discussed leaving for Scarcroft in three days' time only that morning, and she must have the place settings in order.

It had taken all her willpower to pull herself from bed that morning when she discovered her husband to be unusually attentive. If he hadn't had a meeting with his solicitors, she likely wouldn't have made it.

Mr. Hammersmith had once more laid out several choices, and she and Annie hovered over them.

"I like the pale pink one here," Gwen indicated with a discreet finger. "But I think pale pink might be too feminine for a title such as Gracey." She looked up and met Annie's gaze. "They are sheep farmers after all. I want to make sure to clearly represent their strength and determination." She went to look away and pursue the patterns once more but the look on Annie's face stopped her.

It was the same expression her sister had worn when Gwen had relayed the story about helping to deliver the lamb. It was almost as if her sister didn't believe her.

She laid a hand on Annie's arm. "Annie, darling, is there something wrong?"

Annie made a pretense of adjusting her bonnet, but Gwen suspected she just wished to pull her hand away. Annie had withdrawn after her husband's death, and even now, she shirked human contact. Gwen worried her sister may never come out of the place she had retreated to when her husband had died so unexpectedly.

"I'm quite well. Thank you. You should choose the blue pattern," she said softly, indicating the pattern she meant. "I think I'll just take in a bit of fresh air. Is that all right?"

Gwen frowned but nodded as Annie was already turning to the door.

"Lady Gwendolyn?"

Gwen started at the sound of her name and turned to find Rosemary Hayes-Martin, Viscountess Bowes, standing behind her.

She caught her frown in time and bowed her head in greeting. "Viscountess Bowes."

The viscountess smiled softly. "I suppose you're Lady

Gracey now. I apologize for the error. I'm just so used to calling you Lady Gwendolyn."

The woman's eyes were kind, and Gwen felt momentarily unsettled. The animosity between Viscountess Bowes and Gwen's mother was legendary, but Gwen had never really understood it. For all Gwen had heard and witnessed of Viscountess Bowes, the woman was kind, soft spoken, and cared deeply for her daughters. Gwen noted the new strands of gray at the woman's temples and wondered horribly if her mother had caused them.

"Yes, it is Lady Gracey. I hope your daughters are finding some success this season." Gwen quite frankly didn't know what else to say to this woman. She'd never spoken more than a handful of words to the viscountess in the years of their acquaintance, and there was something about the woman's bearing that was strangely foreboding.

The viscountess looked down and licked her lips nervously. Gwen laid a hand on the table behind her as the room seemed to tilt.

"Lady Gracey, if I may, I don't wish to frighten you. It's only…" As the woman's voice trailed off, Gwen inserted any number of things the woman could have meant to say.

It's only that your husband cares more for his sheep than humans.

It's only that your husband was unkind to his first wife.

It's only your husband is a murderer.

She'd heard that one already, and if Viscountess Bowes hoped to frighten her, she was too late.

Gwen raised an eyebrow. "What is it, Viscountess?"

The woman licked her lips once more and took a step closer, lowering her voice. "I only say this because of my connection with your mother. We were good friends once, and no matter what has happened since then I hope she would treat my own daughters with such kindness. Lady

Gracey, do you know of the circumstances of your husband's first wife's death?"

Gwen raised her chin. "If you think I will gossip about—"

Lady Bowes raised a hand to stop her. "It's not gossip I'm interested in, Lady Gracey. It's your reputation. Before her death, your husband's first wife went to great measures to slander your husband's name. It was one thing when you were in Yorkshire, but now that you've returned to London I thought I should warn you."

Slander his name? What was this woman speaking of?

"Warn me of what?" Gwen held firm to the table behind her.

"Warn you that it will be difficult to take your place in society as Lady Gracey. I'm sure you plan to introduce yourself at some point, and I'm afraid whatever it is you plan, your invitations will not be accepted. A great deal of damage was done by that careless woman's tongue, and it will take something monumental to overcome it."

The conversation she'd had with Logan on the window bench the night before came roaring back to her, and she hated how easily Viscountess Bowes's words fit in with what Logan had told her about his first wife.

Someone who was selfish, willful, and unhappy might wish to hurt the person she thought had hurt her.

Gwen let go of the table and took a step toward Viscountess Bowes. "What kind of damage?"

Logan had said himself that his wife had blemished the title, but as the man had also seen no issue with replacing a beautiful rose garden with ram enclosures, she needed to ask the question of someone who would see Catherine from society's perspective. That Viscountess Bowes should have stepped forward was odd, but the woman was doing her an unusual kindness.

What if Gwen had sent the invitations without warning?

She and the title would have been disgraced. And wasn't that what Logan had specifically asked of her? That she represent the title with respect?

Viscountess Bowes hesitated. "You know I don't like to gossip, Lady Gracey. I want to make that perfectly clear. But the nature of the woman's claims…" She trailed off again.

"Please, Lady Bowes," Gwen implored.

Viscountess Bowes looked away before swallowing and meeting Gwen's gaze. "The previous Lady Gracey claimed her husband was cruel. That he mistreated her in the vilest ways."

Gwen was so surprised by the woman's words that she stepped back without thinking, knocking into the table behind her.

Viscountess Bowes reached out a hand to steady her. "I only tell you this to warn you, Lady Gracey." The woman's eyes softened then, and Gwen steeled herself for the woman's pity, but it didn't come. Instead the woman's gaze was filled with only a sad understanding. "I want you to have a chance, Lady Gwendolyn. Of anyone, it's you who deserves one the most."

Before Gwen could say anything further the woman turned away and headed for the door, nearly colliding with Annie reentering the shop in her haste to get away.

"Were you speaking to our mother's nemesis?" Annie asked.

For a moment, Gwen was distracted upon seeing the confused look gone from Annie's features, her normally pleasant demeanor returned. When she realized her sister was waiting for an answer, Gwen said, "Yes, I was. I'd better tell you in the carriage home."

She finished her business with Mr. Hammersmith as quickly as possible, selecting the blue pattern as Annie had suggested, and within moments they were back in the Bounds carriage headed to Stoke Bruerne House.

"Well?" Annie prompted when they'd settled into their benches.

"Lady Bowes says Logan's previous wife slandered his name through society. That should I try to introduce myself as the new countess, my invitations will be declined."

"Has Lord Gracey said as much?"

Gwen's frown was immediate. "If it did not take place in the barns, he would be wholly unaware of it."

Annie's frown was eerily similar. "I see. So what are you going to do?"

"I can hardly host a dinner now and have no one come. The Gracey title will surely be relegated to the rubbish heap then."

Annie leaned forward and gripped her arm. "Mother will know what to do."

But upon returning to Stoke Bruerne and finding their mother along with Grandmother Bitsy in the shared courtyard, the first thing Nancy said to Gwen after hearing about her encounter with the viscountess was, "I'm disowning you."

Grandmother Bitsy shook her hand at her daughter-in-law, the same hand that held what looked to be a glass of sherry, and it had only gone half-eleven. "Come now, Nancy. It's not as though Gwennie has joined a quilting circle with the woman."

Nancy acted as though her daughters weren't standing in front of her as she continued to arrange a bouquet of cut roses on the wrought iron table on the terrace. "She didn't need to speak in return. Now did she, Mother? A firm chin and a stiff nod of dismissal. That's all it would have taken."

Gwen found a seat, feeling the weight of the day press down on her. She wished she had Felicity with her to distract her, but Rachel had insisted on taking the child to the park.

Gwen would have thought the woman would wish to attend interviews for positions, but she seemed oddly persistent in taking Felicity for the day. She claimed it was to allow Gwen the freedom to spend what little time they had remaining in town with her family, but Gwen couldn't help but wonder if something else were amiss.

Thinking of Rachel had her wondering if Logan were adamant about leaving in three days' time as they had discussed. Gwen could hardly host a dinner at Scarcroft. Not all the way in Yorkshire and in the middle of what was appearing to be a most contentious season. If her invitations would go unaccepted in London, they would be a laughing-stock if sent from Scarcroft.

A pain blossomed in her chest when she thought of letting Logan down, but it couldn't compare to the heart-break she felt for her husband. To have his first wife damage his reputation so, it was unthinkable.

What could the woman have possibly been thinking? What had Logan done to cause her to retaliate in such a way?

Gwen thought of those first days at Scarcroft and knew perfectly well what the woman had been thinking. She herself had nearly left after being married to the man for only one day. But to disparage someone in public was petty and childish, and the picture she was beginning to piece together of Catherine was becoming clearer.

She wished she could speak to Logan about her, but last night had been a breakthrough, and she wasn't about to push it.

"Gwennie, darling, your problem is one with a simple fix."

Gwen looked up, shaking herself from her tumbling thoughts as Grandmother Bitsy's voice carried over the strained voices of her mother's rebuke to Annie's attempts to defend Gwen.

"What is that, Grandmother?"

Gwen had to wait for the answer as Grandmother Bitsy downed the rest of her sherry. "You must have a ball. Here. At Gracey House in London."

"That's a lovely idea, Grandmother, but no one will come." Gwen eyed the sherry glass and wondered how many the woman had already had.

"They will come. Mark my words they will." She shook the empty sherry glass in the air to emphasize her point.

"And just how is that going to happen, Mother?" Nancy said, her hands still full of cut roses.

Grandmother Bitsy's eyebrows traveled straight up to her hairline. "They'll come if the dukes come."

Gwen felt the moment her thoughts stopped racing, latching on to the idea.

"How is she to get the dukes there if Lord Gracey has been so disgraced?" Nancy asked.

But Grandmother Bitsy didn't need to answer because everyone on that terrace knew precisely how to get the dukes to attend. At least one of them, anyway.

Slowly all eyes turned to poor, quiet Annie who had tried to put the wrought iron table between her and the other members of their gathering.

Gwen surged to her feet, going directly to the table. "Please, Annie. You must speak to him. He'll listen to you. I know it will be painful, but he was Roger's most trusted confidante."

Annie stared at the spirals of iron under her fingertips, and Gwen's heart squeezed at the lost look in her sister's eyes.

"Oh Annie," Nancy breathed, her hands dropping so the roses crumpled against her skirts.

When Annie looked up, there was a haunting emptiness in her gaze. "I can't, Gwennie. I want to, but..." Her voice stopped as if her throat had suddenly gone dry.

Gwen circled the table, but Annie dodged away from her. "Please, Annie. I would never ask if it didn't mean a great deal to me, but Grimsby will surely do anything you ask of him."

If Gwen hadn't been watching her sister so carefully she would have missed the flare of something in her eyes. Was it surprise or fear? There was such a fine line between the two it was difficult to tell.

"Annie, I know you can do this," Gwen said then, something calm washing over her at seeing her sister cower on the other side of the table. "I've always known you to be able to do the things I can't. I think you've just forgotten that."

Annie's eyes flashed up, and Gwen saw the recognition there. Of the three sisters, it had always been Annie who was the most confident. It was likely why she'd secured a husband so quickly after her debut. It was only that Roger's death had stolen her confidence from her. Now it was her chance to reclaim it. Gwen knew it even if Annie didn't.

This time when Annie spoke, her voice was more certain. "I'll do it."

Gwen smiled until she realized getting Annie to agree to her scheme wasn't nearly the most challenging part of this whole endeavor.

It would be getting her sheep farmer husband to stay out of the barn long enough to attend a ball.

CHAPTER 14

$\mathcal{L}$ogan returned to Gracey House after his meeting with his solicitors in the early afternoon, hoping to find his wife and instead nearly colliding with Miss Haversham, who also held Felicity. He wasn't sure who was the more surprised of the two of them, but Felicity was certainly the most excited. She let out a squeal, and then most surprising of all, she reached for him.

The strangeness of the situation was compounded when he took the child naturally into his arms, cradling her against his chest as though he had done the same every day for the past two years. Felicity gurgled something that seemed surprisingly close to actual words and then pressed her palms to his cheeks and then to her own.

He found himself smiling, bouncing his daughter on his hip just to hear her laugh. When he turned back to Miss Haversham, she looked as though she had found a troll in the foyer instead of an earl.

"Miss Haversham," he said, adding a note of concern to his voice to hopefully shake her from her stupor.

She swallowed and nodded in greeting. "My lord, I wasn't

expecting you. I had hoped her ladyship had returned from shopping."

He frowned at this news. "Lady Gracey hasn't yet returned?"

Miss Haversham folded her hands in front of her. "No, I'm afraid not, and I've received a note requesting my presence for an interview this afternoon for a governess post. I shan't wish to miss it, and the nursemaid has the afternoon off. I was hoping her ladyship would return in time, so I may—"

"I can care for Felicity." The words slipped so easily from his mouth, but what was far more concerning was how sure he was of them.

Miss Haversham clearly was not as her mouth fell open, and her hands clutched at her skirts. "You'll care for Felicity?"

He adjusted the girl on his hip. "She is my daughter, Miss Haversham. I assure you I'm more than capable of caring for her. You may have the afternoon off to see to your interview." He had taken two steps in the direction of his study when he paused and turned back. "I wish you luck this afternoon, Miss Haversham. Should you require a reference, I should be happy to write one for you. You possess a certain stamina not seen in many people, and it is rather a good quality for a governess."

He left her standing in the foyer, mouth agape, as he made his way to his study.

Nearly two hours later, he was prepared to write a treatise on how sheep were easier to care for than toddlers. Felicity proved a fearsome opponent. She was just ambulatory enough to cause utter destruction to his study but not agile enough to avoid possible harm should her exploration bring her into danger. She pulled every book from every shelf she could reach, toppled the rubbish bin more than once, and played a game of discard with the sofa cushions that only she knew the rules to.

He had lost his jacket, waistcoat, and cravat within a matter of minutes, and by the hour, his shirt sleeves were rolled to the elbows, his back damp with sweat. He vowed to increase the next nanny's pay by ten percent.

He found himself sitting on the floor, his back against one of the sofas as Felicity sat between his outstretched legs, merrily gurgling to herself as she flipped the pages of a book on the complexities of the relationship between sphagnum moss and a quaking bog. At any moment he expected her to declare herself an expert in the earth sciences.

He watched her, feeling the funny twist in his chest grow, the same funny twist that had started the moment he had first seen her in one of the gowns Gwendolyn had chosen for her. Her pale blonde hair was brushed now and curled against her ears, and he knew soon they would need to trim it, and the thought of losing those curls pained him. He would keep a lock of it and press it into this book on bog ecology and treasure it forever.

She flipped the page again, revealing a detailed illustration of moss and let out a noise of appreciation, tapping his leg with her hand in excitement. She looked up briefly to make sure he was watching, and he rewarded her with a smile just as the door to the study opened.

His wife entered at a clip, and for a moment, concern flashed through him at what might be causing her to rush so when Felicity looked up and clear as though a bell were ringing said, "Mama!"

Gwendolyn froze, and Logan was absolutely certain his heart stopped beating. Gwendolyn's lips had parted as though she had meant to greet them, but she stood there, just inside the door, her lips pressed into a strange *O* as Felicity clapped her hands in excitement before reaching for her.

The moment was shattered as soon as Felicity struggled to gain her feet, using Logan as a means to aid her, and he did, holding her steady until she was standing and could better hold up her arms for Gwendolyn. His wife came forward, and he noticed now her eyes were wet with unshed tears, and his heart stopped all over again.

Instead of picking Felicity up, Gwendolyn dropped to her knees and scooped up the child, pressing her into a hug. He watched as Gwendolyn closed her eyes, as the tears fell softly down her cheeks, and he knew more than he knew anything else that he loved this woman.

This woman who had defied every expectation he'd ever had of her since the day he'd met her. This woman who continued to test him, this woman who dared him to be a better man.

This woman whom he loved.

Felicity squirmed, clearly done with the constrictions of emotion, and Gwendolyn set her back down next to the book. The toddler happily went back to turning pages, and Logan reached up and tugged his wife to him. She fell against him, and he held her there long enough to capture a kiss.

When he finally let go of her, she collapsed against him, nestling into the crook of his arm. He used his free hand to wipe away her tears as he said, "Well, Mama, I should like to know where you've been." He smiled softly.

Her smile wobbled a bit, but she met his gaze as she said, "I've been planning a ball with my mother and sister."

His smile evaporated. "What ball?"

"The one we are hosting in three days."

He straightened, holding her away from him so he could properly see her face. "We're not hosting a ball in three days. We're returning to Scarcroft in three days."

Gwendolyn bit her lip, the first time he had ever seen her unsure, and he wanted to stand up and pace the room, but it would have disturbed Felicity, and he would never consider such a transgression.

"I thought you might say that, and I know I had promised just this morning that I would need only two more days to finish my business here in London, but I received a bit of information today that has changed that."

Was there a hesitation in her voice at the end of her sentence, or was he hearing things? "What sort of information?"

If she worried her lip anymore, she would damn near chew it off.

"Gwen," he said softly, and her face relaxed instantly, the corners of her mouth twitching as if holding back a smile.

He'd been right about that. She liked it when he called her by the shortened name. But stranger than that was the fact that he liked making her smile.

She wasn't distracted for long though as she settled beside him, facing him this time and idling stroking Felicity's hair.

"I know you do not like to speak of your previous wife, Logan, and I shouldn't wish to cause you pain or make you do something you don't wish to, but a woman of some acquaintance approached me today to inform me of something your previous wife had done."

Logan felt the momentary pleasantness of sitting on the floor, his wife at his side and his child playing happily on the carpet, disappear like smoke in the wind.

"You were gossiping about me?" The words were out before he could stop them, and he felt like hardly more than an ignorant boy as soon as he'd said them.

Her frown was fierce. "In case you forget, we've already played this game, and I won. Do you wish to retract your question?"

He swallowed. "I very much do, and I apologize." He laid a

hand on the arm she rested on his leg and squeezed gently. "I really do apologize, Gwen."

She smiled in understanding. "I know you have trouble trusting, and I know it will take some time, but do try to hurry, will you?" Her smile turned playful, and he found the tension in his chest easing.

"Now then," he said. "What salacious gossip were you spreading about me in the shops?"

She raised an eyebrow. "Is that sarcasm?"

"Yes, it is. Am I doing it correctly? I haven't much practice with it."

She nodded slowly. "It's a fine showing for starters."

He smiled and beckoned her to go on.

"An acquaintance of the family suggested that should I try to hold a function to use as an introduction my invitations should not be accepted."

"I'll force people to attend then, or we shan't have the introduction at all."

Her eyes widened before she frowned. "Really, Logan. You asked for a wife that would represent the title in the best light. It's required of me to make an introduction as the new Countess of Gracey, and if I do not do so, it shall be frowned upon." She swallowed and dropped her gaze momentarily, and he steeled himself for what she might say next. "The acquaintance suggested your first wife said things about you in society that were not to your favor. That your reputation was—"

"Utterly destroyed," he interrupted, feeling an odd tingling start in his arms and work its way up toward his neck. "Catherine destroyed my reputation with her lies. What of it?"

He'd never spoken so freely both his wife's name and what she had done. Hatrick knew, of course, and Mrs. Rehnquist had been forced to deal with some of the fallout when it came to managing Scarcroft after Catherine's death. The staff in London he'd managed to shield by closing up the house. The result was he hadn't spoken of the things Catherine had done since her death, and yet somehow simply speaking the words sent a rush through him, like opening the windows after a long, cold, raw winter.

Gwen shifted against him. "Catherine's lies have been accepted as truth apparently, and you're not seen in the best way to society. Apparently favor is with Catherine on this front, and if I have any hope of making a proper introduction, it must be done here in London."

Her words stopped abruptly, and he knew the worst was yet to come. "And?" he prodded.

"And we must get one of the dukes looking for a wife this season to attend."

He blinked. "I'm sorry?"

She waved a hand. "It's a silly thing really. There are two dukes on the Marriage Mart this season, and all of society is agog over it. If I can make sure at least one of the dukes shall attend, I can nearly guarantee it will be a success."

"And how do you plan to do that?"

"One of the dukes is a dear friend of my sister Annie's late husband. She's agreed to speak to him."

"I shouldn't wish to make your sister do anything that might cause her pain."

Gwen's features changed then, slipping into a curious mix of disbelief and disappointment.

"What is it?" he finally asked.

"You're terribly empathetic, but you do a remarkable job at hiding it."

"Empathy makes you vulnerable. I wouldn't want it to get out."

Her face fell, but she said, "I wish Catherine were alive so I could give her a stern talking to."

He held back a laugh as he tugged her toward him. He nestled her into the crook of his arm and put one finger under her chin, lifting her face to his for a soft kiss. "If Catherine were alive I likely would never have met you, and the very thought frightens me," he whispered against her lips.

She touched his face, gently, and he'd never been so moved by anything so whisper soft.

"Does that mean you'll let us stay for the ball?"

He growled and kissed her for a very long time. When he finally released her to take a breath, he caught the flash of movement out of his eye and reached out just in time to keep Felicity from pulling a book off of the nearby table and directly onto her head.

Fright lanced through him, and he pulled Felicity back against his chest as if by merely hanging on to her, he could protect her.

"Does it ever get any easier?" he asked as Felicity squirmed to be let free, obviously wishing to find more trouble.

"I'm afraid not," Gwen replied, taking Felicity into her arms and showing the child the bows of ribbon that held her sleeve to her elbow. "As they get bigger they only encounter greater danger."

The very idea left him paralyzed.

* * *

EVERYTHING WAS PERFECT.

The staff had done a remarkable job of opening the ballroom, dusting the chandeliers, stocking the refreshments, and preparing the room to receive a crushing number of guests. To say nothing of the mastery Cook had pulled off to feed all of those guests. Gracey House in its entirety seemed more cheerful, the servants smiling in her direction, and light filled every room. Perhaps the ball would be a good thing for more than one reason.

As Gwen stood in the center of the ballroom, taking in every detail, ensuring each was absolutely as she had wished it, she only had one worry.

Whether or not Annie had convinced the Duke of Grimsby to attend.

Her mother and Eloise had been charged with spreading word of the duke's attendance at the Gracey ball, and with three days of events at the height of the social season in which to do it, the odds had been favorable everyone who was anyone in London would have heard.

Now Gwen had only to wait.

She pressed a hand to her stomach and turned to the stairs where they would receive their guests, but instead of finding Logan, she found Rachel standing halfway down the stairs, a hesitant hand on the balustrade. She was dressed in a soft blue gown with a neckline that framed her features and did marvelous things for her coloring, including setting off the distinct pink in her cheeks.

Gwen smiled until she saw the fractured look on the woman's face. She hurried forward, reaching the bottom step to call up to her. "What is it?"

Rachel hesitated, biting her lower lip, before descending the remainder of the stairs to join Gwen on the ballroom floor.

"It's nothing really, and I shouldn't wish to bother you with it tonight. Not with all of this going on." Here she gestured to the room around them. "It's just that I know you and his lordship wish to depart for Yorkshire as soon as possible, and I just wished—" She stopped and licked her lips nervously, and Gwen felt her stomach tighten even more. "It's just that I wish to return to Yorkshire with you and remain in my post as nanny to dear Felicity."

She had spoken so quickly, the words falling out in a torrent, that it took a moment for Gwen to decipher what exactly she had said.

"You wish to remain in your post as nanny?" Gwen finally managed.

Rachel nodded, and in doing so, the light caught in her eyes, revealing the dampness there. Only then did Gwen notice how the woman wrung her hands together in such a way that endangered the fine kid of her gloves.

Gwen snatched at the poor woman's hands, pulling them into her own. "Oh Rachel, we would be delighted to have you return with us to Yorkshire." She tugged the woman into a hug, only to push her away again to study her face as she said, "This wouldn't have anything to do with Reverend Simons, would it?"

Rachel's gaze darted to the left as she pressed her lips together, and Gwen couldn't stop the smile that came to her lips.

"Oh Rachel, it does, doesn't it?" Gwen breathed.

The governess could only nod, and Gwen couldn't help but giggle like a debutante and squeeze her friend's hands.

"Oh Rachel, I'm so very happy for you." She looped her arm through Rachel's and steered her back toward the steps. "You must tell me all about it and distract me from the dread that is threatening to fill my lungs."

It was Rachel's turn to give her comfort. "You mustn't worry. Your sisters will come through for you."

Gwen appreciated Rachel's meaning, but she knew it wouldn't be as easy as that.

Logan finally appeared at the top of the stairs, and for a moment, Gwen was struck by the sight of her husband. She'd never seen him dressed for a ball before. She'd very rarely seen him in so much as a coat let alone a dinner jacket and a cravat that matched his waistcoat. He looked almost like an earl instead of a sheep farmer.

She wasn't sure how long she stood there and stared until Rachel excused herself to check on Felicity, and Logan suddenly looked as though he might follow her.

"Is there something amiss with Felicity?" Logan asked as soon as Rachel was out of earshot, and Gwen caught his arm as she tried to hold him back.

"Felicity is fine. Rachel is only seeing to her duties as nanny."

"I thought she was a governess," he returned.

Gwen frowned. "I'll explain later," she murmured. "You look lovely tonight," she said more clearly.

"Aren't I supposed to tell you that?" he said, a line appearing between his brows.

"You may except I already know I look lovely." She ran a hand down her torso where the deep blue gown fitted every one of her curves. She looked up in time to see the heat flare in her husband's eyes, and she smiled. "But say it anyway."

Instead he growled and kissed her.

They were interrupted by the clearing of a throat some moments later, and Gwen broke away to find her father glaring in her direction while her mother's eyebrows appeared to be trying to climb off her forehead.

"Father." Gwen smiled.

"Are you Gracey then?" her father demanded.

Gwen peered around her parents to find Annie with Grandmother Bitsy. She made to smile again in greeting, but the look on Annie's face had her stepping away from her husband to go to her sister.

"What is it?" she whispered at the same moment she saw Logan bow in greeting to her father.

There was an exchange of titles at her back, but Gwen

could only look at poor Annie whose face had lost all its color.

"Was he hurting you?" Annie whispered back as Grandmother Bitsy began to hum in tune with the orchestra that had begun to warm up.

For a moment, Annie's words got lost in the commotion, and it was a beat before Gwen could straighten them out.

"Oh no," she said, shaking her head, trying to imagine what Annie must have seen. "He wasn't—" But then her words went away entirely as she caught sight of Eloise coming along the corridor with not one but two gentlemen in tow.

She smiled pleasantly and walked in a rather normal, sedate fashion but there was something strangely nervous about her eyes. Gwen forgot Annie's pallor in an instant, her mind focusing on the strange behavior of her other sister.

What was going on here?

"Gwennie!" Eloise said far too brightly when she reached their group. "May I introduce his grace, the Duke of Ardley?"

The buzz of conversation about them stopped suddenly as Nancy had been peppering Logan with questions, but at the introduction of the duke, Logan was all but forgotten. Even Grandmother Bitsy stopped humming.

Gwen realized she should curtsy in greeting and dipped awkwardly. "Your Grace, I'm terribly pleased you've come. May I introduce my husband?"

"Gracey," Ardley said before Gwen could make the connection. "I've heard a great many things about you, and I hope none of them are true."

Gwen blinked, realizing what the duke had said, but then she saw he was smiling. He was tall and fine boned and had the carriage of a man born to authority, but his eyes were warm, and his smile was sincere, and Gwen found herself liking him immediately. She glanced at Eloise, but her sister's gaze was oddly on the floor.

"I'm happy to help in dispelling any rumors the *ton* has decided would make good fodder." Here Ardley nodded in Eloise's direction. "Lady Eloise informed my cousin of your endeavors tonight, and I can only hope my presence here will aid you in your quest." His smile kicked up on one side in a grin.

"Your cousin?" Logan asked.

Ardley gestured behind him. "May I introduce my cousin? The Honorable Mr. Tucker Ryan."

Gwen's eyes drifted to the second man. The man was of similar build and coloring to the duke, but whereas the duke was refined this man had a more solid presence about him in both manner and structure. The spark of recognition hit her then, and she couldn't stop her eyes from moving to her sister. This was the man Gwen had been certain was searching for Eloise at the Mattersly ball.

The man bowed politely and when he straightened he smiled, but Gwen caught the smallest movement of his eyes in Eloise's direction. It wasn't a glance, per se. It was almost as if he had to stop himself from looking at her.

Gwen opened her mouth to ask more, but the tuning of the orchestra was overcome by a sudden commotion in the corridor.

Guests.

Lots of guests were pushing through from the foyer into the corridor that led to the ballroom. The soft notes of the orchestra were obliterated in seconds as shouts—shouts?—echoed down the corridor.

There was a second for Nancy to grip her hand and whisper, "Good luck," before she escaped down the stairs and out of the way of the coming mob.

Gwen watched as women jostled women out of the way,

elbows flying, and skirts hefted far higher than was proper. Gentlemen struggled to keep up, but it was clear the marrying mamas and debutantes were taking the lead.

"Dear God," Gwen heard Ardley mutter before he too fled.

Gwen was not so preoccupied as to miss the way Mr. Ryan took hold of Eloise's arm, nor the protective look he gave her as he ushered her down the stairs. Gwen watched them go until Logan took her arm.

"Lady Gracey."

She turned at the note of uncertainty in her husband's voice and patted his arm reassuringly. "Don't worry," she whispered. "You'll do just fine."

"It's not me I'm worried about. It's whether or not we'll be fetching a doctor or a bobby by the end of the night."

Gwen held back a laugh as the first of the guests arrived before them then. She struggled to hold a polite smile even as she tried to tame her laughter.

It wasn't until the first marrying mama reached her that Gwen realized what she'd done. Her hands began to tremble, shaking the skirts of her beautiful, blue gown as she stared down the line of guests waiting to be greeted. She must stand there and allow all of these people to stare at her, to see her scars, to whisper—

Fear gripped her heart in icy fingers as the Marchioness of Whitshire curtsied and rose, already pulling her daughter in the direction of the ballroom, but the woman stopped and turned only her head to grin in Gwen's direction. "Well played, Lady Gracey," the marchioness said for only Gwen to hear.

Gwen remembered to smile before the marchioness could disappear down the stairs.

Perhaps it was an anomaly. Surely the rest of the ladies would—

Viscountess Bowes was next, and she merely gave Gwen a knowing smile before towing her daughters along to the ballroom floor below. Next came a countess and a baroness, and both passed by without staring, without whispers, without knowing glances.

And then Gwen froze, her eyes falling on the next woman in line.

She curtsied first. "Your Grace," she said, dipping her head in greeting.

When she rose, the Duchess of Ravenwood was smiling, a generous, warm smile, and Gwen wondered why she should have been so afraid.

"Lady Gracey, thank you so much for having us this evening." The duchess leaned in. "You're far braver than I am. Inviting *both* of the dukes here tonight." The duchess straightened and her smile had turned into a grin. "Well done, Countess."

And then the duchess was gone, replaced by another viscountess and then the wife of a shipping magnate, and then…

And the night went on like that. Minutes turned into an hour, and they were still standing there greeting guests. Surely no more people could fit on the ballroom floor. The terrace doors had been opened at the start of the night, and Gwen saw people drifting into the garden in search of more room.

Logan turned a questioning eye in her direction, but she could only shrug.

She had grown tired, and her knees and feet ached from curtsying. There was a small break as a commotion further along the corridor stopped the line of guests progressing. It appeared one debutante had trod on the foot of another, and this had resulted in seconds being called by their respective mothers and the gentlemen were trying to calm both parties.

This dueling for dukes nonsense was getting out of hand.

"Lady Gracey," Logan said loudly beside her, for one had to speak loudly to be heard just then. "I declare you an unquestionable success. May we now retreat to the ballroom floor and disappear in the crowd?"

"I haven't heard a finer idea uttered all evening." She took his hand and made to escape down the stairs.

They had only just reached the ballroom floor when Nancy stopped them, her hand on Gwen's arm.

"Gwennie, darling, Grimsby's arrived. There will be no accounting for behavior now."

Logan stopped beside her, and she turned in time to see an older gentleman descending the stairs.

"That's Grimsby," Gwen explained as she too watched the man approach. "I almost feel guilty now for doing this to him."

The debutantes that had been quarreling at the top of the stairs poured down them now and surrounded the poor duke. Ever the gentleman, he merely exchanged polite pleasantries with them and continued his way down the stairs.

He greeted Henry first, who stood closest to the stairs when Annie suddenly turned, her eyes bright.

"Grandmother Bitsy, I think you could do with a glass of lemonade."

Grandmother Bitsy was holding a glass of lemonade. "Dear, I'm quite all right—"

"No, no. You mustn't get parched. I think I'll just go and—"

"Lady Anna and Lady Gwendolyn."

Annie froze, and Gwen couldn't help but get the sense her sister was like a rabbit that knew she had just been scented by a hound. She turned a polite, trembling smile on the duke.

"Your Grace," she said with a nod.

Grimsby returned the greeting before turning to Gwen. "I understand it's Lady Gracey now."

Gwen smiled. Gabriel Phelps, the Duke of Grimsby, was likely ten or more years Gwen's senior, and gray already liberally colored his otherwise black hair. He had chiseled features, a broad forehead, and a smile that was always warm. Gwen had always liked Grimsby, and she thought it was about time the man found companionship in marriage if not love.

"It is, Your Grace. May I introduce my husband?"

Pleasantries were exchanged before the duke leaned close to Logan and said, "If you were to take a turn about the room with me and tell me everything there is to know about sheep, I would be eternally grateful, Lord Gracey."

He cast a glance at the debutantes hovering at the edge of their group like wolves at the edge of a fire, waiting for someone to stray so they could pounce.

"I know enough about sheep to entertain you for two laps I should think, Grimsby," Logan said and drew the duke away from the hovering debutantes.

Annie seemed to deflate the moment the duke walked away, but before Gwen could ask her sister if she was all right, Grandmother Bitsy said in far too loud of a voice, "Annie, darling, have you ever noticed how Grimsby looks at you like he wants to eat you?"

CHAPTER 15

Gwen moaned and let her head loll back against the pillows, letting her eyes drift shut from the sheer pleasure of it.

"All right, do this one now," she said, extracting her foot from her husband's hands to replace it with her other one. She wiggled her toes in invitation, and she could almost feel the sardonic look he cast in her direction, but he continued with his ministrations. "Oh," she breathed. "That's much better."

"I didn't realize you could be so demanding," he said.

She opened one eye. "I thought I made that obvious from the beginning."

Now she could see the sardonic look. "I had hopes you would become more biddable with time."

"Biddable, really," she murmured. "I hardly think it suits me."

"It doesn't."

They had retreated to their room at nearly half four, and she felt an overwhelming sense of guilt at leaving the servants to the disaster that was the ballroom, the gardens, the corridors, the retiring rooms…but as Logan had pointed out, Felicity would be awake in a matter of hours, and they would both need their sleep to deal with matters when the sun came up. She had promptly collapsed on their bed and bid her husband massage her aching feet.

Now she had nearly laid her head back down, but his words had her studying him again. He massaged her foot methodically, his gaze intent on his endeavor, and he looked almost…sad.

Shifting the pillows behind her, she propped herself up so she could see him better. "You seem rather melancholy. Did the evening not go as you desired?"

The guests had only left after the Duke of Ardley had made it clear he was departing for the night. He'd had to announce it from the ballroom stairs as he was leaving, and it was rather good of him. By that point it was nearly three in the morning, the buffet had been overrun so only scrapes remained of Cook's beautiful bounty, and the gardens had nearly been trampled by the overflow of guests.

Gwen had lost track of the number of society ladies who had congratulated her on the evening, but more importantly, every time she had caught a glimpse of Logan it was to find him deep in conversation with everyone from dukes to bankers to shipping moguls. It seemed society had been quick to change its mind about the Earl of Gracey once it became apparent the sheep farmer was not at all what he had been rumored to be.

But the thing she would remember most about the evening was not her triumph in society, not how she had vanquished Catherine's specter from the minds of the peerage.

It would be how she had triumphed over her own fears.

For so long, she'd been focused on the external, on finding the thing to fulfill her after overcoming smallpox.

She'd never realized how much damage the smallpox had done inside of her. For the first time since she'd first stepped into a ballroom as her mother's companion, Gwen had felt perfectly at ease. In her own body, in her own skin, in her own place.

She had wanted a second chance but this, this seemed too good to be really true, and she waited now, wondering what could have put such a look on her husband's face.

"It exceeded any expectations I might have had for the night," he said, but his words hung as though there was something he wasn't saying.

She prodded him with her foot. "But?" she asked.

He met her gaze, his mouth tipping up on one side. "How is it that you can read my mind so easily, and yet I can never predict what it is you'll say or do?"

She smiled encouragingly. "You'll get there one day. I promise. It only takes time." She prodded him with her foot again. "Now tell me what's put that look on your face."

He massaged her foot for a few seconds more. "You seemed to enjoy…it," he finally said.

She frowned. "Enjoyed what? The ball?"

He had been looking down at what he was doing, but now he looked up again, and that line had appeared between his brows. "Yes," he said simply. "You…" He shook his head as if he couldn't quite find the word. "Flourished."

The word landed on her like a bucket of icy water, waking her from a stupor she hadn't known she'd been in.

"Flourished?" she repeated.

He nodded. "I've never seen you more animated. At least not when you were at Scarcroft. I just hope—" Now his voice cut off, and she felt a flutter of panic, wondering if this was it. If this was the cause of the niggling sense of dread she'd been feeling.

She sat up and laid a hand on his arm. "Just hope what?"

He swallowed, and it looked like it hurt. The dread in her stomach welled up until she thought she might drown in it.

It seemed to take ages for him to speak, and she wondered how she didn't expire from lack of oxygen by the time he said, "I just hope you won't find yourself preferring to stay here in London." Her mind went utterly blank, but he went on. "I understand if you would prefer to be in London. Your family is here, and I understand now how close you are to them." He hesitated, and his gaze dropped to her foot again as if he couldn't look at her when he said, "It's just that I am needed at Scarcroft, and I will miss you if you're not there."

There was a beat of silence as his words filtered through the dread that had taken over her mind, and then—

She laughed. It was a great bleating sound that startled him into looking up, his eyes wide and mouth grim, but she couldn't stop. His face grew grimmer, and with it a sudden realization formed in her head.

Her laughter stopped. "Oh God, you don't understand," she breathed.

His face remained unchanged, and she tugged her foot from his grasp so she could sit up and move closer to him, taking his hands into hers.

"Do you know tonight was the first time I attended a ball as myself and not as my mother's companion?" His features softened, but his eyes remained hard. "Every ball before this I spent at the edges of the dance floor with my mother, keeping my head down so I didn't see the way others stared at my scars."

His face transformed then, and her heart skittered at the sight of real danger in his gaze. Danger for whoever might stare at her apparently.

She squeezed his hands. "I didn't feel that way tonight. Not with you by my side. But truly I do not wish to linger in

London any longer than necessary. Society may have forgotten about my scars tonight, about how they made me an outcast, but when I no longer have dukes to give them, they'll remember, and I do not wish to be here when they do." She hesitated, but the words were already on her lips, and she knew they were the right ones. "I want to go home, Logan. With you and with…our daughter."

She felt the risk hanging in the air between them, but she'd had to take it. It was as though her second chance meant nothing if Logan didn't confirm it. It was ridiculous really. Logan's confirmation had nothing to do with how she felt inside. How her heart had raced when Felicity had called her Mama. How she felt when Kent had started packing her trunks the previous day for their departure to Scarcroft. How she had felt in her husband's arms, dancing for the first time with someone other than her sisters.

Somehow it mattered. It mattered what he thought and said right now.

But Logan's face remained unchanged, his eyes hard and mouth unforgiving when he said, "Even if your chances of being mauled by a ram increase considerably?"

It was a moment before she realized he was making a joke, and her heart stuttered at the realization. How could this man have changed so much in the past months? He never would have jested with her in such a manner before. She could remember too clearly that first day they'd met when he'd questioned her senses. This was the same man who now teased her about mauling by ram.

She tried to hide her smile. "Even then."

He raised an eyebrow. "I'll take that into consideration, but I reserve the right to question you further the next time a ram tries to accost you."

"Agreed," she said and took his hand to shake it formally as though they had negotiated a business deal.

She thought her heart couldn't beat any faster with joy, but he laughed, the sound full and wondrous, and the breath caught in her throat. He kissed her then, and she forgot everything else.

It was much later as she fell asleep in his arms that she finally knew in her heart that tomorrow they would leave for home.

CHAPTER 16

*S*unshine poured through the windows of the breakfast room, bathing the space in a warmth and glow that did not match the mood of the interior.

Now that they had returned to Scarcroft Manor, Gwen had decided it was time to continue Felicity's development, and this morning that meant introducing the child to new foods, an experiment the child in question appeared not to enjoy.

When Gwen had first arrived, Felicity had been on a rather bland diet of porridge and mashed vegetables, and really the child should have been introduced to more foods by now.

Just as she had done with getting the child to walk and speak, Gwen started small. This morning it was eggs. She had never seen a child have a stronger opinion about eggs than the one Felicity demonstrated.

Rachel had stepped up to the task after Gwen had been the victim of an unfortunate incident with apples the previous day. Eggs appeared to be in the same category of distaste for Felicity as she pushed the little bit Rachel had fed her out between her lips, so it oozed down her chin, the chin in such a state of pout, Gwen had never seen the like.

Rachel turned a pained glance in Gwen's direction.

Gwen set down the morning's post a footman had left beside her plate and returned Rachel's expression. "Should we try pears instead?"

Rachel wrinkled her nose. "I'm afraid the poor child has gone too long without an expanded palette. The damage may never be undone."

Gwen frowned. "We must keep trying. She really must have the best chance of growing strong. There are only a few bites left anyhow." She'd placed only a small amount on Felicity's plate, worried the child might prove physically opposed to the new food and not wishing to subject her to a large amount should she grow ill.

Rachel pushed back a strand of hair that had fallen over her forehead with the back of one hand. "I must say I shall not be trying turnips on her. I'll leave that to you, my lady." Rachel cast a grin over her shoulder at this, and Gwen felt the contentment of the morning fall around her like a warm shawl.

They had returned home nearly a week ago, and she hadn't realized she had been bracing herself for their return until she had felt the tension ease from her shoulders, the breath fill her lungs when she understood things would not be so terribly different.

She had been afraid the magic and bustle of London would have meant something different for them, for Logan and Gwen and Felicity, but it hadn't been so. They'd slipped back into life at Scarcroft as though they had never been gone.

Except everything was different now.

For one, she never slept alone.

Although Logan checked on the barns late after supper,

he would always return to the manor house while she was still awake. He invariably went to check on Felicity, but she had noticed he no longer stayed in the nursery as he had done when she'd first arrived. He would slip into bed beside her, pull her against him, and she'd ask him how the lambs were.

Hatrick had proved more than competent at managing the lambing and seeing to the care of the flock while they were gone, and Gwen could sense Logan understood the same. He left the barn more for one. He visited tenants and met with the builders on the ram enclosures. He even spent entire days away visiting neighboring farms and meeting with other farmers to discuss herd health and changing trends.

She couldn't help but feel he'd been released from some sort of web he had wound around himself after the damage Catherine had done.

Yet she still noticed his careful ways. The way he surveyed the lambs, the way he kissed her softly every morning before going out to the pasture to be among the herd first thing in the morning, the way he still watched Felicity with a sharp concern that was more than doting parent.

And she couldn't stop that niggling sense of dread she had first felt in London. Logan may have opened up to her, but he still wouldn't speak of his first wife easily, and the cautious nature of the servants when Catherine was mentioned left a lingering doubt in Gwen's mind.

That morning in the breakfast room though she tried to push it away. Everything was well, and the weather was fine. If they could get Felicity to try a little of her eggs, the day would be off to wonderful start. She had only to keep the proper mindset about it.

She picked up her post again, noting the letters from the Duchess of Ravenwood and the Marchioness of Whitshire.

"I think I shall walk to the village this afternoon while Felicity has her nap. I should like to purchase a better bonnet for walking Felicity in the park. All that sun, you know," Rachel said, spooning another bite of eggs into Felicity's mouth.

This time the child chewed, but her squished features suggested she didn't care for it.

Gwen set down the post carefully. "A walk into the village? That sounds lovely. I suppose Reverend Simons will be making his usual rounds this afternoon as well. Perhaps you shall run into him."

Gwen knew perfectly well Rachel could have purchased a bonnet in London, and Rachel likely knew it, but this was the game they had been playing since their return to Scarcroft, and Gwen found it rather amusing.

Rachel would pretend to require something in the village, and Gwen would pretend that it was, in fact, a necessity. Gwen only wondered how long the charade would continue until Reverend Simons declared his intentions.

Gwen's heart sank at the thought as she watched Rachel make Felicity laugh by twirling the spoon of eggs in front of her. They would need to find a new nanny should Rachel marry the reverend, and while she would be happy for her friend, the thought of finding a new nanny was daunting.

As she watched Rachel entertain Felicity with the spoon, Gwen caught sight of a small red mark low on the child's cheek. She wondered if Felicity had bumped into something now that she was so steady on her feet, her confidence growing as she toddled about the nursery and park. But then Gwen saw another small red mark higher up the girl's cheek.

Panic set in before she drew her next breath. She was out of her seat in a flash, plucking Felicity from her highchair.

"Don't touch her." The words shot from Gwen's mouth, startling Rachel into dropping the spoon and knocking the plate of eggs to the floor.

The china struck the carpet beneath the table with a dull thud as Rachel scrambled to her feet to get out of Gwen's way.

Gwen held Felicity in the direct sunlight to better see her skin, and there it was.

A telltale line of small red circles traveling down her cheek and disappearing into the neckline of the gown. She clutched Felicity to her and spun about.

"Don't touch anything. Go directly to the kitchen and get the hottest water you can stand and wash your hands. You'll need to change clothes as well. You may need to discard your gown. I'm sorry. It's the only way to be certain. Tell Mrs. Rehnquist to send for the doctor and have a footman fetch Logan." She was already turning to the door. "I'm taking Felicity to the nursery. No one is to enter except the doctor and Logan. Do you understand?"

Rachel's eyes were wide, her lips parted, and Gwen realized she likely sounded like someone bound for Bedlam. She slowed long enough to turn Felicity and show Rachel the trail of angry red circles down the girl's cheek and neck.

"I'm afraid Felicity contracted smallpox while we were in London," she said and fled the room.

* * *

LOGAN HAD BEEN in the western pasture attempting to locate Sheep Forty-two—or Mabel if his daughter and wife had their way—to see if a repair to the sheep's hoof had taken and if the laminae was beginning to heal itself. Sheep Forty-two—Mabel—was proving difficult to find, and he hoped that meant she was healing well and felt confident to wander in the pastures.

He'd just crested the hill and was coming down toward the barn when a commotion by the fence first told him something was wrong. Hatrick was pulling himself over the enclosure, waving one hand wildly as if to get Logan's attention. In doing so, the man fell more than climbed to the other side and landed in a heap on the ground.

He sprang to his feet though and waved madly with both hands now, shouting, "My lord! You must come at once!"

Logan was already trotting down the hill, going as fast as it was safe in the scrub grass. He reached the steward in seconds.

"What is it?" In his mind flashed through a thousand reasons Hatrick should be so concerned. An illness spreading through the ewes, failing lambs, or—

Without notice he was back in the rain, the dark of the night swallowing them as he pushed his horse faster, as he begged Catherine to stay alive.

He blinked and the image was gone. "What is wrong?" he pushed when Hatrick seemed unable to form words.

"It's Felicity, my lord. She's—"

He didn't hear the rest of his steward's words. He vaulted over the enclosure, landing on the other side at a run. He was through the front door of the manor house in less than a minute, only to be forced to sidestep should he crash directly into Mrs. Rehnquist.

She held up both hands. "I've sent for the doctor already. Her ladyship is in the nursery with her."

He started up the stairs, devouring them two at a time even as Mrs. Rehnquist called out, "Your lordship, wait!"

He gave her no heed, the need to get to Felicity fierce and unrelenting. He surged up the stairs until he broke through the doorway to the corridor leading to the nursery. How many times had he traversed this hallway in the dark? Why did it seem so endless now?

He never should have let his guard down. He knew what had started to happen ever since he had gone to London after his wife, had felt it slipping like ice melting from a lock. For a moment he thought he could stop it, but he knew now there was no stopping it.

He'd let someone else in, and now something had happened to Felicity.

The door to the nursery was shut, but he didn't bother to knock. He simply plowed through it so quickly the door bounced against the wall as he flung it open.

Gwen stood in the middle of the room, rocking Felicity in her arms, and she spun about at the sound of the door hitting the wall.

He was next to her in three strides, his hands reaching for Felicity. Later he would wonder what had overcome him, but in that moment, at the sight of his daughter in someone else's arms—this *stranger's* arms—for really what did he know of her? It swamped him until he saw nothing but danger.

Felicity let out a startled cry, but her smile was quick once she turned her eyes on him. He didn't take the time to look her over. He couldn't spare it. He could only hold her, press her to his body to assure him she still breathed.

"Logan, you mustn't. I think—"

He turned on Gwendolyn. "You don't get to think. Not when it comes to *my* daughter. What have you done to her? Why is the doctor coming?"

The words flowed out of him as if the very beat of his heart pumped them from his lips. One condemning word after another, words he didn't mean but needed to say as if they could protect him.

Gwendolyn's arms were raised like the echo of Felicity still lingered there, and he felt the first stab of caution.

Maybe he was overreacting. Maybe nothing was amiss. Maybe—

The rain was coming too quickly. There was no moon, no stars. He couldn't see where they were going. Catherine. Catherine. He couldn't feel her breath any longer. Was he already too late?

He blinked, and it was Gwendolyn before him not Catherine. He couldn't make sense of anything. Felicity was crying now. When had she started crying? He loosened his hold on her, and the tears eased.

"I haven't done anything," Gwendolyn said, her eyes—Oh God, those bottomless brown eyes—there was pain in them. Pain he'd put there.

What was he doing? Why wasn't he acting rationally?

Felicity was crying. Was she hurt? How hurt was she?

"Get out." Once more the words shot from his lips as if pushed, and Gwendolyn's eyes went cold.

He saw the moment it happened. How quickly he had snuffed out the concern, the worry, the very life of her in two small words. But once started he couldn't stop.

"Get out. Get out of his room. Get out of this house. You're not welcome here. You'll never touch my child again. Leave Scarcroft before I throw you out." He shoved each word at her as if by doing so he could stop himself from drowning because surely that was what was happening. He was drowning. Drowning in his own memories, in his own fears, in his own insecurities, and he was making everything worse, but the conscious part of his brain couldn't understand that. The only thing he understood was protecting his daughter.

The worst of it was Gwendolyn didn't even fight him. She said nothing. She closed her mouth on whatever she'd been about to say, and with one last painful look—a look that would haunt him for the rest of his life because the look wasn't for him, it was for Felicity—she walked away.

He went to the chair in the dormer where he had spent so many sleepless nights and sat, pulling Felicity impossibly closer. He held her, stroking her back as she cried into his shoulder. He may have murmured intelligible words, he didn't know. He couldn't remember.

He could only recall the sheer terror that gripped him as he waited for the doctor to come.

CHAPTER 17

He didn't know how much time had passed before footsteps in the corridor alerted him to the doctor's arrival. Logan stood, Felicity in his arms, as Dr. Rivers came through the door.

The man was getting on in years now, but Logan could still remember him from years past. He still had the same hulking presence, height and broadness, that made a person trust him immediately. His hair had gone white several years ago, and he kept his mustache neatly trimmed.

He placed his bag carefully on the floor as he reached for Felicity. "What seems to be the problem with the little one, Gracey?"

Logan relinquished his daughter but followed the doctor to the bassinet now shoved into the corner to make room for the crib Gwendolyn had ordered, keeping careful watch as he placed Felicity inside. "She's—"

He didn't know what was wrong. He shook his head, trying to clear his thoughts, but the past several minutes— had it been an hour now?—was all jumbled in his mind.

Dr. Rivers didn't wait for him to say anything further and

began undoing the buttons along Felicity's collar, revealing a trail of small red welts along her jaw and neck.

Dr. Rivers looked back at Logan. "Has the child been in contact with anything new? Anything she might not have had cause to experience before now?"

Logan's mind was completely blank. Gwendolyn would know. His wife. He needed his wife.

"Just a moment," he said to the doctor. "I'll get my wife." He made it to the corridor and prepared to call down for someone to fetch Gwendolyn, but he stopped at the sight of Miss Haversham cowering in the hallway with—

"Reverend Simons? What are you doing here?"

Simons exchanged a puzzled glance with Miss Haversham, and then strangely, the vicar put a reassuring hand on Miss Haversham's shoulder. "Miss Haversham sent word that the little one had fallen ill. I've come to offer my support in any fashion that may be helpful."

Logan frowned, hard. What the devil was the man about? Felicity needed a doctor not a vicar. He hadn't time for the man anyway.

"Miss Haversham, you were with Felicity this morning, yes?"

The woman only nodded, and Logan wished to scream at her to use her tongue, but then he noticed she was crying. Crying? What was the matter with everyone?

"Come at once," he said and retreated back into the nursery.

He found Dr. Rivers still examining Felicity. He'd removed the girl's gown and was working on her thick wool stockings, making faces at the girl and making her giggle as he continued his examination. Logan leaned over the man's shoulder and peered down at his daughter, his stomach tightening as he saw the red welts continue down her legs.

"Well, my oh my, what have we here?" the doctor said in a

singsong voice that made Felicity gurgle with happiness. "What kind of trouble has this little one gotten into today?"

Trouble? What kind of trouble? Logan was going to be sick. He turned away and nearly collided with Miss Haversham.

"Dear God woman, make a noise when you enter a room."

She looked as though he'd slapped her, and he immediately regretted his tone.

"You must be the nanny," Dr. Rivers said, ignoring Logan entirely it seemed.

Miss Haversham wrung her hands in her skirts. "I am. Is it bad, Doctor?"

"Bad?" Dr. Rivers repeated. "Why, not at all. It seems to be a mild reaction. Nothing she won't recover from." He tickled her feet, and Felicity sent up a cascade of giggles.

Logan spun about. "Reaction? Reaction to what?"

Dr. Rivers's smile was warm and knowing as if he'd faced the same question from countless overwrought parents before. "That's what I'm hoping Miss Haversham can tell me. Has Lady Felicity encountered anything new recently?"

The woman opened her lips and shook her head mutely, and Logan wanted to wring her neck if only to pry the words from her tongue.

"We've been trying new foods with her," Miss Haversham finally said. "We tried eggs this morning, but she didn't like them. She refused most of them and then—" Her voice caught, and she pressed her hand to her mouth, tears springing to her eyes and overflowing.

Logan frowned. He hadn't the time for such hysterics. "And then what?" he pushed.

Reverend Simons stepped into Logan's field of vision, causing him to startle backward. What on earth was the vicar doing here? The man was of no help.

"I think a more understanding tone would be best right

now, my lord," Simons said, that damn comforting hand going to Miss Haversham's shoulder once more.

Miss Haversham pointed to Felicity. "And then her ladyship saw the smallpox blisters." Her eyes were pained as she looked to the doctor. "Is it wise for us all to be in here? Lady Gracey said I must wash my hands and get rid of my gown. It seemed she thought the disease could easily spread."

Smallpox? Good God, his nanny had lost her senses.

Dr. Rivers laughed softly, a sound comforting and warm. "Oh no, no, no. This isn't smallpox. This is but the child's natural response to something her body found displeasing. From what you told me, I think the culprit is the eggs." He wiggled Felicity's foot and adopted that singsong voice again. "It was the eggs, wasn't it, darling?" he cooed, and Felicity laughed.

"Eggs?" Logan said.

"It was the eggs?" Miss Haversham echoed, her voice disbelieving and wet with tears all at once.

Dr. Rivers tickled Felicity's foot one more time and turned to collect his bag. "That would be my guess. You should avoid giving her eggs in future." He gestured to the red welts marking Felicity's body. "These are nothing but hives, a reaction to something she encountered or ingested. Give her a good soak in an oatmeal bath, and she'll be right as rain before you know it. Children can and do grow out of reactions such as this, but I would wait a while before trying the eggs again." He bowed his head slightly in Logan's direction. "If that is all, my lord, I shall be on my way. Please do send for me if her condition should change." He touched the brim of his hat. "Miss. Vicar," he said and left.

Logan approached his daughter's bassinet, placing both hands on the side of it as he peered down at her. She gnawed lazily on her fingers, gurgling happily to herself, but Logan couldn't help it when his stomach tightened at the sight of the hives.

"Miss Haversham, will you please see to an oatmeal bath for Lady Felicity?"

"Of course, my lord," the woman said, her voice sounding stronger now.

"Thank you," he said distractedly and then—"Miss Haversham." He turned to find the woman at the door, the vicar just behind her. "Why did you think it was smallpox?"

Miss Haversham flinched as though struck. "Lady Gracey thought it was smallpox. It was she who first saw the red welts at breakfast and stopped me from feeding Felicity any more of the eggs."

Lady Gracey.

His wife.

Gwendolyn.

Dear God, what had he done?

Terror, fear, and complete loathing for himself spread through him in a sickening wave. Gwen had thought it smallpox. God, what had she felt when she saw those red welts? What had gone through her mind? She must have been so scared. And he'd—he'd—

He pinched the bridge of his nose. "If you'll excuse me, Miss Haversham. I must speak with my wife." Neither the vicar nor the nanny moved. "Miss Haversham?"

The woman had gone back to quietly crying, and it was the vicar who answered. "She's not here, Gracey. She left hours ago just as you commanded."

She'd left.

Hours ago.

What in heaven's name was the man going on about?

"I hardly think it's been hours, Simons." Logan gestured to the window to prove his point, only to find it dark with night. He dropped his hand.

Simons took a step forward, putting himself between Miss Haversham and Logan. "Lady Gracey left this morning as you commanded. She's likely halfway to Leeds by now."

Halfway to Leeds?

"Will you please excuse me?" He pushed past the vicar and the nanny without waiting for their reply.

He didn't stop at his rooms. He didn't have time, and luggage would only slow him. When he reached the foyer, he wasn't surprised to find an assembly waiting for him.

Hatrick, Mrs. Rehnquist, Piven, Cook, Kent, and even the damn groom, young Ian. His footsteps slowed as he made his way down the last of the stairs, feeling every inch the cad as his own servants gave him a dressing down with only their scornful looks. Each of them glared, their hands in fists, their elbows asunder as if they meant to do battle. Logan deserved whatever it was they would throw at him.

It was Hatrick who approached him, Logan's greatcoat and hat in his hands.

"I've done something unforgivable," Logan said even though the man had not uttered a single accusation.

"That's up to her to decide," he said, giving Logan his things.

He shrugged into them and headed for the door, wrenching it open just as the darkness split, and rain poured from the sky.

* * *

SHE WAS COLD, colder than she'd ever been, so cold, in fact, that she felt nothing.

She tried. She pushed at the blackness that had engulfed her mind, but there was nothing there. Logan's words came back to her, over and over again. She knew they were there, and yet no matter how she prodded she felt...nothing.

She was numb.

She couldn't even cry.

She stood before the small fire in her room at the inn outside Leeds. Although they had had a late start, the driver had been efficient in getting her as far from Scarcroft as possible in a single day. It was faster without her trunks, she knew that. She'd left Kent in near tears as Gwen had rushed about tossing things into a carpetbag. Her trunks would be sent along later.

The carpetbag sat on the chair by the door now untouched. She hadn't even removed her cloak when she'd entered the room. She'd simply walked over to the fire, drawn to it as if it could give her blood life again. If she stood any closer to the thing, she would set her skirts aflame.

Yet she still felt nothing.

She thought she should feel some sense of irony in the fact that her second chance had ended in the same way all of her chances had been stripped from her. Banished. Blamed. Outcast.

She wasn't sure when it had started raining. They had stopped shortly after teatime, the driver wrongly assuming she would wish to eat before retiring for the evening, and she'd been safely inside before the weather had turned.

She could hear the rain now though, slashing at the windows, and unbidden, she remembered the night she'd first made love to her husband. The pain was crushing, and she forced away the memory if only to breathe.

Here she was in a nameless inn on a road that looked like any other road, once more banished from the place she called home.

A woman she assumed was the proprietor's wife had brought up a tray some time ago, and it sat untouched on the table by her elbow. She had no hunger or thirst. She had nothing.

She was nearly startled into the fire when a knock sounded at the door. She shifted, finding her feet had fallen asleep from standing still for so long, and she reached for the chair by the fire to hold herself up.

"Yes?" she called.

"I'm terribly sorry, milady," came the familiar voice from the proprietor on the other side. "But there's a gentleman here what says he's yer husband. I'd tell him to sod off—er, that is—I'd ask him to leave, but he looks like a right gentleman, ma'am."

The proprietor's words made little sense, but she went over to the door and unbolted it. She eased the door open enough to take in the proprietor's bushy mustaches and the stained apron that strained over his bulging stomach.

"My husband?"

The proprietor nodded, his eyes round with concern. "Oh aye, my lady. Big bloke that seems real angry like?"

Gwen frowned. "That would indeed be my husband. You can allow him up."

She left the door slightly ajar and went back to her place by the fire. Her heart should have been hammering in her chest, but as before, she felt nothing, just the numbness that had crept over her body when her husband had banished her from their home.

She heard his pounding footsteps on the stairs, and still her heart did nothing. The sound of the door swinging open and then shut, the bolt sliding home reached her, and still nothing.

"Gwendolyn."

Finally her heart broke at the sound of her name on his lips. She didn't turn around. She only squeezed her eyes shut and steeled herself for the worst.

For why had he come? Was he not done dressing her down? Would he blame her for Felicity's illness? Would he think she had given the child smallpox? She squeezed her eyes shut tighter.

There was a step behind her, and then, "Gwen, I've come to beg your forgiveness, but I must tell you first what happened to Catherine."

She couldn't have stopped herself from turning around. It happened so quickly, his words registering and her body moving so swiftly she might have fallen into the fire.

He was wet, soaking wet, and grim looking with his frown and his hard eyes, and she'd never seen anything so perfect.

She reached for the stack of fresh towels on the chair by the fire and went to him before she realized what she was doing. She stuffed the towel in his hands and backed away, pulling her cloak more tightly together.

"You'll catch your death," she muttered and scuffed her feet along the hearth, trying to look at anything but him.

He didn't use the towel to dry himself off. He simply held it as he said, "Felicity doesn't have smallpox, Gwen. It was only a reaction to the eggs she tried this morning. She's going to be fine."

Gwen looked up at this, a strange effervescent relief rushing through her. "It's not smallpox?"

"No, it's—" He shook his head as he took an aborted step toward her, and she thought his voice might have cracked, but that was impossible. This was Logan Bender, the Earl of Gracey, the man who had terrified her at their very wedding. Surely emotion held no power over him.

"It's not smallpox, I assure you," he went on at some length. "The doctor said she should recover soon but probably shouldn't have any more eggs."

His coat dripped rain onto the floor as he continued to hold the towel unused in his hand. She wanted to take it from him, pull his jacket and hat from him, and towel dry his hair before he caught cold.

But she didn't. She just stood there, feeling as though she had stepped wrongly in the garden and fallen through a rabbit hole. No, that wasn't right. He wasn't here about her. He'd only come to tell her about Felicity.

"Thank you for coming all this way to let me know. You shouldn't have taxed yourself so." Again her hands moved as if to take the towel from him, and she stopped herself by gripping the edges of her cloak.

"I didn't only come here to tell you that. I acted reprehensibly, and I owe you the sincerest of apologies, but I must tell you something first. It's not an excuse." He shook his head. "I would never try to excuse what I did. It's more an explanation, so when I do the same thing in future, you will understand and can tell me when I'm being an idiot."

In future? The words bounced around in her head like sunlight in a pool of water. Was there a future for them?

He moved so quickly then she didn't have time to stop him. Dropping the towel to the chair by the fire, he stripped off his gloves, letting them fall to the floor as he reached out and gripped her hands.

His eyes had been on her face, but as soon as he touched her, his eyes widened and fell to her hands. "Gwen, you're like ice. Are you ill?" He pressed a hand to her forehead, and she was shocked at the warmth of his touch. "You're freezing."

He moved quickly then, shedding his hat and coat even as he pulled a quilt from the bed. Dragging the chair closer to the fire, he wrapped the quilt about her shoulders and picked her up without ceremony, sitting down in the chair and holding her on his lap.

She wanted to protest. He couldn't do this to her simply because his size allowed him to manhandle her thusly, but she couldn't find the will to form the protest. His hard body pressed against hers, and heat suddenly filled her, from within more than from without, and she wanted to sit there forever and push him away all at once.

But instead she let him speak.

"Gwen, I must tell you what happened to Catherine."

She closed her eyes against the echo of pain in her chest. It had been months that she'd been waiting to hear those words, and now, when she was so numb, he would choose to speak them.

"Gwen." He spoke her name like an oath and his hand was against her cheek. "Gwen, I want you to look at me when I tell you. Please."

She forced her eyes open, too tired to hope for anything else. A second chance? A third? She'd wasted so many; she couldn't possibly be given any more. But she would give him this. She would meet his gaze when he extinguished the last of her hope.

"I know the servants at Scarcroft would never have spoken about Catherine, but you learned her name from someone and even about the lies she spread about me, so I know you know something of her. I myself have told you how she was willful and selfish, but there was more to it than that." He swallowed, his eyes moving over her face, and she wondered what he saw there for she still felt nothing. "Catherine was the youngest daughter of Lord Kendall," he said, and the name caught in the web of her mind.

"The neighboring estate?" she asked, surprised at the scratchiness of her voice.

His eyes widened ever so slightly when she spoke, and she hated giving him any kind of hope like that. "Yes, Kendall's estate borders Scarcroft. Our fathers arranged the marriage when we were still quite young, and I—" He closed his eyes briefly, and she wondered what pain he was hiding from. "I thought nothing of it. I went off to school, and when I returned, we were wed." He paused, but Gwen already knew the next part of the story. It was inevitable.

"She didn't want to marry you," she said and watched as her husband's eyes widened in surprise again.

"I suppose it was obvious to everyone but me." He shook his head. "She was upset from the start. She acted out, demanding things of me I couldn't give her, and one day I discovered she'd gone home to her father and complained about my treatment of her."

"What happened?" Gwen asked, wondering how he could speak in such an emotionless tone.

A shadow fell over his face as he said, "Her father dismissed her, sent her back to Scarcroft, which only angered her. Apparently such behavior was common from her, and he no longer listened to her complaints."

"But others didn't know how she behaved," she said.

He shook his head again. "No, so she took to spreading rumors about me in the *ton*. I think it was the only way she got any satisfaction in her believed hopeless state. I stopped allowing her to go to London. It was the only thing I could think to do. She was harming the title and the estate and too many people depended on it. I couldn't let her do it. It only made her angrier. So she took a lover."

The words were spoken so plainly she almost missed them, but as they hammered against her breastbone, she unconsciously reached out, pressing a hand against his chest in comfort. "Oh Logan, no."

He shrugged. "Her infidelity mattered little after all that she'd done. I thought perhaps if she found something to occupy her, she may be less dangerous. But then I found out she was pregnant with Felicity."

Her lips parted, the question pushing inside of her, but it wasn't for her to ask.

She didn't need to though.

"She was already pregnant when she took a lover only she didn't realize it. I forbade her from endangering the child, but it mattered little. The pregnancy was difficult, and the doctor ordered bedrest. It only served to infuriate her." His eyes deepened then to a mossy green, and she placed both hands against his chest, no longer in comfort to him but as if to brace herself. "She started to hurt herself. She threatened to throw herself down the stairs, her and the baby. We took turns staying with her, Mrs. Rehnquist, Hatrick, and even Piven and myself, and she'd behave as long as someone was watching. But then Felicity was born, and—" His voice broke off, and he looked away.

"She was free," Gwen whispered, the horrible truth sinking deep within her.

His eyes moved back to hers and in them was a quiet recognition. "Yes. She was free." He closed his eyes briefly, and when he opened them, Gwen saw the rawness there. "She was still weak from the birth, but it didn't stop her. She waited until I was in the barns doing the nightly rounds, and she went to the stables and made Piven give her a horse. He did as she bade because he was a servant, and she the master. There was little he could do, and I don't blame him. She rode off into the dark without a lantern." He stopped speaking, and in the quiet, Gwen heard the words of the seamstress's assistant from so long ago.

Catherine's death was brutal and devastating, that much Gwen knew, and she curled her hands around the lapels of her husband's coat.

"I followed her. I couldn't let her go into the night alone, not when she was so weak and careless. I was hardly out of the gates when the storm broke. It was relentless, and before long, it had swamped my lantern, and I was without light. I followed the road, hoping she wasn't foolish enough to try to find her way across the fields in the dark. And that's when I found her." He clenched his jaw, and she saw a muscle moving there as if he were gathering strength.

She pressed her hands into him. "You mustn't tell me any more. I don't need to know."

His eyes flashed to hers, and he reached between them, wrapping his hands around hers. "Yes, you must know. I know today won't be the only time I push you away. I know I will try to do it over and over again, and I don't want you to ever think that I'm doing it because of you or because of Catherine or because of any number of excuses. I'm doing it because of me."

She sat, speech having left her, and she simply nodded.

He looked away then but went on. "It isn't fit for anyone to hear what happened, but I want you to know because that night still haunts me." His voice had gotten softer, and she leaned forward, reassuring him with her weight. "She must have fallen from the horse, and in the dark, the animal was spooked. She—" He stopped, licked his lips, swallowed. "She had marks on her face and hands like hoof prints, like she had tried to shield her face from the prancing feet of the horse as if she were—" His voice all but stopped, the sound painful, and then he spoke a single word. "Trampled." There was a pause of complete silence, and the terrible word settled between them before he went on. "She was hurt, badly, but she was still alive when I found her, and I got her onto my horse and went straight for the doctor." He paused, but she already sensed the rest. "She died in my arms." Only then did he return his gaze to her. "I wasn't fast enough, Gwen. I couldn't save her. I failed." His voice broke off then, and his face went blank.

Hushed noises of comfort and rebuke sprang to her lips, but she stopped them, realization dawning. "Oh God, Logan," she breathed, and she wondered what he read in her expression because his changed, lightening, questioning. She shook her head. "This whole time I thought you didn't trust people, but really, the person you trust the least is yourself."

His eyes cleared then, turning from moss to clover. "What?"

She shook her head. "I don't know why I didn't see it. The way you wouldn't hold Felicity. The way you snuck into the nursery at night after everyone had gone to bed—"

"You knew I did that?"

She frowned. "I accidentally came upon you once. I'm terribly sorry. You gave me quite a fright." She laughed then because it was all too much and too terrible, and if she didn't laugh, it would choke her. She cupped his face in her hands. "Oh Logan, you mustn't ever think you failed. That night on the road you could have chosen to leave her. She didn't deserve your compassion. She didn't deserve anything. Her own selfish and reckless decisions had put her there, and you were required to do nothing. The fact that you made a decision that night, a decision to try to save her, that is all that matters. A lesser man wouldn't have had the courage to make that decision, Logan. All that we are left with are the decisions we make, and you made the right one that night no matter the outcome."

She saw the understanding in his features, but then his eyes darkened. "I didn't make the right decision today, Gwen. I didn't listen to you, and I should have, and I'm so so sorry." His voice broke again, but this time not in pain but in sadness. He gripped her wrists with his hands, and she'd never felt so small. "I hurt you terribly. I frightened you needlessly, and I can't—" She let him take a breath. "I can't live knowing I did that to you."

She spoke quickly, hoping her words would erase the pain that still remained in his expression. "Apology accepted, and I forgive you."

He blinked and sat back, pulling his face from her hands. "You forgive me too easily."

She shook her head. "Forgiveness is the easy part, I'm afraid. You're right about one thing. You will push me away again. You will because you can't help it, and I will need to be strong enough to stay when you do so. And you—" Here she tapped him on the chest. "You will need to keep me from running away. I'm so used to being banished that I've come to expect it. I've come to not expect good things to happen to me, and I will always accept the terrible ones more easily. I'm sorry, Logan, but I think we may be a right mess."

His smile came softly then. "So you're saying you'll give me another chance to make a mistake?"

"As long as you give me one." She leaned in, her lips nearly touching his. "I love you, Logan."

He growled. "I love you, Gwendolyn," he said and kissed her.

It was sometime later as he held her on his lap in front of the fire, his hand lazily stroking her hair when he said, "I think I was right the day you arrived. You must have been addlebrained to marry me."

She laughed and nestled her head against his shoulder. "No, not addlebrained. Just curious."

"Curious?" His hand stilled in her hair.

"I had been given some very interesting information about sheep farmers, and I wished to see if it were true."

"Is it?"

She sat up and smiled at him. "Absolutely not," she said and kissed him.

CHAPTER 18

He woke her with a soft kiss one morning that summer as he usually did, but instead of letting her fall back asleep, he bade her follow him. He helped her into her dressing gown, and taking her by the hand, he led her down through the kitchen to the garden door. There he helped her into the same boots she had worn that night in the barn when she'd helped him birth the lamb, and taking her hand, he led her into the garden.

Once outside, he guided her in the direction of the western pasture. The hillside rose up before them, the first rays of sun painting only its crest. He helped her over the enclosure and taking her hand once more, started up the hill.

By the time they reached the top, the sun had broken the horizon, filling the valley below them with warm, soft light. She paused, taking it in, letting it fill her up as the warm, summer air skated across her cheeks. She felt whole and hopeful, and it filled her lungs like never before.

Home.

This was their home, all the ups and downs of it. Felicity

was no longer made to eat eggs although Dr. Rivers had assured them that she was likely to outgrow the reaction, and she should be fine. Gwen was happy to discover Felicity did not feel the same about pears and ham as she did of eggs.

This was confirmed by Felicity herself as she did nothing but spout a stream of conversation nearly all day long now. Her favorite word being *Papa,* which she proclaimed the moment she woke up in the morning until she fell asleep in her papa's arms at night. Gwen couldn't even be jealous because she knew what Logan had gone through to simply be with his daughter.

Rachel had married the reverend the previous month, and they were currently on holiday in Augsburg where Dudley was studying some Lutheran texts while Rachel, proclaiming in every letter she wrote to Gwen, was eating her way through all of the Continent.

Delilah, Dudley's sister, had announced she was needed as a traveling companion to a dear old aunt and departed immediately after the wedding.

For America.

According to Delilah, this was not far enough away from the Earl of Gracey, but it would do.

Gwen expected Logan to let go of her hand once they'd crested the hill, but instead he took her other hand in his and turned her to face him.

"Gwendolyn," he said, and she raised an eyebrow at the growl in his voice. She did so love that growl. "Do you recall the day of our wedding?"

She returned his raised eyebrow with one of her own. "Yes, it was when I was first introduced to your charm."

She expected a grin that suggested his lack of guilt at his behavior that day, but instead, he almost appeared to turn red. Her stomach tightened.

"Yes, I did behave rather poorly that day. That is why I've brought you up here this morning."

Her lips parted. "What do you mean?"

"I disappointed you that day. I know I did, and I should like to make it up to you. Right now. Marry me."

Something odd happened in her chest then as though her heart had performed a kind of somersault. "I'm already married to you."

He squeezed her hands. "Yes, I know, but marry me again, and of your own free will."

Yes, her heart was definitely somersaulting in her chest.

She raised her chin. "All right, Lord Gracey. I consent to marrying you. Again. Except—" She shook her head. "I shan't consent to do so again without a ring." She grinned to let him know she was teasing.

Their wedding had been so hasty she hadn't had time to think of a ring, and now so much had happened that a ring was the last thing from her mind.

But he surprised her yet again by letting go of her hands and reaching into the pocket of his waistcoat, withdrawing a slender ring of warm gold topped by an exquisite opal.

"A ring like this?"

She could feel her mouth open but knew she couldn't speak for anything in the world. She reached for the ring, but he pulled it out of her reach.

"You're skipping ahead, Lady Gracey."

She blinked. "You would deny me this ring?"

"I would force you to declare here on this hillside how much you love and adore me before I give you this ring."

She had never seen his expression so playful, and her heart nearly leapt out of her chest.

She dropped her hands. "You wish for me to declare my love for you?" She took a step closer to him. "But how can I put into words what I feel when I watch you rock Felicity to sleep? Or what I feel when in the dark of the night you somehow know to pull me close? Or what I feel when I wake next to you and know that I will do so every day for the rest of my life?" She watched his eyes grow dark through all of her words, and her chest squeezed with love for him. "I can't put those feelings into words, Logan. I can only feel them and cherish them and you." She paused and took another step forward. "Forever."

He picked up her left hand and poised the ring at the top of her third finger. "Gwendolyn Bounds, I didn't want a wife, and after a day with you, I didn't want you either."

She laughed, and it felt impossible that now he could make her laugh so easily, but when she saw the love in his eyes, she knew it couldn't be any other way.

"What I wanted was a partner, someone to stand with me, beside me, and most importantly, in front of me when I needed it most. What I wanted was you, and I could never have believed I could be so lucky." Here he slid the opal onto her finger and held her hand clasped between both of his. "An opal gets its color when gases become trapped in the rock." He rubbed his thumb over the opal gently, making it catch in the sunlight and sparkle. "It's a gem that's coveted for the mistakes it's made and the flaws that have been formed because of them." He met her gaze then, and she thought she would never be more in love with him than in that moment, but then he said, "I hope you'll love me for the mistakes I've made and the flaws they've left behind."

"Only if you'll love me for my flaws, the ones on the outside and the inside," she said.

"I will," he said, the words soft with sincerity, his eyes filled with love.

She had no more words to give him then, so she just said, "And I will too," and kissed him.

She stood there as the sun broke over the horizon,

flooding the pastures below them with the light and hope that only comes with the breaking of a new day. She stood there as she kissed this man she loved, as impossible as he was, and as impossible as it seemed, and finally understood there were no second chances or third or fourth ones. There was only life, and she was finally living it.

ABOUT THE AUTHOR

Jessie decided to be a writer because there were too many lives she wanted to live to just pick one.

Taking her history degree dangerously, Jessie tells the stories of courageous heroines, the men who dared to love them, and the world that tried to defeat them.

Jessie lives in New Hampshire where if she is not at her desk writing, she's probably letting the dog out. Again.

For more, visit her website at jessieclever.com.

www.ingramcontent.com/pod-product-compliance
Lightning Source LLC
Chambersburg PA
CBHW020147310726

48970CB00006B/2044